Love's Beginning

"This is marvelous!" Seth exclaimed involuntarily. "It seems a shame that all this should remain hidden here, unseen. It should be shared with the world."

Eden blushed as though unaccustomed to compliments on her paintings. "This is very kind of you, Mr. Lindow, but as I have explained, very unlikely to come to pass." She stood and moved toward the door. A muted sound floated up from the distance below them. "Goodness, there is the dressing gong already!" exclaimed Eden. "I had no idea we had spent so much time up here."

Seth placed his hand on her arm and she whirled to face him, seemingly startled as though she had forgotten his presence. "Thank you for showing me your work, Miss Beckett."

"Why—yes, yes of course." With that she hurried down the corridor, leaving Seth to stare after her. Good Lord, Eden chastised herself, what was the matter with her? She was pleased, of course, that he seemed to like her work. She halted suddenly, in the process of ringing for her maid. His good opinion of her painting mattered. Or was it his good opinion of her that she sought?

Coming in September 1999

Miss Haycroft's Suitors by Emily Hendrickson

Against her will, a lovely young heiress is about to get married off to a man she doesn't love—to satisfy her uncle's gambling debts. All seems lost until a dashing lord takes interest in her plight. Lord Justin creates make-believe suitors for the woman to keep her uncle at bay, but the true feelings in the lord's heart are all too real....

0-451-19834-4/$4.99

The Misfit Marquess by Teresa DesJardien

While fleeing the embrace of a false lover, a beautiful young marquess is rendered unconscious in an accident. Discovered by a handsome lord, the marquess fretted over her reputation and pretended to be a little daft. The lord's suspicions of her arose with his desire to help her...and to have her. But the villain who pursued her would not surrender without a fight....

0-451-19835-2/$4.99

The London Belle by Shirley Kennedy

When her father gambles away the family fortune, a beautiful young lady must decide whether to marry a wealthy man whom she does not love or accept a position tutoring the son of a notorious rake. But even as she helps a lonely boy emerge from his shell, she also melts the heart of her employer....

0-451-19836-0/$4.99

To order call: 1-800-788-6262

A Man
of Affairs

Anne Barbour

A SIGNET BOOK

SIGNET
Published by New American Library, a division of
Penguin Putnam Inc., 375 Hudson Street,
New York, New York 10014, U.S.A.
Penguin Books Ltd, 27 Wrights Lane,
London W8 5TZ, England
Penguin Books Australia Ltd,
Ringwood, Victoria, Australia
Penguin Books Canada Ltd, 10 Alcorn Avenue,
Toronto, Ontario, Canada M4V 3B2
Penguin Books (N.Z.) Ltd, 182–190 Wairau Road,
Auckland 10, New Zealand

Penguin Books Ltd, Registered Offices:
Harmondsworth, Middlesex, England

First published by Signet, an imprint of New American Library,
a division of Penguin Putnam Inc.

First Printing, August 1999
10 9 8 7 6 5 4 3 2 1

Chapter One

Someone was scratching at the door, disturbing the afternoon silence. Heretofore, the only sound in the room had been the hiss of pen on paper and the whisper of one ledger pushed against another. Seth ignored the interruption, knowing full well that it would be repeated within a moment or two.

"Come," he called in some exasperation when the sound could be ignored no longer.

An elderly butler entered. "It's His Grace, sir," he said before Seth could utter a reprimand for fracturing his concentration. "He wishes to see you in the library, at your convenience."

Seth said nothing, but nodded and rose at once. Setting aside pen and ledgers, and pausing only to rub his fingers on the tails of his coat, he hastened from the room.

Seth's office lay in the rear of the Duke of Derwent's elegant town residence in Grosvenor Square, and the distance to the library was considerable. Still, it took Seth only a few minutes to reach the quiet, book-lined chamber.

The duke was slumped in a leather chair near the fire, his fingers cupped around a snifter of brandy as though to draw comfort from it. He lifted the glass in a curt gesture and, turning to the decanter that stood on a small table at his side, poured another. A thin smile creased his long face, still relatively unlined at the age of eight and fifty. His hair, combed back severely from his temples, showed but a few strands of gray.

He handed the snifter to Seth.

"Your Grace," murmured Seth, accepting the brandy. He seated himself in a chair opposite the duke.

"I wish you'd stop that 'Your Grace' nonsense, Seth. You'd think you were one of the footmen."

Seth smiled ruefully and glanced down at the ink-stained

coat he wore for the days he spent at the ducal accounts. "Behold my livery—Father."

"Tchah!" exclaimed the duke distastefully. "I don't know why you don't push all that nonsense off on one of the people we pay for that sort of thing. Young sprout like yourself—should be spending the day at White's, or at Gentleman Jackson's."

Seth smiled inwardly. How like Father. His foster son was to serve competently as business and social manager, but would be chastised for not living as a gentleman. "Gambling in the middle of the day does not appeal to me, Father, as you well know, and I visited the Gentleman just yesterday at his saloon. In fact, he let me pop a hit over his guard."

"Let you, did he?" The duke rubbed his nose. "At any rate, that's more like it."

The duke paused to sip at his brandy and sank into a meditative silence.

"Was there something you wanted, Father?" Seth asked at length.

A frown creased the duke's aquiline features.

"Yes, I'm afraid so," he said, his expression one of unwonted gravity. "Seth, I'm afraid it's time to do something about Bel. I know." He lifted a hand as Seth opened his mouth. "We've spoken of this before, but the situation has become urgent. Now, a wedding has become imperative. You must find a bride for your brother."

"But, Bel does not wish—" Seth whispered. A sour taste flooded his mouth as it always did at the mention of Charles Lindow, Marquess of Belhaven.

"I know that," interrupted the duke harshly. "But if we wait any longer, God knows what irrevocable mischief he'll get up to. One day he'll kill himself—or someone else." The duke's eyes narrowed. "Look at the mess you just pulled him out of. Besides that, he's six and twenty. He's my heir. It's time he settled down."

Seth almost laughed aloud. The prospect of Bel's settling down, in or out of the bonds of matrimony, was extremely dubious.

"Yes, I know," agreed the duke, as though reading Seth's mind. "He's said often enough that he doesn't wish to marry, but . . ." His expression hardened. "His wishes in the matter have ceased to interest me. Frankly, I very much fear that if we don't line up an eligible *parti* for him soon, there won't be a female in the realm who will have him."

Seth raised his head to encounter the duke's gaze, dark and implacable.

"Yes," continued the older man, "I've heard the rumors—his groom beaten almost to death—the unspeakable sexual practices—the drunken spectacle he makes of himself in public." He shifted his shoulders. "I've tried to excuse him at every turn, but there's no doubt the boy is wild to a fault." He laughed harshly. "And that's dishing it up with sauce."

"Father, no. You must not talk this way. As Bel grows older, surely—"

The duke lifted a hand to silence him, saying harshly, "As he grows older he becomes more unmanageable. Good God, Seth, he almost ended up on a marble slab this last time. If you hadn't pulled him out of that stable, he would have been consumed in the flames—to say nothing of the serving wench he'd taken out there for a bit of dalliance."

"He was drunk, Father. He kicked over the—"

The duke lifted his hand to make a chopping motion. "Yes, I know what he did, and I see no point in discussing his flaws any further. He must have a son to carry on the line. You will find a bride for him, and I shall persuade him to marry her, even if I have to bind and gag him."

Seth clenched his fists. He knew very well that if any binding and gagging were required, the binder and gagger would be he. For, having found the perfect dogsbody in the person of his adoptive son, the duke had no compunction in relegating his life's most distasteful tasks to him. Dear God, Seth wondered, as he seemed to do so often of late, how had things come to such a pass? He had once idolized this man, and now he could barely stand to be in the same room with him. He had always known he had no right to the love the duke lavished on his other children, but he had worked so hard—and to no avail—for something more than the careless affection bestowed on him by His Grace when the mood struck him. The slights, the indignities, the neglect had taken their toll over the years. Was it merely habit that kept him in the duke's service?

No, he thought, it was more than that. He had made a promise, and his mother, whom he remembered only as a small person with a sweet voice, had taught him that a promise must be kept for all one's life, no matter what the cost.

Seth swallowed. "Very well, Father," he said simply. "I shall set about it immediately."

"You will make it your first priority," the duke commanded.

Seth had no desire to fulfill the onerous task that had been set for him, but if that was what the duke desired of him, he would, as he had done since he was a child, bend heaven and earth to grant him this wish. Had he not vowed many years ago to give his life, if need be, to secure the old man's happiness? God knew it was a vow he'd since regretted, but it was iron-clad, nonetheless. He nodded and in a few moments left the duke, returning to his office to stare at the wall opposite his desk.

Some hours later, Seth Lindow, adopted son of the Duke of Derwent, stood before the cheval glass in his bedchamber. Near him, several strips of linen in his hand, stood a short, rather stumpy personage garbed in the somber raiment of a gentleman's gentleman. With due care, he handed Seth one of the linen strips and watched with solemn attention as Seth folded it about his neck, transforming it at last into a complicated arrangement known to the informed as the *Trone D'Amour*.

Jason Moppe, whose plebeian antecedents were distressingly obvious in aspect and speech, scarcely fitted the role of gentleman's gentleman. He had been hired some ten years before on a murky evening in London's Limehouse district. Seth had unwisely ventured into that area on business in a hackney driven by Moppe. When a group of thugs had set upon the vehicle and the toff inside, it was Moppe's quick action that had helped Seth save them both. Seth had taken on the underfed Cockney out of gratitude, and because his erstwhile valet had departed the week before for employment elsewhere. To his surprise, the little man proved himself as adept with a sadiron and boot polish brush as he had been with a team of horses. He was Seth's most dedicated employee and loyal supporter, but this did not preclude a salutary lecture now and again when the valet thought it necessary, or a judicious interference in his master's affairs when circumstances demanded.

On this occasion, Moppe surveyed his master with a well-concealed affection. Mr. L. was a well-set-up fellow, sporting a fine crop of dark, curly hair. He was lean as a whip, but required no padding about shoulders and calves. His eyes were darkish as well and gazed at the world with an authoritative, damn-your-eyes stare that usually brought instant obedience from any underling unfortunate enough to find himself under its glare. Sure to God, concluded Moppe with a sour grin, he looked more the duke's heir than the heir hisself.

"So, what's the mort's name? The one you're off to snabble for the markee?"

"I'm not looking for a mort," replied Seth frostily. "And I'm not going to snabble anyone."

"Ho, that's not the word going about belowstairs."

Seth growled inaudibly. Good Lord, he might have known that word of his quest would have flown about the duke's household like a winter megrim. Hell, the servants had probably known of his conversation with the duke before it was concluded. Gloomily, he made a last-minute adjustment to the *Trone D'Amour* and left his chambers.

Although the Season would not be in full swing for several weeks, there was a sufficient number of prominent families in town to make his efforts worthwhile. Mentally, he perused his list of young females worthy of the title, Marchioness of Belhaven and ultimately Duchess of Derwent. To be sure, the duke's heir had damaged himself almost irreparably in the eyes of the *ton*, but it might be assumed that for at least some families, Bel's title and wealth would outweigh any of his more unpleasant character flaws.

Seth had danced with Lady Winifred Woodhouse and Miss Charlotte Grey. He had fetched punch for the Misses Gilbert and Houghton and had been introduced to Miss Zoë Beckett. Under ordinary circumstances, the latter would be far down on any roster of potential mates for the heir of the Duke of Derwent. Though she was the daughter of a lord, the peer was far from wealthy and dwelled for most of the year on his small country estate. Miss Zoë had thus not been invited into the sacred precincts of Almack's. However, she had caught Seth's attention. She was beautiful, a critical quality if she was to interest Bel. After some minutes in conversation with her, and after a quiet chat with her parents, Frederick, Lord Beckett, and his lady, of Surrey, he concluded that Miss Zoë was the ambitious sort. He hoped she was also the sort who would be willing to accept almost any flaw in a husband as long as it was accompanied by a title and wealth.

Seth ordered a discreet investigation of Lord Beckett and discovered that the gentleman was a rarity among the English peerage; he was virtually landless. Several generations before, a feckless Lord Beckett had let the entail lapse, and his son, falling victim to gambling fever, sold off the family holdings to feed his habit. A once wealthy and powerful title fell into disrepair, and it was not until the present Lord Beckett acceded to the title that matters began to look up. Though regarded by his neighbors as little more than a country squire, Lord Beckett was fiercely ambitious and determined to return the family name to its former status. Through hard work and shrewd dealings, he had, bit by bit, purchased land from the surrounding holdings and was now living comfortably, if not lavishly. His progeny consisted of five daughters, three of whom had made advantageous marriages. The oldest was a spinster of twenty-six summers, and the youngest was Zoë. From all reports, both her father and mother were eager for Zoë to marry well. Precisely how eager remained to be seen.

Now, several evenings after his first encounter with Miss Zoë, Seth stood on the perimeter of yet another ballroom—this one in the town home of the Earl and Countess of Saltram—searching for his quarry. Ah, there she was, near the refreshment table, surreptitiously adjusting the neckline of her silk gown so that it revealed another inch or two of pretty bosom and flirting enthusiastically with the Earl of Breecham's cub. He grinned cynically as the boy's mother approached, rather in the manner of a bitch defending her pup, to pry him from Zoë's beguilements.

As he watched, another figure intruded on his view. He was a little above medium height and muscular. His features were regular, and the smile that crinkled eyes of a pale, almost milky blue was charming in the extreme. His careless style of dress and the golden thatch of hair swept into an untidy Brutus proclaimed him the complete Corinthian. As he made his way through the room, several women drew their skirts aside.

Seth drew in a sharp breath. Good Lord, what was *he* doing here? Cravenly, he turned to bolt into the card room, but it was too late. Bel's eyes met his across the throng of guests, and, his mouth twisted in a crooked grin, he sauntered across the room.

"What, ho, brother mine?"

"Hello, Bel," replied Seth calmly. "What brings you here?"

"I've been trying to connect with Beaumont for the last two weeks. He owes me money, and he's never at home when I call. Heard he's making up to the Danvers chit, so thought he might be here. Don't see him, though. I might ask the same of you, by the by. Reduced to trolling among the virgins, are you?"

Seth breathed a sigh of relief that Bel appeared to be in one of his sunnier moods. Unwilling to let his brother know how close he'd come to the mark, Seth merely smiled. "Aunt Blessborough is sponsoring the daughter of a neighboring squire. She asked me to come by tonight and do the pretty. Stand up with her once or twice—take her into supper—that kind of thing."

"Of course. Saint Seth at work again."

A spurt of irritation prickled through Seth at these words, and he forced an expression of placid cordiality to his features.

"Not at all. I always feel a stab of pity for these infants, pitchforked into society without the slightest notion of how to go on. This particular babe in the woods is a taking little thing, and I don't mind doing her a spot of good if I can. Besides," he added, drawing cautious aim, "I've been rather enjoying my little survey of this Season's buds of promise."

Bel's flat gaze swept the room. "Really? But, brother dear, you cannot be thinking of marrying one of them—even if you could convince any of them to overlook your, er, plebeian origins."

Seth forced himself to relax. He had long since learned not to rise to Bel's baiting. "No, of course not. I am well aware of my origins. But, you see," he said gently, "I don't care. I have no particular desire to marry at all—after all, I need not concern myself with getting an heir—and I particularly do not wish a union with a pampered damsel of the *ton*."

"Ah. Don't fancy prominent teeth, do you? Or spots, or the occasional squint. You might—I say, who is that? Don't tell me she's on the block?"

Concealing his distaste, Seth followed the direction of Bel's languid gesture. His eyes widened. Well, well, Bel found the little Beckett attractive, did he? This was promising, indeed.

Bel's rather narrow mouth quirked cynically. "I see she practices the old strategy of mingling with the ape-leaders and anti-dotes in order to enhance her own charms."

Seth eyed the woman to whom Miss Zoë was talking animat-edly. She was some years older than Zoë, and, though next to the dazzling young beauty, she must be considered plain, the approbation "antidote" seemed misplaced. No longer in the first blush of youth, the woman was yet possessed of a trim fig-ure, and her gown, fashioned with neat propriety, hinted subtly at the curves that lay beneath it. Her most striking feature, how-ever, was a pair of speaking gray eyes and dark brows that swept toward her temples like glossy little wings. That she had placed herself among the rank of the spinsters was evidenced in a small lace cap that rested softly on a sweep of mahogany-colored hair.

"The beauty's name is Zoë Beckett, and, although I've not met her, I believe the woman at her side is her sister. I don't re-member her name, something rather exotic, I think. Zoë was presented last Season. Took pretty well, I understand, but has not married." Seth glanced swiftly at Bel, noting the predatory glitter that had sprung to his brother's eyes. "Her father is something of a nonentity, but I hear he's the old-fashioned pro-tective sort."

Bel laughed and turned away dismissively. "You'd best stick with the antidote, boy-o. She looks to be just your type. Sub-missive and virtuous and utterly boring. As for the beauty, she might be amusing for a week or two, but Lord protect me from tedious parents and their shabby genteel morality."

With an impudent wave, he sauntered away. Seth exhaled a long breath. He wondered for what seemed like the millionth time how the Duke of Derwent and his lovely, loving duchess could have produced the disaster that was Bel. Self-centered, venal, and with a cruel streak the size of Hadrian's Wall, he took delight in causing pain to others. In Seth's case, this had taken the form of a constant denigration of Seth's status in the household. Almost since Bel had been old enough to talk, he had pointed out at every opportunity to any who would listen that Seth was low-born, and not really the son of a peer. He had implied on many occasions that Seth was a bastard. Seth, a few years older, several sizes larger and many decades wiser, had refrained from putting a stop to these calumnies until the day at Eton Seth realized that his younger foster brother had at last grown to match him in height. After Bel had been ducked repeatedly and with great thoroughness in the River Isis, the lies had stopped, but the sly digs and innuendos continued to the present.

And would probably do so until the day one or the other of them died.

Seth sighed and set a course for Zoë Beckett.

Eden Beckett absently noted the approach of the conservatively garbed gentleman, his gaze on Zoë. Eden's mouth curved in a tolerant smile. Lord, how many times had she found herself in this situation? No matter how often she tried to cry off from these interminable social functions, she inevitably found herself acting as backdrop for her beautiful little sister. She did not begrudge Zoë her charm and the skilled flirtatiousness that came as naturally as her breath. However, she was heartily bored with the stultifying conversations to be endured during these occasions, to say nothing of the artificial pleasantries exchanged with persons about whom one neither knew or cared. Hmm, she was unacquainted with this gentleman. Which was odd, she thought, for, at Zoë's side, she must have met every single male in London by now, and somehow, she believed that she would have remembered this tall, angular stranger. Among the jeweled fribbles that crowded the ballroom, he stood out like a raven among peacocks. He wore no fobs and did not carry a quizzing glass. His raiment was superbly tailored, but modest, and his only adornment was a sapphire pin nestled in the folds of his cravat. He could not be called handsome—precisely—for his features were craggy and somewhat irregular. Yet, he moved with an easy, animal grace, and his eyes were dark and commanding.

Perhaps, mused Eden, he was not an habitue of the social scene—or, for that matter, perhaps he was married. In any event—

Her reverie was interrupted by the sudden apparition of young Toddy Danton at Zoë's side.

"Miss Zoë!" he almost gasped in his eagerness. "Would you honor me with your hand for the next dance?"

Toddy was by no means the most eligible of the young men who consistently besieged the fortress that was Miss Zoë Beckett, but he was witty and charming, and his approval was considered essential for any young miss desirous of making a splash in the social swim. With a flutter of her lashes and an engaging giggle, Zoë swept off on his arm, leaving Eden in uncomfortable isolation.

Though the unknown gentleman was almost upon her by now, she fully expected him to reverse course and leave her to her own devices. However, his dark gaze now on her, he continued on his path. She glanced about in search of some lady with whom she might strike up a conversation, but the stranger did not waver in his progress toward her.

Concealing his exasperation, Seth bent over the hand of the young woman left standing by herself. Rather rude of young Zoë, he thought, to leave her sister in the lurch while she loped off to enjoy the dance. Not that he was surprised. His short acquaintance with the younger Miss Beckett had not led him to the expectation that she would let good manners stand in the way of her own pleasure.

Miss Beckett lifted her gaze to his, and Seth was momentarily startled at the sensation of what he could only call recognition that swept over him. To his knowledge, he had never met this woman, yet it almost seemed as though he greeted an old friend, one not encountered for a long time, but still warmly regarded.

What nonsense. He cleared his throat. "I hope you will forgive my ill manners in approaching you before we have been formally introduced. I am Seth Lindow, and I am known to your sister—and your parents. I wonder if I might beg your hand for this dance."

To his astonishment, Miss Beckett's response was a negative shake of her head that set the ribbons on her lace cap to quivering.

"Really, Mr. Lindow, I am, of course, pleased to make your acquaintance, but this is not necessary. I'm sure Zoë will return momentarily, and she will be delighted to dance with you."

As though reading Seth's disapprobation in his eyes, her own widened and she added hastily, "That is, I do not dance."

She turned away as though to escape, but, nettled, Seth grasped her wrist.

"You would leave me standing alone like Horatio at the bridge?" *As your sister did you*, he added mentally. "Come, this is only a country dance. I am not suggesting we perform the *pas de deux* from *Medée*."

Without waiting for an answer, he swept her out onto the dance floor. The movements of the dance prevented further conversation, which was just as well, Seth noted in some amusement. A most becoming flush had risen to Miss Beckett's cheeks, and her eyes fairly sparked with indignation. He could imagine the set-down that trembled on her lips.

"You spoke an untruth," Seth said calmly at their first opportunity for speech. "You dance remarkably well."

Well, of course she did, reflected Eden. She'd had lessons from an accredited master who had said the same thing. Mr. Lindow was merely chiding her for her earlier rudeness. As well he might, she conceded ruefully. Even as she had spoken her rejection, she almost gasped at her own temerity. How could she, the consummate country mouse actually have refused to stand up with a gentleman of the *ton*? She quailed a little before his disdainful stare. How odd. She had never met this man. Why, then, did she feel she already knew him? To say nothing of the effect his dark gaze produced deep inside her.

However, she said merely, "Thank you, sir," before taking refuge once again in the figures of the dance. When the last strains of the music died away, she kept her gaze downcast as Mr. Lindow returned her to where Zoë posed prettily, talking to their father.

Poor Papa, thought Eden. He had been pleased at their invitation to Lady Saltram's ball, but he was not comfortable at such functions. He stood now, looking hot and harassed as Zoë spoke to him, obviously trying to wheedle him into something.

Upon being introduced to Mr. Lindow, Zoë's expression grew blank, but she was perfectly willing to agree that they had probably met before. Eden stood back to let Zoë take charge, which she did, of course, with her usual ease and confidence. After one sweeping glance over Mr. Lindow's person, she bestowed on him the brilliant smile she bent on any male—followed almost immediately by an expression of courteous disinterest.

"Mr. Lindow," she murmured, whereupon she transferred her attention to a young gentleman standing by. Lord Willipott, if Eden was not mistaken. Mr. Lindow turned to her father, whose greeting was only marginally more cordial.

"Lindow? Yes, we met at some confounded soiree or other, didn't we?"

"Yes, sir," replied Mr. Lindow courteously. "We discussed your string of Thoroughbreds. I believe it was Sir Robert Oakaton who was telling me just the other day that your stud is the finest this side of Ireland."

Not unnaturally, these sentiments caused her father to beam expansively. She glanced at Mr. Lindow, only to intercept his gaze as it slid from her father, back to Zoë. She found it oddly compelling—and unsettling.

Smiling slightly, Mr. Lindow begged Zoë's hand for the next dance. As they moved away, Eden thought she caught a speculative glint in the gaze he bent on her little sister.

Eden frowned.

Chapter Two

The air on a March morning a few weeks later was chill, as though winter protested its slackening grip on the countryside. But as the sun climbed higher in the sparkling Surrey sky, it was evident that spring was ready to take the upper hand. A certain softness blessed the breeze that flirted with tentative, new-green leaves and sighed over budding orchards. Birds chirped ecstatically as though affirming the advent of the season.

The beauty of the day was lost on Seth as he made his way along the Portsmouth Road in a light traveling coach. Sprawled on the forward-facing seat of the vehicle, frowning in abstraction, he was oblivious to nature's beguilements and the splendor of the Surrey landscape. Across from him, Jason Moppe sat rigid and prim.

Seth had procured an invitation to Lord Beckett's estate with laughable ease. Once he had conveyed the information that he was representing the Duke of Derwent in his search for additions to his stables, the man was all beaming joviality. He fairly begged Seth to visit. "Do come along any time, sir. Stay as long as you please. We can promise you some fine fishing." Seth grimaced distastefully, and looking up, noted Jason Moppe's grin.

"It's been a long trip, Moppe," he responded, shifting his shoulders under a modish coat of superfine. "I'll be glad when we reach—what the devil is the name of the place?—Clearsprings. Although, glad is not precisely the *mot juste*. Relieved, perhaps."

"Well," countered Moppe, his eyes, black and bright as shoe buttons, snapping mischievously. "Y'could have traveled a bit more plumpish. His Grace wouldn't object if ye—"

"Yes, I know. We could have arrived in a style more appropriate to His Grace's man of affairs."

"Or, ye might say, to his son," admonished Moppe severely.

"Adopted son. In any case, it's not *my* style, Moppe."

"Hmph. Half the Polite World don't even know you're something more than his man of affairs. Y'never show up at any of the nobs's parties or flirt with the pretty little maids on the marriage mart."

"And that's how I prefer it. I have never endeavored to hide the fact of my adoption, but I have no wish to bray out my connection with His Grace. The fact that I'm known to handle his affairs gives me all the clout I need in dealing with his associates. As for the, er, maids, I am a commoner, Moppe. I could never aspire to the hand of a lady." He smiled sardonically. "Would you have me horsewhipped at the cart tail?"

Moppe grunted. "Y'got plenty o'blunt o'yer own. It's been my observation that most of them fine leddies would be happy t'overlook you not bein' a duke nor a earl, fer the jingle in yer pockets."

"Moppe," declared Seth sternly, "we will not speak of this further. I am content with what I am, and that's all there is to it."

Moppe sighed. Indeed, Mr. Seth was not the top lofty sort to enjoy swanning about the countryside in a plush carriage with a crest emblazoned on the side. Which, to Moppe's mind, was a blinkin' shame. If a bloke was lucky enough to be took up by a duke when he was a nipper, din't it behoove that bloke to take advantage of the situation? Partic'larly when the duke had used Mr. Seth all his life like a faithful hound—of little account, but handy to have around when needed.

"Is this Beckett female the mort yer tryin' t'bring to harness for 'is lordship?"

Seth grunted in irritation. "I told you, I'm—" He halted and flung up a hand in defeat. He could rely on Moppe for discretion, and a confederate with access to servants' gossip would probably prove helpful. Damn, he hated this smarmy subterfuge. He wasn't cut out for such Byzantine negotiations.

"Yes," he admitted shortly.

Ah, well, he reflected, with any luck this girl would suit his purpose. He'd settle the matter with her father and be off within a few days, returning to his snug suite of chambers in Derwent House, the jewel of Grosvenor Square.

He swayed as the carriage turned from the main highway onto a secondary road. In a few minutes, the vehicle changed direction again, this time to pass between a pair of slender pillars. Moppe glanced briefly out of the window.

"Ump," he grunted. "Looks like we're 'ere."

Seth followed his gaze to observe a pleasant Georgian building, crafted of local stone that glowed pleasantly in the late morning sun. As he looked, the front door opened and a stout figure in breeches and boots emerged. The man descended the steps and waved vigorously at the approaching carriage.

"Ah," murmured Seth, "a welcoming committee."

He surveyed his host assessingly. Lord Beckett was not a tall man, but he made up for his lack of height in an impressive breadth. Thinning brown hair liberally sprinkled with gray sprouted in wisps above a florid face in which two small eyes fairly glittered in anticipation.

Moppe snorted. "Ain't surprised, are you? How often d'you suppose somebody like the Duke o' Derwent's son shows up on that feller's front steps? Or no," he added after a disgusted glance at Seth, "I suppose you din't mention that fact, didjer? Well then, the duke's personal represent'tive."

"Good God, Moppe, I'm only here to buy some horses—at least as far as Lord Beckett is concerned. I hardly think that's enough to send him into alt."

"My eye and Betty Martin! You c'n tickle me with a barge pole if he don't plan t'show you off to the neighbors like a prize pig and winkle an invitation t'Derwent House for the next time he's in Lunnon, besides."

Unknown to Seth and his henchman, the same sentiments were being uttered—in slightly more genteel terms—in an upstairs chamber.

Eden stood at the window, observing the carriage as it swung up with a flourish before the front door. She watched her father's burly form as he hastened down the steps, almost tumbling headlong in his eagerness.

She curled her lip. Lord, one would think Mr. Lindow had come to Clearsprings with the express intent of placing all the Duke of Derwent's wealth and power at her father's feet. Although . . . She examined the thought that had been nibbling in the back of her mind since Papa had announced the imminent visit of Mr. Seth Lindow, ostensibly to look over a string of horses Papa hoped to sell to the duke. Why had it fallen to such an exalted personage as the duke's man of affairs to see about the purchase of horses? Was this not the sort of thing to be handled by His Grace's steward? Or even his head groom? She recalled the expression of assessment she had caught in Mr. Lindow's gaze the night of Lady Saltram's ball.

On the other hand, she certainly could not think of an ulterior motive for Mr. Lindow's visit. The idea that the duke wished to curry favor with an obscure country lord, or to beg an indulgence from him was too ludicrous to be considered.

Eden shrugged. Perhaps Mr. Lindow had other business in the neighborhood and had deigned to perform this small task for his master—or no, wait a moment. Had she not heard some time ago that Seth Lindow was the duke's adopted son? If this was the case, it made his visit here more mystifying. In any event—

"Is he here?"

The lazy voice spoke from behind her. Zoë had ambled into the room, and as she had done so often in the past, Eden marveled at the cosmic accident that had dropped two such dissimilar offspring into the same family. Eden knew herself to be tall and thin and plain, her hair a nondescript brown, her eyes a very ordinary shade of gray. It was no wonder she had remained unmarried at the advanced age of six and twenty. On the other hand, Zoë was a certified beauty. A petite blonde, her hair curled naturally in appealing ringlets, set off by eyes the color of a fathomless sea. Her features were dainty and flawless, and her complexion encouraged comparisons to cream and rose petals.

"Is he here?" repeated Zoë. "Ah." She answered her own question as she moved to the window to stand by her sister. "That must be he. I cannot think who else Papa would be making such a cake of himself over."

"Zoë," murmured Eden in gentle remonstrance.

"Well, just look at him, almost licking the man's boots." She flung out her hands. "And I don't understand why. Mr. Linden, or whatever his name is, is merely a hired servant, isn't he? I mean, he sounds like little more than a glorified secretary, even if he does work for a duke. And why Papa insisted we all had to be on hand to greet him—"

Obviously, Zoë was unaware of Mr. Lindow's more personal relationship with the duke. Eden saw no reason to enlighten her.

"Mmp," continued her sister. "I vaguely remember meeting

him, but I . . . oh, my . . ." She craned to obtain a closer look.
"I'd forgotten. He's not bad looking, is he? In an odd sort of
way."

Zoë hastened to a mirror to run a practiced hand over the
golden perfection of her curls.

"He seems relatively well set up," agreed Eden placidly.

Zoë grinned saucily. "Are you saying that in order for me to
find a man unattractive he would have to possess a second head
or an extra foot?"

Eden returned the grin. "Of course not. He'd have to be fat
and bald—and as poor as an apple seller, besides. Come along,
then. We might as well get this over with. Papa will probably
whisk him out to the stables after a decent interval, and we can
get on with our day."

Grasping Zoë's arm, she propelled the younger girl into the
corridor and down the sweep of stairs that led to the manor's
Hall. The two arrived as the newcomer was being ceremoni-
ously ushered inside the house by Horsley, their butler, with the
assistance of Lord Beckett.

Another man, presumably Mr. Lindow's valet, entered as
well and was turned over to a footman for delivery, along with
Mr. Lindow's portmanteau, to the chambers that had been set
aside for them.

"Ah!" cried Lord Beckett to the sisters, rubbing his hands together briskly. "Just in time to greet our visitor. Mr. Lindow,
you've already met my daughters, Miss Beckett and Miss Zoë
Beckett." He chuckled obsequiously as the ladies curtseyed and
Mr. Lindow removed his hat with a bow. Lord Beckett beamed.
"My two girls were constant gadabouts the whole time we were
in London."

As he spoke, Lord Beckett drew the group into the drawing
room, which led from the salon. Awaiting them there, seated in
a wing chair of yellow-striped satin, was a lady of some forty-
five summers. Her graying hair was curled in a style perhaps
more suited to a younger woman, but the cap that rested on
them was propriety itself, as was her gown of pomona silk.

"And here is Lady Beckett."

"So very pleased to make your acquaintance, sir." Extending
a plump hand, Lady Beckett spoke in a high, breathless voice.
"Do sit here by the fire. I declare, when I arose today and saw
the sun fairly bursting through the curtains, I thought we would

have a warm day, but no, there's still a bite to the air. I said to
Beckett, 'You mark my words, dearest, we'll be needing a fire
in the hearth for many a day to come.' Such a trial, when we've
all been longing to pack up our winter things into a trunk and
deck ourselves in our new spring finery. Eden, do ring for tea.
Or perhaps you would prefer a glass of wine, Mr. Lindow?"

Her hands fluttered like startled birds as her husband moved
to a nearby decanter.

Eden fancied she could see an expression of contempt on Mr.
Lindow's face, and her cheeks grew hot as she moved to the
bellpull. Poor Mama had a tendency to rattle when she was ner-
vous, and this morning her tongue was running on wheels.
Even so, Eden reflected angrily, it was not for the likes of Mr.
Seth Lindow to pass judgment. She shot him a darkling look.

Seth intercepted the glance with some puzzlement. Lord, the
rest of the family had fallen on his neck. What in God's name
had he done to earn the disfavor of this unprepossessing female?

"I recall the dance we shared at Lady Saltram's ball, Miss
Beckett." He noted the look of surprise that flashed in her face.
He seemed oddly attuned to the mood reflected in her misty
eyes. She had not expected to be remembered, then? He turned
to the younger girl. "As well as Miss Zoë, of course."

Eden was indeed astonished. She had been sure the gentleman would have no recollection of her. Certainly, they had exchanged little more than a few words. To be sure, he had
dutifully solicited her hand for a country dance, and she had
been aware of that peculiar sense of connection with him, but
his mind had obviously been concerned with matters of more
import.

She smiled inwardly. Give Mr. Lindow marks for thinking on
his feet. No doubt, he was merely making the assumption that if
pretty Miss Zoë had come to his notice, the elder Miss Beckett
must have been lurking in the background—ranged among the
matrons and the potted plants.

Conversation languished then, or at least it would have, if not
for the stream of inconsequential chatter flowing from Lady
Beckett's lips like water rippling over brook stones. Eden knew
a stab of gratitude for her mother's voluble, if scattered discourse.

She eyed Mr. Lindow surreptitiously, noting again the self-possession in his gaze. There was something else, as well. To her, it seemed as though she beheld a dangerous man. His eyes were not simply compelling, they were, she felt, distinctly predatory. She wondered again, this time with a flutter of panic, what was he doing at Clearsprings?

She chastised herself for her foolishness. Was she a fearful rabbit, then, cowering beneath the shadow of a swallow, mistaking it for a hawk?

At length, Lord Beckett rose and tossed back the last of his wine.

"Well, sir, I'm sure the ladies will forgive us if we repair to the stables. I know you did not come all this way to fritter away the hours as they do in idle chatter."

If the ladies took umbrage at this categorization of their daily routine, they made no sign. Instead, Lady Beckett said brightly, "Of course, dearest. Mr. Lindow will think our wits have gone begging. Do go along and take care of your business, and we will meet again at luncheon."

With this, she rose as well, brushing muffin crumbs from her skirt. Placing a hand under his guest's elbow, Lord Beckett moved him purposefully toward the door, and the last words Seth heard as they strode down a corridor toward the rear of the house was Lady Beckett's breathless voice.

"Eden, that puts me in mind . . . I wish you will tell Cook that if she's going to serve her special trifle for dessert, she must make plenty of it this time. Last week when the vicar was here . . ."

Seth breathed deeply when they reached the outside. *Phew!* What a feather-wit! For that matter, what a family. The *paterfamilias*, grasping and ambitious, the lady of the house with more hair than wit, a gray eyed spinster daughter who obviously had taken a dislike to him on sight, and a flirtatious beauty who might or might not be the solution to his problem. Zoë had spoken little this morning, but so far he had no reason to revise the impression he had gained at their meetings in London. Here was a young lady aware of her marketability, who would have no qualms about using her charms to advantage.

Lord Beckett would not likely put a spoke in his plans. He had married off three daughters and no doubt had given up on sending off the oldest. Surely, he would be nothing less than ecstatic to be presented with an eminently eligible *parti* for his

youngest—if he could be persuaded to overlook the prospective
groom's shortcomings. It seemed like a nasty trick to play on
the girl, but, as he had observed before, there were many
women who would put up with almost anything, including a
husband who was a degenerate rake, for security and social position.

"Yessir, my little Zoë's a real beauty, ain't she?"

Seth started. Good Lord, had the man been reading his mind?
Lord Beckett's bray of laughter sounded loud in the sunny
kitchen garden.

"Couldn't help notice you noticing her, young feller. You
may be the duke's man—but you ain't no different from the
young sprigs hereabouts. Yessir, I've turned down many an
offer for that hand—some of 'em very tempting. She had a
London Season, y'know. Every one of my girls did," he added
with obvious pride. "Every one of 'em took, too—except for
Eden, o'course. Zoë could have had her pick of the dandies and
the bucks on the strut."

Seth suppressed his distaste at the man's vulgar revelations.
After all, he had not expected to enjoy becoming acquainted
with the girl and her family.

"And yet, she did not marry?" he probed.

"Ump," replied Lord Beckett. "The gel knows her own
worth. Said none of 'em was good enough—even Lord Speck-
rill's boy. And to my mind she's right. I can't say as I blame her
for setting her sights on the moon, but without vouchers for Almack's . . ." He frowned. "Not that she didn't try—and her
mama, too, but none o'them highborn ladies would give my little girl the time of day, just as though she wa'n't the daughter of
a lord." He turned a speculative gaze on Seth. "What she needs
is a sponsor, Mr. Lindow."

Seth almost gasped aloud at the man's blatant merchandising
of his daughter's charms. In the next moment, he nearly
laughed. Did Lord Beckett look on him as his daughter's entrée
into Almack's?

"I'm sure she will find one eventually," he said.

Lord Beckett looked somewhat chastened, but his demeanor
brightened as he flung open the gate to the paddock, where several horses could be seen, exercising under the care of their
grooms. Seth listened absently as his host enumerated the many
and varied points of these animals. To be sure, he was no expert

on horses. He fully intended to buy Lord Beckett's string, but could only hope he wouldn't be inflicting a pack of bone-setters on the duke.

"You see that filly? She's out of Rainbow—over there—by Gosweetly. A smart man would snap her up, as the line is pure and strong."

Seth smiled. It was another sort of filly altogether that engaged his interest. He would stretch out his visit to . . . oh, possibly a week. That should be sufficient time to assess Miss Zoë's suitability to reign as the next Duchess of Derwent.

"I can see," he said smoothly, his hand on Lord Beckett's shoulder, "that I shall have to make a careful examination of all your cattle, so that I won't miss any prime 'uns."

Chapter Three

Lord Beckett gleefully took Seth at his word, and the rest of the afternoon was taken up with an exhaustive exploration of his lordship's estate.

"Too bad it still gets dark so early," said his lordship as they turned their horses toward the house. "Tomorrow, perhaps we'll visit the tenant cottages. I've some work going on there that needs seeing to."

"I look forward to it," murmured Seth, his mind on the evening ahead, to be spent in furthering his acquaintance with Miss Zoë.

At the manor house, Eden's anticipation was less than enthusiastic. It was with some relief she had stood at her mother's side to see her father and Mr. Lindow off on their expedition. Zoë had not waited for their departure before hurrying off to her own pursuits.

What was Mr. Lindow's interest in her little sister? wondered Eden as she busied herself with her own daily routine. She had watched with increasing concern the speculative glances that he had cast in Zoë's direction that morning. Could he possibly be in the market for a wife?

She wished now that while she was in London she had paid more attention to the gossip that drifted through the great houses like an unending strand of beads, bright and inconsequential, binding the upper strata of society together with a thread of iron. Her father had said Mr. Lindow served as the duke's man of affairs, and as such—overseeing His Grace's social, financial, and personal interests—wielded a great deal of power. She had heard nothing of his search for a bride.

The only other member of the duke's family of whom Eden had heard was the duke's heir, the notorious Charles, Marquess of Belhaven. Even a mention of the man's name caused a shiver of horror to flutter in the bosoms of the gently bred ladies of the *ton*. The marquess was not just a profligate and a womanizer; he was known to indulge in the most depraved pursuits. He was unable to keep his servants because of the savage beatings he inflicted on them when in a temper—which was most of the time. Not that the gentleman could not be charming. He was eminently personable, and his success with women of every social station was legendary. When he first appeared on the marriage mart, he had been welcomed with open arms by mothers of eligible damsels. Every ball and soiree and musicale that took place in Mayfair was graced by his presence. Unfortunately, he soon revealed himself to be faithless in his loving, and false in his promises. When the lovely young daughter of the Earl of Bainbridge put an end to her life, it was rumored that Lord Belhaven had proposed marriage, seduced her before the settlements were signed, and then transferred his fickle affections to another.

When the girl's brother had called him out, he killed the young man at dawn in Hyde Park.

Such was the influence of the Duke of Derwent, however, that, though Bel, as he was called, was forced to leave the country for a short period, no charges were brought against him. Had the indispensable Mr. Lindow handled that matter? wondered Eden distastefully.

The ladies of the house lunched alone, and, not surprisingly, the conversation revolved around their guest.

"I have heard little of Mr. Lindow," said Lady Beckett thoughtfully, "for he is not often spoken of. It seems to me, however, that I heard that he is not just the duke's man of affairs, but his adoptive son, as well. Something about owing Mr. Lindow's father a favor."

"Really?" gasped Zoë, wide-eyed. "The duke's foster son? Well," she added speculatively, "that certainly makes a difference. That means he's the Marquess of Belhaven's brother."

Lady Beckett started visibly. "The Marquess of Belhaven?" she exclaimed. "Where did you hear that name?"

"Why, I expect everyone has heard of him," said Zoë with a giggle. "He's the most notorious rake in London, isn't he?"

"Yes, he certainly is," responded Lady Beckett repressively, "although his name is hardly mentioned these days in polite company."

"My!" Zoë's eyes glistened. "What's he done?"

Lady Beckett pursed her lips, but Edèn replied prosaically, "If rumor is to be believed, he seems to have gone down the list of deadly sins and committed each of them with a great deal of care and thoroughness."

"My," breathed Zoë, obviously much impressed.

"But, I'm sure," added Eden, "that half of what's been said about him isn't true. Well, I don't see how it could be. A man can only fit so much debauchery into his schedule."

"Eden!" remonstrated Lady Beckett. She turned to Zoë. "Suffice it to say, young lady, that the Marquess of Belhaven is not a fit subject for discussion in a decent home."

"Yes, Mama," said Zoë with a demure smile, bending her attention to her salad. A moment later, she lifted her head. "But wait. Sally Brevers mentioned him just last week. Something about his setting fire to Lord Church's stable."

Despite herself, Eden gasped. "Set fire to a stable? Why would he do that?"

Lady Beckett shifted in her chair. "Never mind."

Zoë, who knew her mother well, merely giggled again. "Of course, Mama. I suppose you would not be in the way of knowing of the affairs of such an exalted personage as the Marquess of Belhaven. I'll ask Sally. Perhaps her mother has heard something."

Lady Beckett stiffened. "None of your sauce, young woman. As it happens, I heard of the incident at the Tellisand's soiree, just before we returned home. Lady Winterhaven told me. And she, as all the world knows, is of the highest *ton*. I should not be repeating such a tale, particularly in front of you two, but—" She laughed self-consciously. "It seems the marquess had brought one of the earl's housemaids out there for a . . . well, an assignation. He'd been drinking heavily and somehow managed to kick over a lantern. As you can imagine, the whole place went up like a tinderbox, but the marquess was too dr—indisposed to get himself and the maid to safety."

"Lady Winterhaven told you all this, Mama?" asked Eden curiously.

"Indeed, she did. Apparently, the maid screeched her head off after she was rescued. The whole neighborhood was privy to the scene."

"Rescued?" Zoë dropped her fork into her salad, now forgotten. "Who rescued her? Did the marquess get out, too? Never tell me he perished!"

"No, of course not. A passerby happened to notice the smoke, or perhaps the flames. At any rate, he dashed into the stables and pulled the two to safety."

"An intrepid passerby," murmured Eden.

"Yes, indeed," agreed her mother breathlessly. "At any rate, no respectable female will give him the time of day."

"Well!" declared Zoë with an impish smile. "He sounds perfectly fascinating."

"Zoë!" exclaimed her mother, an almost ludicrous expression of horror on her face.

"Mmm," interposed Eden. "He sounds a dead bore to me. I encountered his like a few times in London, and they were invariably set up in their own estimations and could speak of nothing but their own scandalous exploits, which were generally highly varnished."

"I suppose," said Zoë casually, apparently dismissing the subject. However, Eden detected an ominous gleam in the girl's cerulean eyes.

Eden changed the subject with a deftness born of long practice, but an explanation of Mr. Lindow's interest in Zoë had entered her mind. Papa seemed to think that Mr. Lindow might be on the hunt for a bride. Certainly someone in Zoë's position might be considered the proper pride for an untitled gentleman of unimpeachable connections but limited means. However, it occurred to Eden that the gentleman's interest in her sister was appraising rather than amorous. Still, Mr. Seth Lindow had put in an unwonted appearance at Lady Saltram's ball.

Goodness, might he have formed a *tendre* for Zoë? It did not occur to Eden that she, too, was gently bred and that Mr. Lindow might be looking at both Beckett sisters in his discreet quest for a bride. Eden had long since abandoned any idea of marriage for herself. Indeed, though she was not opposed to the institution, and she had received one or two offers in her salad days, her heart had never been touched. She did not regret her single state. On the other hand, men were invariably attracted to Zoë, and it had been to Zoë that Mr. Lindow's attention had gravitated as naturally as a needle turning to a magnet.

Whether Zoë would see the austere Mr. Lindow as a possible mate was another matter. Pretty, flighty Zoë dreamed foolish dreams of capturing the heart of a nobleman, whereupon she would live a life of "happy ever after" in beautiful gowns and expensive jewels with all of London at her feet. Mr. Lindow could not know that Zoë lusted to be called "my lady," or even "Your Grace," and was unlikely to be satisfied with life as a mere "Mrs." To be fair, it must be said that, beneath the frivolous exterior, Zoë held some unexpectedly old-fashioned notions about loving and cherishing, and "till death do us part."

Ah, well, Eden concluded briskly, perhaps the gentleman had come to Clearsprings for the reasons he had stated. He wanted to buy some horses.

The rest of the luncheon passed with no further reference to the Lindow family, and after the ladies had risen from the table, Eden hurried to her chambers to collect a rather ungainly satchel. This she took from the house and set out on horseback for one of her favorite spots on her father's estate. It lay in a forested area just beyond the immediate environs of the house near the curve of a small brook. Dismounting from her mare, Hyacinth, she turned to delve into the satchel, from which she brought out a paint box and a small canvas. Reaching for the small easel strapped to her saddle, as well as a folding stool, she made herself comfortable. She had chosen as her subject a young, bare-branched tree that stood alone in sharp contrast to the new green of the budding trees behind it. As she arranged paint bladders and palette knives, Eden felt a surge of excitement. Would Mr. Rellihan approve of this work? She recalled the interview with the small, excitable gallery owner, not six weeks ago, in London.

"Sure, Miss Beckett, I like what I see, but . . . well, t'be honest, it's not what is selling now. Your paintings are too . . . too bold, particularly for a lady. Folks want their flowers to look like flowers, not like splashes of fire and lightning leaping out of the forest."

Eden had barely managed to conceal her disappointment at his words. She had been irresistibly pulled toward art since, as a four-year-old, she had been scolded for scribbling pictures in the back of her copy books. Consideration of any talent she might possess had not entered into her passion. She knew only that sketching and painting were as necessary to her as the air she breathed.

"I can't *not* make pictures," she explained to her family when they ridiculed her hobby horse. She had hoped that her paintings might prove salable, thus providing her with a possible independence from her family. The thought of dwindling into spinsterhood, at the beck and call of her relatives in times of petty crisis, she found depressing in the extreme. She hoped to put by some money unknown to her father—money that would allow her to live her own life in dignity.

At least Mr. Rellihan had encouraged her to continue her painting, and said he would examine them again the next time she was in town.

Unmindful of the passing hours, Eden worked steadily. It was only when the slanting rays of the afternoon sun began to lose their warmth that she returned to her surroundings. With an exclamation, she restored brushes and palette to the satchel and mounted Hyacinth.

Lord Beckett and Seth, returning from their own excursion, intercepted Eden as she left the stable. Lord Beckett waved absently. Seth noted with interest the paint-stained satchel, but said nothing. By the time the two men had been relieved of their mounts by stablemen and had taken a restorative glass of good Irish whiskey from the desk in Lord Beckett's office next to the tack room, Eden was nowhere to be seen.

Pleading the need to remove the dirt of the day's explorations from his person, Seth hurried to his chambers, where he found Moppe awaiting him.

"So, how was yer day?" queried the servant as he assisted his master our of his top boots.

"Actually, I quite enjoyed myself," replied Seth in some surprise. "Lord Beckett is something of a bore—I don't think he ever entertains a thought beyond the state of his crops—but he has a beautiful place. It made me long for Highacres."

"You ain't thinkin' of goin' up there, are you?" Moppe asked in an ominous tone.

"No, you hopeless city grubber, not in the immediate future, but once I get this business of Bel and his future settled, I may well retire to the country for an extended period. I could use some time in God's clean air and sunshine. In addition, I've left Highacres unattended for too long—and I miss it," he added in a low voice.

"You say that," returned Moppe, "but you've lived most of your life in the city. You dream of fresh air and sunshine and birds twitterin', but a few weeks o' talkin' to nobody but the cows and you'd be ready for Bedlam."

Seth laughed. "Perhaps. At any rate, I hope to get a chance to find out. I pray Miss Zoë turns out to be Bel's redemption."

Moppe snorted.

"Ain't a female alive who can redeem that makebait," he muttered, ducking his head before Seth's minatory stare. At the sound of a muted gong from belowstairs, he straightened hurriedly. "There now—it's time t'dress for dinner. And you needin' a reg'lar sluicin' down after your day jaunterin' about in God's clean manure."

An hour or so later, Seth strolled into the small salon where he had been told the family would await dinner. There he found Eden, alone, seated at a tambour frame near the fire. This evening she was garbed in a simple, rather shapeless gown of dark blue silk, adorned only by a small locket about her neck. She lifted her head at his entrance and flushed becomingly, though he could not ascertain whether she was unaccustomed to entertaining gentlemen without the protective bulwark of her family, or if she was still offended with him.

"Mama and Papa will be here shortly," she said quickly. "And Zoë as well. Won't you be seated, sir? M-may I offer you some wine?"

"Thank you, but I'll wait for your father," he replied, after which an awkward silence fell between them.

"Did you enjoy your outing with Papa?" Eden ventured at last.

"Indeed," replied Seth gratefully. "Clearsprings is beautifully situated, and must certainly be one of the most productive estates in the area."

"And the horses?"

"The—? Oh, yes, the horses. They, too, were most impressive. His Grace had expressed an interest in purchasing just two or three, but I'm sure he will be pleased to acquire all that Lord Beckett might be willing to sell."

Eden's laugh lit her gray eyes in a manner that touched her features with an undeniable beauty.

"I must warn you, sir, that my father is a shrewd dealer. I hope His Grace expects to pay a pretty penny for horses from the Clearsprings stud."

"What terrible things are you saying about your poor old

papa?" bellowed a jovial voice, and Eden and Seth turned to observe Lord Beckett entering the room. "Pretty penny, indeed. You must be aware I'm known far and wide for the fairness of my dealings."

"That's very true, my lord," agreed Seth, smiling. "Lord Sidmouth—it was he from whom I first heard of your excellent stock—told me that he was much impressed not only with the quality of your cattle, but the openhanded manner in which you do business."

"Quite right," said Lord Beckett promptly. "Of course," he added after a moment, "I always insist on fair payment for fair goods."

"Of course," murmured Seth gravely.

Lady Beckett entered the chamber then, with Zoë at her side. Seth's brows lifted. The young lady had obviously taken pains with her appearance tonight. Over a gown of pale pink sarcenet, she wore an overdress of a darker pink gauze embroidered with a leafy border of spring flowers. Entwined in her golden curls was a wreath of small, delicate roses.

From her place at her tambour frame, Eden observed Mr. Lindow closely. Most men, on beholding Zoë in her battle garb, went slack-jawed with admiration. But once again, in Mr. Lindow's penetrating gaze, Eden could only find that peculiar expression of assessment.

At that point, Horsely entered to inform the group that dinner was served. Eden thrust her needle into her embroidery and rose. Stifling a marked feeling of apprehension, she turned on their guest the most charming smile at her disposal and followed the group into the dining chamber.

Chapter Four

Conversation over an excellent dinner was convivial. Eden noted that Mr. Lindow said very little about himself, but with subtle direction kept the subject on the Beckett family in general and Zoë in particular.

"And did you enjoy your sojourn in London last year?" he asked, accepting another helping of buttered crab.

"Oh, yes!" Zoë cried. "It was everything I dreamed it would be. That is—" she amended quickly, her lashes drooping in a semblance of world-weary sophistication. "It was all a dead bore, of course, but I did enjoy the dancing, and I made some lovely friends."

"And when will you return to the Metropolis? Do you plan to take part in the Season this year?"

"Return to London?" interposed Lord Beckett with a chuckle. "Good gad, we just came home."

"But, dearest . . ." began Lady Beckett, her hands fluttering helplessly.

"Oh, Papa!" Zoë giggled shrilly. "We were in London for barely a fortnight, and you *know* how I am pining to return for another Season."

"I know the reason for that." Her father's small eyes narrowed indulgently. "You didn't find your highty-tighty lord last year, and you're hoping to snabble one this year."

"Papa!" cried Zoë in mortification. She cast a sidelong glance at Seth. "I am *not* on the hunt for a husband. In any event—" She tossed her curls. "You know very well I had several *notable* offers for my hand. As it happens, I merely wish to partake of some of the advantages of city life for a month or two—the museums and libraries—and . . . and . . ."

"The opera and the theater," finished Eden obligingly.

Zoë cast a glance of gratitude toward her sister. "Yes, precisely. And I would so love to celebrate my birthday there. I shall be one and twenty next month," she said to Seth with an arch smile.

"I dunno," mused Lord Beckett. "It may be too late now. Town was just beginning to fill up when we left. We'd never get lodgings now."

"Oh, but dearest," put in Lady Beckett, "my sister would put us up."

Zoë made a small moue. "Aunt Nassington? Oh, Mama, would we have to stay with her again? I don't want to live in poky old Portman Square. Could we not find a more fashionable address this time?"

Lord Beckett evidently thought it time to assert himself. "Now then, Puss. Your aunt's house will do well enough for the time being. She is away from Town at present, visiting her daughter in Hove, I believe it is. She'll be gone for a month or two, so we'll have the place to ourselves. Perhaps next year we will consider something a little more up to the mark."

This was all to the good, thought Seth approvingly. So far, Zoë had not displayed herself to advantage, but he still felt she might be an acceptable *parti* for Bel. In which case, he had planned to arrange the whole business with her father. On the other hand, it might be much better to get her to London, where Bel could actually meet her. He did not doubt that Bel would be attracted to Zoë. She was just the sort of beautiful, feather-brained young miss he found irresistible—and ripe for seduction. This time, however, Bel's big brother would be on hand to hold him to the straight and narrow. Not a finger would Bel lay on Zoë, except in the line of duty.

He turned his attention back to the discussion between Zoë and her father.

At this point, Eden intervened.

"Tell us a little of yourself, Mr. Lindow. Where in London do you reside?"

"Why, I make my lodgings at Derwent House in Grosvenor Square." Out of the corner of his eye, he observed Zoë's pink mouth form an O of surprise. "Since most of my time is spent on His Grace's affairs, I have never sought to remove myself to other lodgings."

"His Grace?" put in Zoë. "But isn't he your father?"

"Zoë!" Lady Beckett exclaimed in scandalized accents.

"Well, but how am I to know anything if I don't ask?" responded Zoë reasonably. She turned to Seth. "I heard that you are the duke's son."

Seth hesitated, startled. Lord, had the chit no sense of propriety? He said coldly, "Yes, Miss Zoë, I am the duke's son—his adoptive son, although I cannot conceive of what possible use this information might be to you."

Eden gasped, and even Zoë seemed taken aback, but she continued her impertinent interrogation. "But I do not believe I ever saw you before the night of Lady Saltram's ball. Do you usually attend such functions? Or go to the opera? Or to Almack's? I suppose you must be allowed there."

By God, this was the outside of enough! Seth opened his mouth to offer the young lady the set-down of her life, but was stayed by Eden's expression of mortification. "No," he said stiffly, "I am seldom out and about except in the commission of my duties."

He glanced up to catch Eden's wide gray gaze on him. The candlelight had turned her eyes to the color of fine old silver, and he thought he caught a glimpse of gratitude—and yes, interest—in their glowing depths. To his surprise, he heard himself continue, "I do not believe it would be seemly to trade on my connection with the duke."

Zoë merely stared blankly. "How long have you been with him?" she asked at last.

"His Grace took me in when I was nine years old." Seth realized with no little dismay that he was speaking solely to Eden now. "He was Lord Hugh Lindow then, a second son, serving in the army. My father—my birth father, whose name was George Winslow—served under him as a sergeant."

Though he must have been aware of the lifted brows this statement provoked, Mr. Lindow remained cool and self-possessed. If, reflected Eden, he felt any stigma in having been born into the lower orders, he had either come to terms with it or was accustomed to concealing his discomfort.

"It was at the siege of Toulon," continued Mr. Lindow, staring directly at Eden, "that my father lost his life saving that of Lord Hugh. When he sold out after being elevated to the title on the death of his older brother, the duke went to visit George Winslow's widow with the intention of providing for her for the rest of her life. When he arrived at Sergeant Winslow's home village, however, he discovered that the young woman had herself perished from smallpox not three months previous. He also discovered Winslow's nine-year-old son, myself, being sheltered by an uncle. I was, by the by, about to be sent to work in a nearby foundry." Mr. Lindow's dark gaze focused on a distant point, and his voice harshened. "I was terrified at the prospect, for I knew boys who had been sent there. Within weeks they were transformed from happy, laughing children to small old men, weary and sullen. The tales they told of abuse and careless cruelty made me shiver with fear."

Eden watched in unwilling sympathy as Mr. Lindow's fingers tightened around his fork. What must it have been like, she wondered, for the small boy, overwhelmed by the enormity of his double loss and obliged to face the vision of hell provided by the youngsters who served as industrial fodder. What must he have felt upon being summoned to meet the Duke of Derwent in all his titled glory. To her surprise, Mr. Lindow glanced at her, and as though reading her thoughts, smiled.

"The duke is a tall man," he said, "and it seemed as though I had to look up to the sky to meet his gaze. He stood in a shaft of sunlight. The jewels he wore in his cravat and on his fingers were set ablaze, and I thought I was in the presence of God.

"Before I knew what was happening, he whisked me up on his shoulder, and bade me call him 'Father.' Subsequently, he arranged for—" Mr. Lindow halted suddenly, and his eyes sought Eden's. "My father had been buried in foreign soil, and my mother had been put in a pauper's grave. This last was a matter that weighed heavily on my spirit. The duke saw to it that Mama was reinterred in a proper resting place with a fine headstone." Mr. Lindow stared off again for a moment before concluding briskly, "Not long after that, he took me from the house, never to return again, and brought me into his own home. I was raised as one of his own family."

"My," breathed Zoë, "it's almost like a fairy tale. You must be ever so grateful to the duke." She smiled pertly. "And did you live happily ever after, Mr. Lindow?"

Eden thought a strained expression flashed momentarily in his eyes, but Mr. Lindow smiled again, this time indulgently, as Lady Beckett made another futile attempt to quell her daughter. "Yes, I did, Miss Zoë, inasmuch as any of us can be said to reside in complete happiness. And, yes, of course, I owe the duke an enormous debt of gratitude. I . . ." He paused, then spoke slowly and reflectively, again to Eden. "I've tried to repay his . . . kindness . . . and that of his family, as well."

"What family?" It was Zoë again. "Do you mean the duke's wife? And his children? How many were there? Goodness, how did they take to the idea of a new child in the household? I'm not sure how I would have liked waking up one morning to be told that Mama and Papa had siphoned a strange little boy into the family. Although," she added thoughtfully, "I've always thought a brother would be nice."

"The duchess was everything that was kind. She took pity on the scrawny little waif who turned up in her drawing room one day and made room in her heart for one more child. I . . ." Once more he hesitated. "I owe the duke and duchess my life.

"As for the rest, I now had a brother and two sisters and they—" Seth paused and concluded austerely, "I was not of their world, and there were . . . contretemps from time to time, but we gradually worked out a living arrangement."

Again, Eden sensed something unspoken, an unpleasantness concealed. Remembering what she had heard of the Marquess of Belhaven, she wondered with what enthusiasm the duke's heir had subscribed to the "living arrangement." And, the duke himself, had he treated the boy with love or the distant forbearance shown a stray picked up on a whim and then forgotten?

"But the duchess," put in Lady Beckett tentatively. "Didn't I hear . . . ?"

"Yes, she passed away from the wasting sickness when I was sixteen. It was a sad time for all of us."

Seth drew in a deep, shaking breath. This was the first time in years he had revealed so much of his past to anyone, let alone a roomful of strangers. Again, he was struck by the notion that Eden Beckett already sensed too much about him, as though she had known him for a very long time.

Eden noted a tightening in Mr. Lindow's jaw muscle. He looked around suddenly and flushed, as though he had just committed a faux pas. He turned abruptly to Eden.

"Tell me, Miss Beckett—when Lord Beckett and I encountered you on our return to the house this afternoon, I noticed that you were carrying artists' paraphernalia. Do you paint?"

Now it was Eden's turn to redden. "Oh!" She gasped a little. "Yes . . . that is, I . . ."

She was interrupted by Zoë's giggle. "Some might call it painting. We, however, usually refer to her efforts as flinging paint at a canvas."

Lord Beckett's laugh brayed forth. "Yes, you could say our Eden paints with more enthusiasm than talent."

Lady Beckett's bracelets clinked in distress. "Now, dearest, I'm not sure that's true. Why, I could clearly recognize the work she showed us yesterday as a bouquet of, um, daffodils, I think they were."

Seth absorbed these comments in some astonishment, particularly as it became apparent that Miss Beckett seemed in no way discommoded by this rude disparagement of her efforts. Instead, her engaging smile once again lit her face, and Seth noted with some surprise that the elder Miss Beckett could put her younger sister in the shade were she to dress more becomingly and learn how to flirt, just a bit—and display that magical smile to the world more often.

"In answer to your question, sir, yes, I do enjoy painting—and sketching. As you can see, my genius is not universally acknowledged, but I find it relaxing."

It seemed to Seth that a certain hidden excitement flashed in her expressive eyes, but the next moment, it was gone.

"Do you—?" he began, but apparently Miss Beckett did not wish to continue the subject.

"Do you reside in London all year, then?" she asked, before he could form his question.

Seth stared into her gaze, determined not to reveal any more of himself. What the devil had possessed him to babble on about his relationship with the duke? He usually kept such information buttoned deep within himself, yet tonight he had spilled his most sensitive memories to her and her whole damned family. He was uncomfortably aware that it was the gaze of a gray-eyed witch that had prompted his unwonted monologue, and it was to her that he had been speaking. He had the uncomfortable feeling that she had gleaned much more from his ramblings than had the rest of her family. Much more, in fact, than he intended.

He drew a deep breath. "Yes—I make my home in London, for the most part. When His Grace leaves to spend the summer months at his seat in Wiltshire, I usually accompany him, and spend a few days at The Priory. However, since most of my work takes place in London, that is where I spend the bulk of my time."

"Then, I hope you will take advantage of your sojourn in the country," said Eden. "To be sure, this is a rather slow time. It is too early for fairs and festivals, and too late for sleigh rides and ice skating and other winter fun, but I believe the trout are running in our brooks, are they not, Papa?" She glanced toward her father.

"Aye." Lord Beckett nodded. "And if you would care to take a gun out, sir, I think we can promise you some bird shooting, as well—wood pigeons, perhaps, and a rabbit or two."

"It all sounds enticing," replied Seth, "but I shall not be here for much outside a week, so that—"

"Oh, no!" exclaimed Lady Beckett with a quaver. "I have planned two dinner parties and a musicale, and I have promised several people that I would bring you—that is, we have been invited to gatherings at neighbors' homes, to which I am sure you would like to accompany us."

Lord, thought Seth ruefully, the Becketts were indeed planning to show him off, as Moppe had predicted, like a prize pig. To his surprise, Miss Beckett spoke up at that point.

"Now, Mama, I'm sure our friends will survive without Mr. Lindow's presence at their dinner parties. We cannot expect him to leave His Grace's affairs dangling just to rusticate here."

Seth glanced at her gratefully and nodded his head in agreement. "No matter how pleasant the rustication," he added dutifully.

After dinner, following a mercifully brief session with the port decanter in Lord Beckett's company, Mr. Lindow was entertained musically by the Misses Beckett. Zoë sang in a light, sweet soprano, accompanied by her sister on the pianoforte, after which their positions were reversed. Eden's voice was neither so sweet nor so high as Zoë's, but her tone was true, and she sang one or two country songs with a simple sincerity that greatly enhanced at least one listener's enjoyment.

Afterward, Seth refused Lord Beckett's genial offer of a hand of piquet, pleading the rigors of a long journey and the afternoon's excursions. Embroidering on this theme, he yawned once or twice, and soon declared that it was time he took to his bed.

"Well!" exclaimed Zoë when he had departed. "I had no idea

Mr. Lindow was a gentleman of such importance. Fancy his being a duke's son—almost. It's too bad he is not the heir," she added, "for I think he was rather taken with me."

"Of course he was, dearest," said her fond mama. "And if you ask me, you could do worse. While he doesn't have a title and does not give the appearance of a wealthy man, it stands to reason, if he's made himself so useful to the duke, that he will come in for a tidy inheritance."

"Yes, but—" Zoë pouted.

"Yes, but you'd rather have the heir," finished her papa matter-of-factly. "Well, let me tell you, if you have any intention of sniffing after the marquess, you may as well put that notion in your bonnet and leave it there. The heir to the Duke of Derwent can look as high as he pleases for a bride—even in the royal stable."

"Dearest!" cried Lady Beckett, scandalized.

Lord Beckett shifted uncomfortably. "Well," he mumbled, "I believe in calling a spade a spade. In any event," he continued, his little eyes glittering shrewdly, "if I was you, Puss, I'd set my sights a little lower. An earl would do nicely, and if I'm not mistaken, the Breecham sprout is fair taken with you. Now, wouldn't that make the nobs sit up and take notice? Old Beckett's chick wed to an earl. And with a tidy settlement to go with it."

Eden gasped at the crudeness of her father's remarks, but Zoë merely giggled demurely. "I'll do my best, Papa."

At this, Eden rose to make her way to her bedchamber, reflecting that none of them had heard the last from Zoë on the subject of the Marquess of Belhaven. Zoë was rarely thwarted in her desires, and after meeting a gentleman so closely connected to a duke's heir, it was obvious that she meant to milk the association to the last drop.

Eden found herself ruminating at length on the mysterious Mr. Lindow. During the evening, she had again been struck by the notion that he posed some sort of threat to her well-being— or that of her family. Was it simply because he was so different from any man she had ever met before, with his harsh features and air of authority? Yet, she felt, inexplicably, that she knew him in a strange, impossible way. He had not looked at her often, but when he did, his gaze seemed to penetrate the center of her being. She was sure he was not in the habit of discussing his background or his relationship with the duke, as he had done tonight. All during his discourse, she had the oddest notion that he was speaking just to her.

She was being absurd, of course . . . and yet . . . To her mind, his horse-buying story was a patent fabrication. According to her father, Mr. Lindow was reasonably knowledgeable in equine breeding and knew one end of the animal from the other. However, even if he were an acknowledged expert in the field, it seemed beyond the realm of possibility that a man of his responsibilities would have dropped everything for a week's holiday in the country.

At least, she thought, as she blew out her bedside candle, he would be leaving Clearsprings soon. Once he departed for his home in Grosvenor Square, they would not be likely to see him again and their lives would resume their routine.

Climbing into bed, she resolutely turned her face against her pillow. A harsh, arrogant face seemed to float just under the canopy, however, and it was many moments before her eyes closed in sleep.

Chapter Five

Seth came down to breakfast the next morning to discover that he was to hold center stage at a dinner party planned by his hostess for four days hence.

"But, I do not know if I shall be here then," Seth protested.

"Oh, dear!" exclaimed Lady Beckett. "We have invited all our friends and neighbors."

"Do please stay," said Zoë with an inviting pout.

"O'course, you must stay," put in Lord Beckett. "I forgot to tell you yesterday, but in addition to the stock I showed you, we have some fine Cleveland Bays. You won't see any finer carriage horses in the country."

"Surely, a few days won't make any difference in your schedule." Zoë smiled coquettishly, as though beckoning him to an assignation in the bushes. Lord Beckett beamed jovially.

"Um," Seth replied. He glanced around and, in an effort to turn the subject, asked, "Where is Miss Beckett this morning?"

"Oh." Zoë sniffed. "She probably breakfasted hours ago and is no doubt riding. She always sets out at a frightful hour, while everything is still damp and nasty." She rose from her place to move toward Seth. She fluttered her incredible lashes and wound a golden curl about her finger. "Since my father showed you most of our estate yesterday, Mr. Lindow, would you allow me to give you a tour of the house this morning? After you have breakfasted, of course."

"Ah," replied Seth, perspiring profusely. Lord, he should welcome an occasion to become better acquainted with Zoë, but the minx apparently intended to make full use of him as a path to the upper altitudes of the *ton*. He was not at all sure her methods would not stretch to a full-blown seduction. He rather thought that placing himself in such isolated proximity to her, particularly since they would no doubt be in and out of every bedroom in the house, might prove hazardous in the extreme.

"Actually," he said swiftly, "I usually go for a good gallop myself before breakfast." This was perfectly true, of course, and he blessed the impulse that had caused him to don riding breeches and top boots this morning. "May we postpone the tour until, say, later this morning?"

"Oh." Zoë seemed rather nonplussed. She was no doubt unused to refusals by gentlemen invited to spend an hour or two in her company. "Y-yes, of course. Perhaps later, although by then I may be otherwise occupied." She flounced from the room with a swish of her skirts, followed by her mother, as usual, stirring the air with her hands.

Lord Beckett, still at his place at table, took a noisy gulp of coffee and with a genial nod to his guest, immersed himself in his copy of *The Birmingham Inspector*.

With some relief, Seth left the dining room and walked to the stables. There, the head groom personally saddled the bay gelding Seth had used for his outing the day before. Upon leaving the stable yard, Seth rode toward a forested area he had seen outlined against the horizon yesterday and within some minutes entered the little glade. It was quiet here, the only sound that of birds busy about their routine.

But no, someone was singing—a woman. Not one of the gentle songs she had sung last night, but a rollicking and not-altogether-proper sea chantey. As he moved farther into the woods, the sound stopped. Making his way toward the direction of the song, Seth soon came upon Miss Beckett. She was seated at a small easel upon which rested a square of canvas. In her hand, she held a palette, and her apron of coarse linen was liberally stained with the contents thereof.

She looked up at his approach and jumped to her feet.

"I thought I heard someone." She scrambled to collect her utensils.

"No, please," said Seth, "do not let me disturb you. I was just passing through."

He had intended to retreat gracefully and leave the embarrassed Miss Beckett to her efforts, but, his curiosity getting the better of him, he paused and urged his mount closer. The lady had evidently spoken the truth when she said she pursued her art with some seriousness. Did she have any talent? he wondered, or was her painting merely one of those avocations indulged in by spinsters to give some meaning to their lives?

Miss Beckett, evidently taking him at his word, turned back to her work. When he dismounted and moved toward her, she stiffened and placed a protective hand over the canvas.

"I don't mean to pry," said Seth reassuringly, though that was, he admitted to himself, precisely what he intended, "but I would very much like to see how you occupy yourself in your bower."

Miss Beckett, whom he had previously thought of as eminently self-possessed, blushed furiously and dropped a handful of brushes.

"Oh, no! I am the merest dauber. I'm sure you would not— That is, I do not like to show my work to others, and . . . I was just about to leave." With trembling fingers, she tucked brushes into cases and paints into containers. When she stood to remove the canvas from the easel, however, Seth stayed her hand by the simple expedient of placing his own over hers. He glanced down in surprise. Her fingers, warm and slender, were unusually strong.

He laughed softly. "Now, dear lady, I am not a critic from the Royal Academy. I did some painting myself in my misspent youth, and simply wish to see the work of a fellow dabbler."

So saying, he gently turned the canvas toward him. The next moment, he drew in a startled breath.

"You painted this?" he whispered. He caught himself immediately. "Well, I mean, of course you did, but . . . Miss Beckett, this is positively astonishing."

Reverently, he examined the canvas. The painting depicted a single branch of a young tree. It was gracefully delineated by a shaft of sunlight against the darker green behind it. He turned to Eden. "But you are possessed by a truly remarkable talent."

For a moment, Eden gaped at him, nonplussed. She blushed again, feeling absurdly pleased at his encomium. "Do you really like it?"

Seth examined the sensuous curve of the branch, the swollen buds about to burst into new life.

"One can almost feel the rebirth taking place," he breathed. He swung once again to Eden. "With whom did you study, Miss Beckett? Your use of cyan is somewhat reminiscent of Constable, but your style seems to me unique. The tree is bare and stark, yet so tender."

"Yes, that is the feeling I was trying to convey," she said eagerly. Very few people had seen her paintings, and even fewer seemed to grasp the moods she endeavored to create.

"I have never studied under anyone," she added. "Well, I had a drawing master, when I was young, of course, but he usually laughed at my efforts. Kindly, of course. I have studied the work of others, though, and I purchased several books over the years on the theory of art and painting, which I perused most earnestly."

"My expertise in the field of art is minimal," said Seth slowly, "but to me, your work is extraordinary." He turned to gaze at her, mystified. She was, as he had noted previously, an attractive woman, but in no way exceptional—except for those penetrating gray eyes. She was neat, unobtrusive, and altogether prosaic. Who would guess that beneath this unprepossessing exterior lay the soul of what he suspected was a true artist. "I wonder, might I see more of your work?"

He cursed himself immediately. It was Zoë Beckett on whom his attention should be focused. He did not wish to spend any longer at Clearsprings than necessary and had already avoided an opportunity to pursue his quarry. Was he now preparing to diverge farther from his path to investigate Zoë's older, completely nonessential sister?

Eden considered for a moment before she answered. At last, she said reluctantly, "Yes, I suppose so—if you wish. But, you have so little time. Are you not returning to London soon?"

"I planned to leave tomorrow morning, but it seems your mama has planned a dinner party, more or less in my honor, and—"

He stopped abruptly as Eden smiled. It was more of a grin, actually, and it lit her gray eyes like a warm fire on a winter evening. Seth swallowed suddenly.

"You must know, Mr. Lindow, that we do not often entertain dukes' sons, and when we do, we must make the most of it. Mama has all but posted signs on the front lawn."

"But, I'm not—"

"Your last name is Lindow, and that's what matters." Her face grew serious. "Mama is not socially ambitious—precisely—but I'm afraid when she heard you were coming, she could not resist showing you off—just a bit. And, I'm afraid Papa encouraged her." Her gaze dropped. "He does so wish to appear to advantage before his neighbors."

As though regretting her words, she whirled about and once again she gathered brushes and paints and tucked them into her satchel.

"I fear I shall disappoint when I am put on display," Seth said solemnly, "but I shall try to do my part. I didn't bring any ermine, and I left my satin breeches at home, but I do own a rather fine sapphire stickpin. Do you think that will be sufficient to impress the neighbors?"

Eden laughed. "I suppose it will have to do. You would not happen to have a coronet tucked in your luggage, would you?"

She reflected that Mr. Lindow scarcely needed external embellishment in order to command respect. His height, his rather forbidding features, and above all that assured stare combined to convey the certainty that here was a man to be reckoned with.

Seth joined in her laughter, and the thought occurred to him that his brief period of ruralization might not be so onerous after all. He observed that Miss Beckett had tucked away her equipment and was now preparing to mount her little mare.

"I hope I'm not driving you away from your work," he said diffidently. "I'll be leaving now."

"Oh, no. It's high time I returned home. In fact, it's a good thing you happened by. As so often occurs when I'm out here by myself, I tend to lose track of time."

Seth assisted her with the satchel, easel and stool, then, cupping his hands, tossed her lightly into her saddle. Astride his own horse, he accompanied Miss Beckett back to the house.

They conversed easily and companionably on the way, and when they reached the stable yard, Seth asked, "May I see your paintings now?"

Eden turned to him, startled. "Now? Oh, no. That is, I am promised to the vicar's wife for a meeting on an upcoming church fete. After luncheon perhaps."

"Very well, or—no, I'll be off then for a spot of fishing with your papa. When I return, perhaps?"

"That will be fine." Dismounting, Eden collected her paraphernalia and, with a smiling nod, returned to the house.

Her mood oddly unsettled, Eden went about the routine of

her day in a fog of abstraction. She had been prepared to dislike Mr. Seth Lindow, sure that he was somehow up to no good with his clearly meretricious story of a horse-buying outing in the country. Yet, he seemed harmless enough, although harmless was the last word she would use to describe him. He could be charming, she mused. She had watched the hard gaze soften and the harsh features crinkle into laughter. And he liked her painting—certainly a point in his favor. Or perhaps he was merely trying to turn her up sweet. But why? Lord knew she had little influence with Zoë, or with her parents for that matter. Of course, even if he genuinely respected her art, that did not make his motives any less suspicious—but it certainly made it more difficult to keep her guard up.

After her visit with Mrs. Genther, the vicar's wife, Eden returned home to pursue another favorite hobby, gardening. She was inordinately proud of her roses, and, although at this time of year, her rose garden was bare, there was still much work to be done to assure future blooms of acceptable quality. She did not enter the house again until much later in the day, thus did not see Mr. Lindow until his return from the fishing expedition.

"Yes, we were reasonably successful," replied Seth in answer to her question. "Your papa owns every kind of fly known to man, and he was most generous. When the Jock Coachman failed to produce results, he provided me with a Black-tail Viper and a Wee Grubbie after that. How could I miss? Your cook promised us a fine feast of trout for dinner. Good God, where *is* this studio of yours? We seem to have been climbing forever."

Eden, hurrying to the drawing room after being summoned by a footman, had led Seth to the rear of the house and then up three flights of stairs to a warren of corridors, each more dark and deserted than the one before. At last, she paused before a door and threw it open. Seth blinked in the sudden shaft of light that assaulted him. The room lay across the back of the house, facing north, and it smelled of oil and turpentine. A large easel was set up in the center, catching light from the windows that spread across the chamber. Along the walls stood a number of canvases, stacked one against the other.

"This is part of the nursery wing, which of course hasn't been used for ages. This particular chamber lies just off the school room and was used for games and reading on rainy days. Since it is large and provides a good exposure, it is perfect for my purpose. No one comes up here anymore—in fact, I think Mama and Papa have forgotten its existence—so I can creep up here, and it's as though I've escaped to a hidden lair."

Seth moved into the room and, glancing at Eden, raised his brows in an unspoken request. Eden waved her hand permissively. As he lifted the canvases to examine them, she sat down before the easel, pretending to make minute corrections to an almost-completed work.

Seth's progress was slow, for he became increasingly mesmerized with the perusal of each painting. Most were watercolors, but there were some oils. None of the paintings were large, no grand landscapes or mythological panoramas. Although most of them were outdoor subjects, they portrayed small delights, like the budding tree in the wood. Eden apparently liked to paint flowers, but her subjects were not pretty bouquets of daffodils or formally arranged roses. Eden's flowers cascaded in riots of colors that seemed to spill from the canvas into the viewer's hands. Her daffodils were a glorious burst of gold and green that almost assaulted one with their sensuous beauty. They were formed of strong, almost violent brush strokes, and they suggested rather than took the true shape of the blossoms depicted. Her roses were full and vibrant in their blazing reds and pinks and yellows, and swollen with an almost suggestive passion.

He came across a portrait of Zoë, and almost gasped. It had been painted at night, and the sole source of lighting was a candle, from which the viewer was shielded by a sweep of drapery. Zoë's face was bathed in the warmth of the candlelight, glowing against the darkness behind her. The contrast of light and shadow was dramatic, creating a lush, almost shocking sense of intimacy. Eden had captured Zoë's freshness and the innocence of her youth as well as the mystery of her awakening sensuality. The effect was stunning.

"My God!" whispered Seth. "These are like nothing I have ever seen. Have you considered offering any of them for sale?"

Eden uttered a high laugh. "Oh, no." She dropped her gaze. "At least, not seriously. I have given away some as gifts—although not many people really want them. I have done a few portraits of my friends' children. Those turned out rather well. Papa and Mama and my sisters think my pictures are quite dreadful. They don't understand why I must paint with such . . . ferocity. They complain that my flowers and trees and

whatever else I choose are hardly recognizable—and I daresay
they're right. But I must paint things as I see them. In any
event, Papa would not for a minute countenance my offering
my work for sale. It would smell of trade, don't you see?"

Seth grunted. Yes, he did see. On the other hand, though he
was by no means an expert on art, he could feel the talent fairly
boiling forth from the canvas. He knew only that in these paintings he beheld a vitality, a sureness, a pure virtuosity.

Seth touched one finger to a particularly explosive chrysan-
themum. "Your style is . . . quite original," he murmured.

Eden laughed. "My family would agree—although they
would not put it so tactfully."

"I meant it as a compliment," Seth said hastily. He glanced at
the stack of paintings. "Have you any more portraits?"

"Y-yes—or no, they are not formal portraits. I do have one or
two studies, and a few sketches."

From a cupboard she pulled several sheets of vellum. There
were watercolors and pencil and charcoal sketches, mostly of
children and mostly in preliminary stages. Seth chose one of the
more or less finished products, a charcoal sketch of Zoë seated
at the piano. It seemed to Seth that she had caught Zoë's personality in a few bold strokes. Her impatient verve, as she at-
tacked the keyboard, her enjoyment of the music thus
produced, and the wilful mischief that proclaimed itself in the
very curve of her body over the instrument.

"This is marvelous!" Seth exclaimed involuntarily. Again,
Eden blushed as though unaccustomed to compliments on her
work. "It seems a shame that all this should remain hidden here,
unseen. It should be shared with the world."

Eden blinked. "That is very kind of you, Mr. Lindow, but as I
have explained, very unlikely to come to pass."

She stood and moved toward the door, where she turned to
gaze at him. The viewing was evidently over. As they emerged
into the musty corridor outside the studio, a muted sound
floated up from the distance below them.

"Goodness, there is the dressing gong already!" exclaimed
Eden. "I had no idea we had spent so much time up here." She
hurried down the stairs ahead of him, and when they reached
the floor below, she set off toward the family wing. Seth placed
his hand on her arm, and she whirled to face him, seemingly as
startled as though she had forgotten his presence.

"Thank you for showing me your work, Miss Beckett."

"Why . . . yes, yes of course." Her smile was strained. "And thank you for your kind words. You were most . . . encouraging. I'll see you at dinner."

With that, she hurried down the corridor, leaving Seth to stare after her, mystified.

What the devil was the matter with her? What had there been in his tone to indicate anything but the most sincere admiration of her work? Why was she behaving as though she did not believe a word of it? If he was not mistaken, she resented the interest he had displayed in seeing her paintings at all—as though he had inveigled his way into her studio under false pretenses, and once having got there, had hurled insults at her. He frowned. Perhaps she was so accustomed to ridicule that she could not recognize honest admiration.

In any event, he reflected prosaically, he had satisfied his curiosity, and that would be an end to it. Turning, he strode toward his own chambers.

Good Lord, Eden chastised herself, standing in the midst of her bed chamber. What was the matter with her? The man had merely commented that her style was unusual, and she had flown into the boughs as though he had hurled a paint pot at her. She was pleased, of course, that he seemed to like her work. At least, she thought so. Although he hadn't actually said that, had he? She could only remember the words "astonishing" and "unusual" and . . . and "original." Certainly not high praise. One might say the same thing about a newly discovered species of lizard. Yet, she had sensed a real admiration, and—

Oh, for heaven's sake. What difference did it make to her if he liked her work, or considered her the merest dabbler?

She halted suddenly, in the process of ringing for her maid. But . . . it did make a difference to her, didn't it? His good opinion of her painting mattered. Or was it his good opinion of her that she sought?

She shook herself. What nonsense. She had yet to meet the man whose opinion, well or ill, mattered one whit to her. Not that gentlemen tended to form opinions of her one way or another, at least not once they caught a glimpse of Zoë.

Ringing for Timmons, her maid, she began the laborious process of unhooking the back of her gown.

Chapter Six

Dinner that evening was not so pleasant as it had been the night before. Zoë, perhaps unwisely, aired further plans for the upcoming visit to London. These, apparently, included a whole new wardrobe. Her fond papa saw no reason to expand the superfluity of gowns she already owned, and the discussion quickly grew acrimonious.

"Devil take it, Zoë, you have enough clothes to outfit a sizable village. You wore most of them only once, and when you returned here to Clearsprings, you ordered a pile more just because the London garb was not—you said—fit for country wear. So there they all are taking space in your wardrobe and providing food for the moths. You can very well make do with those. Now, let us hear no more about it." Lord Beckett took a large gulp of wine.

"Papa, everyone has seen those gowns." Zoë's voice rose to an indignant squeal. "You cannot wish me to appear in last year's ensembles. I would be a laughing stock." She drew a deep breath. "I cannot believe you are being so . . . so parsimonious about this. Do you not wish me to make you proud? How do you expect me to attract the most eligible young men if I'm dressed in rags?" She lifted wide, angry eyes to Eden as though for support.

"Zoë!" exclaimed Lady Beckett helplessly, as she seemed to do so often.

"I said," barked Lord Beckett, banging his hand on the table, "we will hear no more about it."

Zoë jumped up from her chair, furious tears glittering in her eyes. "Yes, we will, too! Much more. For, I . . . want . . . . some . . . new *gowns*. And I mean to have them!"

Flushed with rage, she ran from the room, nearly knocking over her chair as she did so. In the appalled silence that followed her exit, Seth was aware that Eden's gaze had fallen to her lap. Her cheeks flamed as well, but not, he felt, with rage. He was seated across the table from her, and he knew an urge to go to her, to take her hands in his. Looking quickly away, Seth glanced at his host and hostess in some astonishment. Was it Zoë's habit to engage in such tactics to gain her own way? And were Lord and Lady Beckett in the habit of accepting such behavior?

Evidently so, as became almost immediately obvious.

"Oh dear," sighed Lady Beckett.

"Unmanageable chit," muttered Lord Beckett.

"Perhaps, dearest," said Lady Beckett after a moment, "since it seems to mean so much to her . . ."

"Tchah!" was Lord Beckett's response. He added after a moment. "I'll think about it."

Good God, thought Seth, was this the young woman he thought to present to Father as the future Marchioness of Belhaven?

Good God, thought Eden. She was ready to sink with mortification. Not only had Zoë treated Mr. Lindow to an outrageous display of temper, but her parents had presented themselves as completely ineffectual in disciplining their youngest daughter. It did not matter, of course, what Mr. Lindow thought of her family, but to so reveal themselves to a stranger was the outside of enough.

She glanced across the table to find Seth grinning ruefully at her. She could find no contempt in his gaze, only a smiling empathy that somehow warmed her. She supposed that the urbane Mr. Lindow must be taken aback by very little, and for this she was grateful.

After dinner, Lord Beckett bore Mr. Lindow away for a game of billiards, leaving Lady Beckett to commiserate with her oldest daughter over the behavior of her youngest.

"I just don't know what will become of her," moaned Lady Beckett. "She thinks to find a lord in London, or even a viscount."

Or a duke's son, thought Eden acerbically.

"She treats the young men hereabouts so dreadfully," continued her mother, "that I just know many of them have already turned away. If she keeps on the way she's going, she will end up without a husband, just like—"

She caught herself, and lifted a hand to her mouth. "Oh, dearest, I did not mean—"

Eden chuckled. "It's all right, Mama. Spinsterhood suits me, but you're right. It would not do for Zoë."

"Mr. Lindow seems quite interested in her. Do you think . . . ?" Lady Beckett raised her colorless brows hopefully.

"I doubt if Mr. Lindow would meet Zoë's criteria for a mate, even if he were to propose tomorrow." Eden was surprised at the uncomfortable twinge that snaked through her at the thought.

Lady Beckett's shoulders sagged, but then she brightened. "But, do you not think he would do nicely for you, dearest? He is lowborn, of course, but I think perhaps we should not let that weigh with us . . . in view of his, er, connections," she finished delicately.

"What!" gasped Eden. She felt herself blushing to the roots of her hair. "Really, Mama! Mr. Lindow has come here in search of horses, not a bride. I'm sure if he were seeking one, our tiny corner of the world is the last place he would think to look. He may be only the adoptive son of a duke, but I'm sure he can look as high as he pleases for a *parti*."

Lady Beckett sighed. "I don't know about that, but—do you think Zoë really has a chance of snaring a peer? That is," she amended hastily, "I would not have her marry for position, but as I've heard it said, one can fall in love just as easily with a rich man as a poor man. Zoë is such a taking little thing, I'm sure—"

"Yes, she might. She might also gravitate toward precisely the worst kind of man." Eden's thoughts again went to the Marquess of Belhaven. "You know the possibilities of getting up to no good in London are almost endless."

"There is that, of course. However, I shall be there, and you . . ."

"I'll do my best, Mama," replied Eden, "but I would so much rather stay here."

"Ah," spoke a voice from the doorway. "You have no desire to partake of the delights of the Metropolis, Miss Beckett?"

Eden whirled to observe Mr. Lindow enter the room, with her father close behind. The gentlemen had concluded their game, he explained, and were now ready for a spot of tea, or perhaps something more fortifying.

"You dislike London, Miss Beckett?" repeated Seth, after the game had been replayed, with vigorous commentary, for the benefit of the ladies.

"Oh, no," replied Eden. "I enjoy the galleries and museums—as Zoë said—and the shopping and the parks. It is the endless social round that I cannot abide. One sees the same persons night after night, and the conversation is always the same, with the result that one stands about mouthing the most tedious nothings to persons who are bored with them before one even begins. I do enjoy the dancing, though," she added as an afterthought.

"Of course," he said softly, and Eden knew without knowing why that he was recalling the dance they had shared at Lady Saltram's ball. She felt her cheeks heat again and reflected angrily that she had blushed more often since the arrival of Mr. Lindow than she had during the entire previous year.

The tea tray made its appearance then, after which the Becketts and their guest sought their beds.

Morning came early, and Seth greeted it less than enthusiastically. He was beginning to have grave doubts about the suitability of Miss Zoë Beckett as a bride for his tiresome younger brother. Moreover, except for Eden Beckett, he was finding the occupants of Clearsprings more than somewhat trying. He would make a decision within a day or two, he decided, and return to London.

After dressing, he made his way to the stables and after an invigorating gallop felt his spirits rise. He rode into the wood, but did not see Eden there. On his return, surprisingly disappointed and feeling rather at loose ends, he headed for the nursery wing. When he reached the schoolroom, he tried the door, only to find it locked. He turned away to retrace his steps to the lower floors, but was stayed by the sound of footsteps approaching. He experienced an odd surge of pleasure as Eden approached. How did she always manage to look so impossibly neat? wondered Seth. Not a hair was out of place, and her simple muslin morning gown of a muted amber, while not particularly becoming, was crisp and fresh.

She lifted her glossy brows on observing him at the door to her sanctum, and Seth launched into an awkward explanation of his presence.

". . . and since your father is busy with a matter brought to him by one of his tenants, I thought I would inflict my company on you for a few moments. I had hoped to observe you at your painting, if that would not discompose you. I know some artists cannot bear to be watched."

"I . . . I don't know," she replied after a moment. "No one has ever wished to do so. But, do come in."

She unlocked the door and ushered him inside. It soon became obvious that she found his presence unsettling. After gesturing him to a comfortable chair near the window, she fiddled with her brushes for a moment and repositioned the easel.

"I would offer you some refreshment, but there is no bellpull in this room—and in any event, I do not like to encourage the servants to come up here. However—" From a small cupboard nearby, she produced a flask half full of a murky liquid. "I do have some lemon water." She eyed it dubiously. "It's been here awhile."

"Mm, yes. I believe I'll pass," he said solemnly. "I am not very thirsty, you see."

"No, I don't suppose you are," Eden returned with equal gravity, glancing again at the lemon water. "Well, then—"

"If you don't mind, I'll just peruse this volume on, ah, *Analysis of Beauty*. Since it was written by Hogarth, it should be worth investigating."

"Oh, yes, Hogarth is one of my favorites. The last time we were in London, I studied his *Shrimp Girl* for hours at the Royal Academy Gallery. He has the most marvelous gift for portraying the character and personality of his subjects."

She turned to arrange her subject, a bouquet of wild flowers that had been thrust with deceptive carelessness into a crude pottery pitcher. As Eden seated herself at her easel, however, an idea occurred to her.

"I wonder . . ." she said to Seth. "Instead of your simply sitting there, occupying yourself with a book in which I'm sure you have little interest, would you consider posing for me?"

Seth gaped. "Me? You want me to pose for a portrait?"

"Well, yes—but I'd like it to be more of a study. In pastels, I think, since there will not be time to do an oil painting. Frankly, I rarely have an opportunity to draw males, and—and oh, the facial planes, the clothing, and even the curve of the hair."

"Of course," said Seth in some amusement. "Would you like me to remove my coat?"

Eden blushed to the roots of her hair. "Oh, no! That wouldn't be . . . Or . . ." She almost gasped at her own temerity. "Yes, that would be most . . . instructive. No, leave the waistcoat," she added hurriedly as he slid out of his elegantly tailored coat of superfine and began on the buttons of a superb waistcoat of mulberry silk. "It will make a nice contrast to all that white. Now, if you will just sit right here. I think we will face you three-quarters away from the light. Yes, just right. With this piece of pasteboard as a reflector. And, if you would not mind, may we dispense with the cravat, as well?"

Once more astonished at her own boldness, she took the cravat from him, and when he put his fingers to the three buttons that closed his shirt, she nodded encouragingly. When the muscular column of his throat was exposed, she gazed unabashedly and reached to grasp him lightly by the shoulders. Seth glanced at her in some startlement, but she merely turned him this way and that until he was posed to her satisfaction.

Really, Eden thought dazedly, whatever did she think she was about—closeting herself with a gentleman not related to her? She had all but forced him to disrobe for her, and she had never been in the presence of a man in such a state of dishabille. If anyone were to come upon them—well, such a circumstance was highly unlikely, but it would be disastrous if she and Seth were discovered behind closed doors. Before seating herself, Eden moved to fling open the schoolroom door. And when, she reflected distractedly, had she started thinking of him as Seth rather than Mr. Lindow? She had been uncomfortably conscious of the warmth of his skin and the taut frame beneath her fingers, a reaction she certainly had not experienced when posing the little Stebbins boy or the Matchingham sisters.

She gave herself a shake and turned her mind firmly to the business at hand. For an hour, she worked to create a likeness of Seth on a square of drawing paper. At her suggestion, he rolled up the sleeves of the shirt, and she marveled at the strength of his forearms, so like and yet so different from the anatomy of the female arm. She even found a certain beauty in the very maleness of his musculature. How wonderfully utilitarian in form, yet how perfect. She would very much like, she confessed to herself, to see Mr. Lindow in the altogether, completely free from the encumbrance of his clothing. What a study that would make! For she was sure the rest of the body so irritatingly concealed by shirt, trousers, and boots would prove every bit as fascinating as those arms and that throat.

By now, she considered, she should have been blushing again, but she felt no shame in her musings. After all, Mr. Lindow was merely another intriguing subject for her art—admittedly a superior specimen, but still—just an object. The human body was beautiful in form. The fact that she wished to see that form whole and complete in its purity she considered in no way shameful. Had she not wished to disrobe the greengrocer's daughter—she of the creamy skin tints and lush figure? That desire, too, had sprung from the simplest of motives. As an artist she was interested in beautiful shapes, and the human body was surely the most intriguing of all.

This, of course, did not account for the sudden warmth that flooded her belly as she gazed on the particular shape seated before her at the moment. Well, she supposed she must take into account a spinster's natural unfamiliarity with a not-quite-fully-clothed male, and the social prohibitions that such a situation implied. That must be what caused her to catch her breath when the sunlight created those marvelous glints in the depths of his dark hair.

After a while, her maidenly flutterings subsided, and she was able to chat easily with her subject.

"Tell me, Mr. Lindow," she said during a pause in the conversation, "do you enjoy living in Derwent House rather than in your own lodgings? You must feel rather limited in your social activities."

"Since my social activities are practically nil, I do not notice much curtailment. Actually, I enjoy living in the duke's home. All my needs are supplied."

"I see," replied Eden, who did not see at all. Most bachelors of her acquaintance preferred living on their own. Mr. Lindow, in particular, was of an age at which he would surely wish to set up his own establishment. A thought occurred to her. "I suppose," she said without thinking, "your father must prefer to have you with him. Otherwise, it would be lonely for him, with all his family gone."

Mr. Lindow stared at her blankly for a long moment before uttering a bark of laughter. "Miss Beckett, my father scarcely knows I'm in the house, except when he wants me for some task."

He had no sooner spoken than he frowned as though he could

have bitten his tongue. He changed the subject swiftly to a more innocuous topic. Eden followed his lead, but kept her own counsel.

They talked of many things after that. Mr. Lindow proved knowledgeable on a remarkable range of subjects, and did not seem to think it odd that she enjoyed talking of something other than the weather or the latest *on-dits* in London. He was also possessed with a sense of the ridiculous, and the hour passed in a companionable conversation on art, literature, politics, and the absurdities of the royal family.

"There," she said at last, stretching her fingers. "It's rather haphazard, but I think it will do."

Seth rose from the position he had obediently maintained for so long. He stretched his long limbs. "Whew!" he exclaimed, rolling his shoulders. "Who would think that merely sitting still could be so fatiguing?"

Curiously, he moved to where Eden sat with her drawing pad. After a moment's hesitation, she moved the drawing so that he could see it. Seth stared at it in bemusement.

"I . . . I don't know what to say," he said at last. "Do I really look like that?"

Trying to divine from his tone whether he was pleased or not with the picture, she decided that he was, if rather sheepishly. The man portrayed in the drawing looked as though he should be garbed in fringed buckskins, for he might have just arrived from the American frontier. His shirt stretched tautly over muscled shoulders, and powerful thighs were delineated by fashionably tight pantaloons. His hair, dark as midnight and slightly disheveled fell over his forehead in a cluster of crisp curls. Those compelling eyes, gazing directly at the viewer, put one in mind of a powerful predator, sizing up its prey.

Seth's glance moved once or twice from the drawing to Eden, and Eden thought she beheld a certain degree of puzzled astonishment in his countenance. Suddenly, she became aware of how it must look to him—the fantasizing of a spinster over a strong virile male. She snatched the drawing from him awkwardly, turning to place it on a nearby table. As she did so, she stumbled a little and fell awkwardly against him.

Catching her in his arms, Seth righted her and released her almost at once. The contact, however, produced an odd effect in him. Her portrayal of him had startled him, for it seemed to him that she had captured a certain wildness in his nature that he had always taken care to keep hidden. In addition, the warmth and softness of her curves could be plainly felt through his linen shirt. He felt an urge to prolong the embrace, to draw her to him and to bury his face in the sweet-scented mass of her hair. Good God, he actually burned to kiss her until she moaned with desire. He could almost picture her, rosy and, for once, disheveled. What the devil was the matter with him? He was not a womanizer, after all, to be stirred to passion merely because he was in a room alone with an attractive woman. He'd been known to engage in dalliance from time to time, but never with a gently bred female of maidenly virtue.

He shook himself, aware that Eden was speaking. Had she experienced a similar reaction to their brief contact? he wondered. A slight blush stained her cheeks, and she seemed a little breathless, but that might be merely from the embarrassment of finding herself in the arms, even if very temporarily, of a strange man.

"Perhaps, some day, while we are in London again, you will permit me to do you in oils," she said, her voice slightly strained.

"Of course. I hope to see you when you come to Town," said Seth retying his cravat.

He shrugged into his coat. Yes, indeed, Zoë would be in London, and soon. A twinge of compunction snaked through him. And she would be walking right into the wolf's den. The chit was a holy terror, but did she deserve a life sentence chained to someone like Bel? And what of her family? They loved her. A vision of Eden's expression of tender exasperation rose before him. She was aware of her sister's flaws, but she loved her anyway.

No, he must not think of that. He had promised the duke a wife for Bel, and what the duke required, he must have, no matter what the cost. There had been many times since Seth had made his vow that he regretted it, but, he reminded himself, that no matter his . . . flaws, this was the man who had given him his life. He drew a breath to steady himself.

"Perhaps we shall meet again, then," he murmured.

Eden nodded noncommittally. "Perhaps."

Later in the day, Seth once more removed the coat, preparatory to dressing for the dinner party that seemed to loom over his head like the sword of Damocles. He was thoroughly weary of the Beckett family and had no desire to spend an evening with a group of persons who would in all likelihood prove to be more of the same. At least, he thought, brightening, he would have Eden's company. He had long since ceased to think of her as one of the Becketts, though he refused to contemplate the absurdity of this view. How could such a family have produced Eden? Unlike either of her parents, she was intelligent, cultured, and possessed of a keen wit—to say nothing of her astonishing artistic talent. In addition, there was that sense, irrational though it might be, of . . . of, well, acquaintanceship with her, as though he had known her since childhood. He smiled as a mental picture flashed before him of a hoydenish imp, dark hair in plaits and gray eyes sparkling with mischief, her skirts no doubt rumpled and stained with berries or stolen sweets.

"So, how goes yer project?" asked Moppe, just entering the room with a freshly laundered shirt.

"My project?" asked Seth frostily, being deliberately obtuse.

"Young Miss Zoë. Though, I'm not so sure that particular miss is exactly what His Grace has in mind for his son."

Abruptly, Seth abandoned his lofty attitude. He realized that Moppe had no doubt gleaned more information on Zoë's character and habits in two days belowstairs than Seth was likely to discover in a month spent in the young lady's company. "What do you mean?"

"Only that she sounds a rare handful. By the by, didjer know yer missin' a cufflink?"

"Mm, yes, I noticed it when I returned from . . . that is, I must have lost it earlier today. I think I know where it may be. But, you were saying? About Miss Zoë?"

"Uh-huh, a decent little thing, but with a temper that would fry eggs, and her tongue can slice leather. She's kind to the staff, but if she don't get her own way, every servant in the house scampers to stay out of her path."

"Mmm." Moppe's words filled Seth with foreboding. It had seemed to him when he had begun his quest in London that Zoë fit his requirements more precisely than any of the other young women on his hurriedly contrived list. Even the duke, when Seth had described her, seemed to think she would fit the bill. Now, however, the more he came to know the young hoyden, the more unsuitable she appeared. He sighed. He could only hope that she would be willing to curb her willfulness and forgo the gratification of temper for the sake of a coronet.

He affixed the rather fine sapphire stickpin to his cravat and, upon being solemnly assured by Moppe that he was presentable, left his chamber and made his way to the drawing room.

Lord and Lady Beckett were already on hand, along with Eden and several guests. Eden, reflected Seth, his breath catching, looked extraordinarily lovely. She was garbed in the most becoming gown Seth had seen her in to date. It was of a deep carnelian, with an enticing décollatage. She had dispensed with the ubiquitous, absurd cap, and her hair, brushed into a delicate Clytie knot caught the reflection of the candlelight, which laced it with gleaming rivulets of fire.

Eden, intercepting his glance, blushed—again. She had spent an inordinate length of time on her appearance this evening, deciding at last on the carnelian silk, purchased in London, but worn only once. On that occasion, Zoë had stared at her appreciatively, noting with a grin that it was about time that she stopped dressing like a governess and started "showing off your wares a bit." Eden, feeling remarkably like a prize ewe at auction, had been uncomfortable all evening, despite the compliments from several gentlemen who had heretofore appeared oblivious to her existence.

On this evening, as she had stared into her mirror, she declined to examine the reasons why she felt it necessary to wear a gown whose color she knew to be more than somewhat exotic, even though it was exceptionally becoming, and which displayed an attractive if altogether indecent display of bosom.

Still aware of Seth's gaze on her, Eden absorbed his own splendor. Though she considered him a well-set-up gentleman in his usual sober garb, the sight of him in evening dress was quite another matter. He was undoubtedly the most handsome man in the room, concluded Eden, her pulse fluttering.

Lord Beckett, fairly bursting with satisfaction, introduced his visitor to his neighbors—those present and those who continued to arrive. It was not until a few moments before Horsley was due to announce dinner that Zoë danced into the room.

At Eden's indrawn breath, and Lady Beckett's horrified gasp, Seth swiveled to face the newcomer. Zoë's gown made her look like a very young girl done up as a bit of muslin—and in her own home.

Lord Beckett advanced on her, his face a disagreeable shade of puce.

Chapter Seven

Lord Beckett set a hammy fist on Zoë's shoulder and opened his mouth in an enraged hiss. At that moment, however, he seemed to recollect the presence of half the county gentry in his drawing room. Instead of shaking her until her teeth rattled, which was plainly his desire, he whispered sibilantly, "What the *devil* do you mean by it, missy? You will go straight upstairs and change into something more suitable!"

Zoë merely laughed into his face, and, shrugging out from under his grasp, she skipped past him to greet her friends and admirers, of which, it must be admitted there was a sizable throng. Thwarted, Lord Beckett sputtered helplessly for several moments before stamping over to his wife, who stood wringing her hands ineffectually. Eden, pale but composed, turned back to the group with whom she had been conversing before Zoë's dramatic entrance.

Zoë, apparently oblivious to the upheaval she had caused in her parents' bosoms, began the always enjoyable task of drawing her usual court to her side. Among these were most of the young men of marriageable age and several damsels who slavishly followed her in manner and dress.

Horsley entered to announce dinner, and with a shrill giggle, Zoë grasped the arm of her nearest swain. Unheeding, she pushed past her father and Lady Pritchett, who should have led the procession to the dining room.

All through dinner, Seth's spirits sank lower and lower as Zoë violated, one after the other, seemingly every rule of behavior known to civilized society. She called to gentlemen seated across the table from her. She confined her conversation exclusively to young Lord Eversley on her right, completely ignoring poor old Mr. Holmes on her left. She spilled soup on a footman, and then berated the fellow on his clumsiness. Worst of all, she drank entirely too much wine and soon became giddy and flushed, her giggles growing louder and more frequent and her conversation becoming laced with improprieties.

Good God, was this what happened to the young woman when she was turned loose in a large gathering? Seth had not observed her at length when the family was in London before. Did she behave as badly, or worse, among the *beau monde* as she did in her own milieu? If so, could she be trained to conduct herself with some degree of gentility?

From her position nearer the foot of the table, Eden watched her sister's antics in growing dismay. Zoë's conduct was never what one could call decorous, but tonight she was outdoing herself. She noted that from time to time, Zoë cast covert glances at Seth. Surely, she was not behaving so outrageously in a bid for his attention! In Zoë's eyes, Seth was almost elderly. He was untitled, and he certainly gave no indication of the wealth that Zoë considered essential to a man's desirability. To be sure, Seth had been taken up by the Duke of Derwent, but Seth apparently had declined to take advantage of this fact, and was known to polite society simply as the duke's man of affairs. He had no claim to the duke's title, nor, most likely, to his wealth. So what could account for Zoë's interest?

Suddenly, Eden recalled the conversation two days before at luncheon. She believed she had succeeded in turning Zoë's incipient admiration for the degenerate Marquess of Belhaven, but—Good Lord! Did the little twit see herself as the future Marchioness of Belhaven, and, following, the Duchess of Derwent? If so, it was reasonable to assume that Mr. Lindow, the marquess's foster brother, could provide a direct path to the fulfillment of her desires.

Mr. Lindow was observing Zoë intently, which seemed to inspire Zoë to even greater heights of bumptious impropriety. Eden noted again, that his sardonic gaze was watchful rather than amorous, and certainly marked with disapproval. That was all to the good, thought Eden, though she squirmed uncomfortably at Zoë's disgraceful revelry.

After dinner, when the ladies proceeded to the drawing room, Zoë's behavior improved. She joined in the gossip that swirled about the room like a scented breeze and laughed unaffectedly with her friends. Later, when the gentlemen ambled into the chamber, she again joined her sister in playing the piano and singing several unexceptionable melodies, as did several of the guests.

Seth, mellowing under the influence of the music and Lord Beckett's fine port, allowed himself to view Zoë's volte-face with a rising hope. He would, he decided, present Zoë to Father as soon as the family was settled in London, for it was His Grace who must make the final decision regarding his son's future bride. He hoped Zoë would be so overwhelmed in the presence of the duke that she would exert herself to assume a demeanor befitting a well-bred maiden, used to the ways of the *ton*.

Seth's rosy vision suffered something of a setback a few minutes later, when Zoë, jumping up from her chair, insisted that sets be formed for dancing.

"We have enough people here," she cried gleefully, clapping her hands together in girlish enthusiasm, "and Eden can play for us."

"Oh, but dearest," breathed Lady Beckett in distress. "The carpets . . . ! And our guests may not wish to—"

Zoë's ingenuous smile was replaced with the mulish expression that by now was becoming all too familiar. "What nonsense, Mama. Everyone loves to dance. Why, Mr. Sedgewick was saying just a moment ago that he wished we could have an impromptu hop." She swept an arm to indicate a blushing youth who appeared to be the center of her court. "Come, let us move the furniture and roll up the carpets."

She gestured to the footmen standing by, who came forward hesitantly.

The next moment, despite Lady Beckett's faint protests and disapproving stares from some of the older guests, the young gentlemen set to work with vigor, applauded by the young ladies. The footmen fell to. Resigned, Eden took her place at the piano. Zoë curtsied roguishly before Seth.

"Will you stand up with me, Mr. Lindow? I vow, as our guest, I believe it must be your duty."

Seth surveyed her with a forced tolerance, and his smile held only a bored amusement. "Oh, I think not, Miss Zoë. I should be slain by the glares of every young man here, and I'm sure you do not wish to disappoint your ardent admirers. In addition, I think, rather, that my duty lies in assisting Miss Beckett. She will require someone to turn pages for her."

With an avuncular smile, he lifted her gloved fingers to his lips in a practiced movement and placed her hand in that of one of the young sprigs hovering nearby.

"Oh!" cried Zoë with an indignant gasp. The next moment, she turned the moment to her advantage by smiling radiantly. "How very gallant of you, Mr. Lindow, to save me from the embarrassment of turning away so many claimants to my hand."

Seth watched for a moment as Zoë made a charming show of accepting her partner for the first set, then he turned away to join Eden at the piano.

"Zoë sometimes allows herself to be carried away by her enthusiasm," murmured Eden awkwardly as she settled herself on the stool.

"Indeed," replied Seth coolly. "Sisters can be the very devil, can they not? I recall the antics of my own at that age." He sifted through the music piled on a table near the instrument and made several selections, one of which he placed on the music rack for Eden's inspection. Eden nodded and began to play.

Seth remained at her side for the next hour. That he was supremely content to do so, caused him no little surprise, as did the realization that he garnered pleasure in watching her strong, supple fingers move over the keys. He found her scent—a blend of flowers with something a little spicier, he thought—almost as intoxicating as the glass of wine he held in his hand. He marveled at the grace of her slender neck as it bent over the keys.

Good God, he reflected at length, he was becoming jugbitten. Abruptly, he moved away from the piano, and Eden looked up quickly.

"My!" she exclaimed, glancing at the clock. "I believe we have indulged the youngsters sufficiently." She finished her song with a flourish and rose from the stool. Overriding cries of disappointment from the dancers, she declared the impromptu hop at an end and signaled Horsely to bring in the tea table.

After another hour of tea and other refreshments, the guests began to take their leave, and at last, yawning behind their hands, the Becketts and Mr. Lindow found themselves alone in the entrance hall, the laughter of the last guests sounding as the front door closed behind them.

"Well, I'm for bed," declared Lord Beckett, lumbering to-

ward the stairs. He gave his arm to his wife. "A successful
evening, I think, Lady B., don't you?"

"Oh, yes," interposed Zoë. "Everyone admired my gown."
Here, she cast a sidelong glance at her papa. "Freddie Barnsta-
ple is on the verge of proposing, I think, although I have no intention of accepting him. As though I would marry the son of a
mere squire." She laughed merrily. Bestowing noisy kisses on
her parents' cheeks, she scampered up the stairs.

As Lord Beckett and Lady Beckett began their own journey
upward, Eden moved to follow them, but was stayed as Seth
laid a hand on her arm.

"I wonder if I might trouble you for a moment," he said. "I
seem to have misplaced one of my cuff links, and I think I may
have dropped it in your studio. Would you mind unlocking the
door to your sanctum so that I might look for it? We can wait
until tomorrow, of course," he added. "I just thought that, while
it is still in my head . . . They were a gift from my
mother . . . that is, the duchess . . . and I'd hate to lose them."

"Of course," responded Eden. She picked up two of the candles set on a table near the stairway, lit for the purpose of guid-
ing the family to their beds. Handing one to Seth, she started up
the stairs. "I'm sure it will take only a moment."

Upon entering her studio, Eden turned questioningly to Seth.
"Do you think you might have dropped your cuff link near
where you were sitting?"

"Undoubtedly." Seth holding his candle high, perused the
chair where he had posed for Eden, and the floor around it.
When this produced no results, he set the candle down and
lifted the cushion. Peering into the depths of the chair's uphol-
stery, he dug his hands into the seams between its back and the
cushion, again without success.

Eden, meanwhile, moved to the table where he had tossed his
coat. A search of the floor proved a failure. Eden rose from her
knees and glanced around helplessly.

"I can't think where else to look," she said helplessly. "I believe we'd best come back in the morning. Perhaps in the light
of day it will turn up."

Seth, clambering to his feet from where he had been examin-
ing the floor near the chair, brushed the knees of his breeches.
"Yes, I expect you're right," he sighed. "Or no—wait." Once

more he lifted the candle. "I think I see something—glittering. See? There."

Hurrying to him, Eden followed the direction of his pointing finger. "N-no, I don't—Oh! yes, there in that crack." She bent for a closer look, as did Seth, and it soon became apparent that the cuff link had fallen into a gap in the floorboards, wedging itself behind a nail that had worked itself loose from its original position.

Eden caught up a palette knife from the table near her easel, and kneeling on the floor, attempted to pry the little piece of jewelry from its hiding place. Her efforts were to no avail, nor were Seth's when he sank beside her and removed the knife from Eden's fingers. At length, he sank back on his heels.

"Whew, it's really stuck." He leaned forward again. "However—" He glanced around and helped himself to another palette knife. "I think with a bit of pressure . . . Yes, by pushing against it, I can move the nail with the point of the knife. While I do that, if you will attempt to pry the cuff link from its place, perhaps we can grasp it."

"Right." Bending close to Seth, Eden watched as he moved the nail ever so slightly to one side. Then, with the point of the knife, she eased the cuff link forward, until with a clatter, it popped from the crack in the floor.

"There!" she exclaimed, scooping it up. "Success at last!"

She slid it into Seth's waiting palm, becoming aware as she did so of their proximity. Goodness, she was closeted in alarming intimacy with a man who was a virtual stranger—sprawled like a hoyden on the floor and pressed close against him.

She struggled to rise, but made the tactical error of glancing up at him. His eyes, hooded and mysterious, were more compelling than ever. His gaze seemed to penetrate her innermost being, and was lit with more than just the candle flame. She trembled, mesmerized, as his hand lifted to brush a tendril of hair from her cheek. He bent his head. He was going to kiss her! The knowledge washed over her like warm rain, but she seemed unable to so much as turn her head.

When his mouth descended on hers, she was shocked at the response that seemed to sizzle in her very nerve endings. His lips were warm and firm, and his touch ignited a fire that swept through her. She felt she might be consumed, and her blood sang in her veins. She sank backward in his embrace, until she felt the polished surface of the floor against her body. She realized she was completely prone beneath him. She should have been appalled, but her only thought was to press closer to him, twining her fingers into the crisp curls that lay against his collar.

His kiss deepened, and he shifted so that one arm lifted her head against his. The other cradled her face for a moment before moving down the curve of her body. She thought she might die of pleasure and the desire to know more of the chaotic, heretofore unknown emotions that surged within her.

From a distance, she heard a soft moan. It was only when she realized that the voice had emerged from her own throat that she came to herself and pulled away, horrified.

No, not horrified—or at least not by what had just happened. It was her loss of control that terrified her. His embrace had seemed too right to be regretted. She had fit against him as though she had been created for just that purpose. Once again she had felt the sensation of familiarity, as though her treasonous body had recognized his touch and welcomed it.

Seth, too, had scrambled to a sitting position. He rose to his feet and, putting out a hand, assisted Eden to hers.

"I must apologize." His voice was harsh. "It is not my custom to . . . to assault gently bred ladies. I . . . I don't know what possessed me. I don't . . ."

Eden paused in the act of restoring her hair and clothing to order. She gazed straightly at him. "Please, Mr. Lindow. You did not assault me—or, at least, if you did, I must confess to being a willing participant. It is not my habit to indulge in dalliance." She almost laughed. She had never been kissed in such a manner in her life! "But, I cannot deny that I found it pleasurable."

She felt heat rise to her cheeks as Seth's brows lifted. "I am trying to dredge up some shred of maidenly outrage here, but I must confess I feel no shame. A kiss is, after all, not an occasion of sin. At least, I don't think it is," she concluded earnestly. She gazed at Seth, searching for confirmation, but he merely nodded bemusedly, and then, in some confusion, shook his head.

"You are not unattractive, Mr. Lindow," she continued, "and I do not imagine I am the first woman to succumb—*begin* to succumb—to your charm, but—"

Seth's bark of laughter interrupted her. "Charm? I've never

been accused of possessing so much as an ounce of charm, Miss Beckett."

Eden merely smiled faintly. "Be that as it may, Mr. Lindow, I am not made of wood. I enjoyed our . . . little interlude . . . but it shall not happen again. I am not a wanton. Therefore, I think it would be best if we were simply to forget what just happened, chalking it up to experience."

Picking up the two candles again, she handed one to Seth and moved toward the door, gesturing to him to follow. She locked the door behind them and turned to him once more.

"I shall bid you good night, Mr. Lindow."

Turning on her heel, she walked smoothly away, leaving Seth to gaze after the straight, slim back vanishing into the darkness of the corridor.

Chapter Eight

What just happened here? Seth wondered dazedly. Had he actually embraced—and kissed for some duration—a gently bred maiden? He had never behaved so in his life. He knew well that the daughters of the Polite World were off-limits to him, and up till now this fact had caused him not a single pang. Yes, he might engage in dalliance with those who sought illicit release from their marriages of convenience, or cared so little for the conventions that their names had become bywords for scandal. When one made advances to a maiden of the *ton*, one had by God better be prepared to marry her. Such an outcome was, of course, impossible for him. He had heard stories of persons of low birth marrying into the peerage, but—he smiled sardonically—never the son of an army sergeant. For an instant, an image of raven curls and sparkling black eyes rose before him, only to be firmly suppressed as it had for so many years. In any case, he told himself firmly, marriage for himself was the last thing on his mind.

What, then, had possessed him to gather Miss Eden Beckett in his arms and kiss her with a passion he had not known existed within him? To be sure, they had been caught together in a scene of unusual intimacy. Their candles had bathed them in a warm, secluded pool of light in a room that, for all intents and purposes, might have separated them from the rest of the house by a hundred miles. He had found himself in such situations before, however, and felt not the slightest inclination to indulge in illicit behavior. Their search for the cuff link had, of course, brought him into an unexpectedly close proximity with Eden, but who could have foretold the effect her scent would have on him, or the candlelight gleaming in her hair and caressing the creamy curve of her breast?

He was astonished at the quiver of response that had shuddered through her at his kiss. It had nearly driven him out of his senses. Certainly, he'd been mad enough not to care that he was compromising a gently bred female. He'd wanted only to press the full length of her slender body into his, to drink in the softness of her lips and to . . . He paused, finding it necessary to physically steady himself against a piece of statuary.

And what about Eden? She had pulled away from the embrace—eventually—but she had exhibited none of the indignation he might have expected. Indeed, her demeanor was surprisingly matter-of-fact. She had even admitted a certain enjoyment at their encounter. Was she, then, one of the wild ones? Such a delineation scarcely seemed to fit her character.

No, it was as though she had been as taken aback as he, and was trying to analyze the scene honestly. Could she possibly be that rarity, a woman who sought to look objectively at life's circumstances? She had said the incident must not be repeated. There, he fully agreed with her. He had no desire to find himself on the business end of her father's horsewhip.

Lord, the sooner he got back to London, the better.

Eden walked resolutely until she was sure she was out of sight and sound of Seth Lindow. Then, picking up her skirts in one hand and clutching her candle in the other, she began to run and did not stop until she had reached the sanctuary of her bedchamber. She blew out the candle and flung herself on her bed.

Good God, what had possessed her? She had embarked on a midnight quest with a stranger and then allowed him to kiss and caress her as he might a flirtatious housemaid. To make matters worse, she had enjoyed the whole thing! Lord, his mouth on hers had set her aflame, and she had writhed against him like a mink in heat. What kind of woman was she? She had always thought of herself as cool and reasonably self-possessed. She had never regretted the fact that she was not the sort to inflame a man's passions, particularly since she had never met a man whose attention she desired.

Until, that is, Seth Lindow had requested her hand for a country dance. He was far from handsome—in fact, a perfectly ordinary specimen, she told herself, if one discounted his height, and his damn-your-eyes air of authority, and that compelling gaze. Why did she feel that sense of communion when they were together, that comfortable familiarity as though there was never a time she had not known him?

She had been kissed before, of course—not often, and certainly not with any degree of passion. Those brief encounters had been as different from Seth's searing kiss as a child's sparkler was from an erupting volcano.

In any event, it would not happen again. Even if Seth should wish to repeat the occasion, she could manage to stay out of his way, and he would be gone in a day or two. They might meet each other in London, but such a circumstance would be purely social and would take place, no doubt, in a roomful of people. She rose and, without ringing for her maid, prepared for bed. She would chalk up her midnight encounter to experience. She might in later years draw it out from some dusty corner of her mind to savor, for she was sure nothing like this would ever happen to her again.

After brushing her hair with unwonted briskness, she retired, but it was many minutes before she was able to compose herself for sleep.

Eden saw little of Seth the next day, for he went out again immediately after breakfast with her father. At luncheon, she searched Seth's face, but could find nothing in his expression to indicate that he bore the slightest memory of the kiss that had left her trembling and disoriented, like a leaf blown from its branch in a winter storm.

That evening, Lord Beckett proclaimed with some satisfaction to his family that Mr. Lindow had agreed to purchase for the duke's stable two hunters, a hacking mount, and six carriage horses. The portly peer was cordiality personified to his guest at dinner, and when Seth announced his plans to leave for London the next day, he rubbed his hands with satisfaction and expressed a proper regret for Mr. Lindow's imminent departure.

"Oh, but I do hope we'll be seeing you in London, sir," put in Zoë, her lashes in full flight.

"Indeed, Miss Zoë, I trust we shall encounter each other frequently." Seth turned to Lady Beckett. "When will you be arriving in the Metropolis?"

Lady Beckett lifted her hands. "Why, I'm not sure. I have written to my aunt in Portman Square, but—"

"We should be in residence in a fortnight or so," interrupted Zoë eagerly.

"Splendid! The ambassador from Portugal is arriving in England for an extended stay, and the duke and he are longtime acquaintances. His Grace is planning a dinner party in the ambassador's honor in the first part of April—the sixth or seventh, I believe. Perhaps you and your family could join us? I believe there will be dancing."

Lady Beckett appeared to be robbed of breath by the heavenly vision provoked by this query, and for some moments gabbled speechlessly. Zoë, laboring under no such hindrance, spoke up quickly.

"Why, that would be lovely, would it not, Papa?" Clapping her hands prettily, she swung to face Lord Beckett. That gentleman, satisfaction written in every line of his face, harrumphed and said he supposed so.

Eden, seated nearby in a cherry-striped wing chair, straightened. "No!" she whispered involuntarily.

The others swiveled to face her.

"What?" asked Zoë.

"Surely," she continued hastily, "the duke will not want a parcel of strangers intruding on a private dinner party. We must not—"

"Oh, Eden, don't be tiresome!" interposed Zoë. She inclined her head toward Seth. "We'd all love to attend your papa's party."

"Excellent!" declared Seth, casting a sidelong glance at Eden. "I shall have an invitation sent to your aunt's house if you will give me the direction."

No more was said on the subject, but Zoë fairly simmered all through dinner and the rest of the evening. Seth excused himself early, citing his day of travel ahead, and Eden sought her own chamber a few minutes later.

So, thought Eden as she climbed into her bed, she would not be seeing the last of Seth Lindow once he clattered away from Clearsprings tomorrow. She firmly suppressed a twinge of anticipation. She shook herself. She did *not* wish to encounter Seth again. She had spent most of a lifetime building her facade of amiable composure, and now she had met someone who possessed the ability to shatter that composure into a million lightning shards of passion. As such, he was a person devoutly to be avoided.

Mr. Lindow left Clearsprings shortly after breakfast the next day, accompanied by the beaming good will of Lord Beckett and his lady. Zoë, too, stood on the front steps, waving him off with a graceful sweep of her arm. Eden, however, chose to say her good-byes at the breakfast table, civilly wishing him a pleasant journey home. If, in issuing his own farewell, he kept her hand in his a few moments longer than was entirely proper, she made no mention of the fact. If she blushed just a little when he held her gaze, he said nothing. Nor did he give any indication as he made his way to his carriage that he was aware of her presence at an upstairs window.

On Seth's arrival in London, one of his first priorities was to apprise the duke of his recent mission.

"She sounds perfect!" exclaimed His Grace, his relief patent. "Her birth is unexceptionable, and, from what you say, she would very much like to be married to a marquess—particularly one who will someday be a duke. Er, has her father heard of Bel?"

"I believe so," replied Seth cautiously. "We did not discuss him, but Lord Beckett did not seem the sort who would cavil at—" He stopped abruptly, flushing.

"At marrying his daughter off to a degenerate rakehell?" finished the duke dryly. "No need to wrap it in clean linen."

"Er, yes. As far as I can tell, Lord Beckett is extremely anxious that his daughter marry well. He is a baron, and he's tired of being treated like a country squire. As for Lady Beckett, the mere mention of the Marquess of Belhaven puts her in a flutter. While mention of the Duke of Derwent," he added with a cynical grin, "renders her positively speechless."

He then went on to tell the duke of the invitation he planned to send to the Beckett family for the Portuguese ambassador's dinner party.

"Splendid!" declared the duke, rubbing his hands together. "I think that wraps things up then. It remains only for you to begin negotiations with the little baron to arrange the marriage between his daughter and my son."

Seth shifted uncomfortably. "I would not be so sure, Father, until you have met her. She's a taking little thing, but her manners . . . leave something to be desired."

"I suppose that must be true," replied the duke expansively, "being raised in the country and all, but I'm sure you or one of m'sisters can give her a coating of town bronze. I've asked Horatia to be hostess for the ambassador's dinner party, so perhaps she might be willing to take Miss Zoë in hand."

Seth nodded dubiously. Horatia, Countess of Shipstead, was the most formidable of the duke's sisters. A matron of impeccable *ton*, she ruled her household, including the hapless earl, four children, and seven grandchildren with an iron hand. "I should imagine," he said, "that after a few weeks under Aunt Horatia's tutelage, Zoë will become either a model of deportment or be driven into a state of complete rebellion."

The duke only laughed dismissively. "Well, we shall see what we shall see," he said before turning away to examine the snuff box he had purchased that day.

Seth stared coldly after him for a moment. Then he shrugged and left the room.

He found himself faced with a number of tasks that had accumulated during his absence; thus, after directing the duke's secretary to send a card of invitation to Lord and Lady Beckett and their daughters to the upcoming dinner, he was fully occupied during the interval of time between his return home and the party.

Still, the fortnight did not pass so quickly as he might have expected. His thoughts drifted frequently to the Beckett family. Or no, if he were to be honest, his anticipation centered solely on the idea of seeing Eden Beckett again.

Would the stolen kiss in the midnight silence of the old nursery be uppermost in her mind when they met again? Or perhaps she had already forgotten the encounter. He thrust such maunderings from him. Lord, he was behaving like a smitten schoolboy.

He would be occupied in seeing to the enjoyment and comfort of the duke's guests. He would have little time for socializing with a minor peer from the country and his family. Courtesy, however, demanded that he be on hand to greet them, since, in all likelihood he would be the only person present with whom they were acquainted. He would bid Miss Beckett welcome, along with her tedious family. He might exchange a few pleasantries with her over the course of the evening, and that would be it.

When the night of the dinner party arrived, he stood at the top of the stairs, not a part of the receiving line composed of his father and his aunt, but nearby. As the guests were ushered into the house, one by one, and directed up the stairs, he found himself scanning each group expectantly. When, at last the Becketts arrived, accompanied by a footman to the drawing room, his gaze went immediately to Eden. She was dressed with her usual propriety in a gown of a deep peach satin, trimmed around the hem and bosom with gold, embroidered acorns. Around her slender neck she wore a single strand of pearls, and another was woven in her hair, caught up with small rosettes. Drifting in a soft cloud about her shoulders was an Indian shawl, also embroidered with gold thread.

Next to her, thought Seth, Zoë and her mother looked like partridges done up as peacocks. Lady Beckett's gown of puce satin put one strongly in mind of a theater curtain, burdened by swags of fringe and tassels. In addition, she had apparently draped the entire contents of her jewelry box around her plump arms, neck, and fingers. Zoë wore a robe of a startling green, whose décolletage was completely unsuitable for a young girl on the fringes of the *ton*. Lord Beckett, himself, looked in imminent danger of choking from a very high, tight collar, whose points were already wilting under the heat of the room and the awkward consequence of its wearer.

Seth presented the Becketts to the duke and to Lady Shipstead. This lady, whose ponderous mien and imposing shelf of bosom tended to put persons who met her in mind of a ship of the line, raised her lorgnette and subjected the Beckett ladies to an examination. The entire process took only a few seconds, but not one of the examinees failed to realize that she had been surveyed from head to toe, every facet of her ensemble noted and evaluated. Lady Shipstead extended two fingers to Lord Beckett and acknowledged with a thin smile Lady Beckett's curtsey and those of her daughters.

His Grace was all cordiality as he shook Lord Beckett's hand and bowed over those of the ladies. Brushing his lips over Zoë's gloved fingers, he gazed with particular intensity at her, and the girl responded with a coquettish smile.

"I trust you are all settled comfortably into your town lodgings," he said.

"Yes," replied Zoë, a flush of excitement tinting her cheeks. "I am so glad we came!" She giggled confidingly. "I had *such* a time talking Papa into a new wardrobe, but I finally succeeded."

She pirouetted the green gown before His Grace.

Lord Beckett laughed uneasily. "I'm afraid our little puss is badly spoiled, Your Grace."

Zoë inclined her head with another giggle, as though she had just been paid a compliment. "Yes, I am. Papa always gives in—for I must admit, when I want something very badly, I refuse to take no for an answer. At any rate, we have already been invited to several balls and soirees, not including this one, of course." She fluttered her fan.

The duke frowned a little, but said in an avuncular tone, "Ah, Miss Zoë, you enjoy the empty frivolity in which we social beings indulge ourselves?"

Zoë simpered. "I know it is considered farouche to admit it, but I adore London. The shopping, the parties, the theater! And the young men can always be relied upon to simply drown one in compliments."

The duke's returning smile was, perhaps, not so admiring as she might have wished, nor did he make the rejoinder that might have been expected. Instead, he turned to Eden and said, "And you, Miss Beckett? Do you find London to your liking?"

Eden's eyes lit with her lovely smile. "I'm afraid I am more of a country mouse, Your Grace. There are aspects of city life that I enjoy—the museums and the galleries and, yes, the theater, but I must confess, I would rather be home among more familiar delights."

"Well said, my dear." The duke's gaze widened to include the others in the family. "At any rate, I do hope you will all enjoy yourselves tonight."

At this point, another contingent of guests toiled up the stairs to be greeted by the duke and his sister, and the Becketts moved into the drawing room. Seth accompanied them, introducing them to some of those already gathered in the chamber.

Among these were such exalted personages as Lord and Lady Sefton, Lord Castlereagh, and other prominent social and political figures. As was his custom, Seth did not remain in conversation with the company, but excused himself after a few moments to see that things were progressing properly in the kitchen. He realized full well that this was unnecessary, since the Duke of Derwent possessed an excellent staff that could certainly be relied on to handle a dinner party without his supervision. However, he considered it as part of his duty to keep a personal eye on all aspects of any entertainment undertaken by the duke.

Eden's gaze followed him as he left the room, and she felt oddly bereft at his departure. She had spent the previous fortnight in a state of anticipation that she found annoying in the extreme. The house had seemed inordinately empty following Seth's departure, and she found herself reflecting far too often on the enjoyment she had taken in his company.

She refused to dwell on those shattering few moments in his arms, but it cost her a great deal of self-control not to do so.

On seeing him this evening, her pulse had raced and her breath had caught in her throat as though she were the maiden in a Gothic novel, beholding her hero. Certainly, she reflected, Seth Lindow was in no way heroic, being very much an ordinary man. Resolutely, she turned away from the sight of his broad shoulders vanishing through the doors and swung back toward her family.

The important personages to whom they had been introduced soon drifted away to seek other more compatible company, and the Becketts were left standing alone in a corner of the room. Lord Beckett gazed a little wildly about the room and, spotting a gentleman who was known to him, hastened to his side. Lady Beckett rather desperately struck up a conversation with a woman standing nearby. She introduced Zoë and Eden with marginal success. Eden contributed her mite, but Zoë peeked over her fan in a covert surveillance of the population of younger, hopefully wealthy and titled gentlemen.

When the last guest arrived, the duke circulated about the room, introducing his friend, the ambassador, to those not already acquainted with him. Thus, it was not long before he appeared once more before Lady Beckett and her daughters. He chatted with them for some minutes, during which time Zoë's behavior was all that her mother could have wished. She laughed charmingly at the duke's witticisms, and the rest of the time kept her pretty mouth shut, except to answer the oddly penetrating questions put to her by the duke.

Seth returned to the drawing room just before dinner was announced, and he accompanied Lady Beckett and her daughters into the dining room. To Eden's surprise, she found herself seated next to him, near the middle of the table.

Catching her expression, Seth lifted his own brows quizzically.

"It is nothing," said Eden, "only I would expect to see you seated nearer your father." She gestured toward the duke, who presided, of course, at the head of the table with the ambassador at his right.

"Actually," he said somewhat stiffly, "I rarely sit at table at one of these functions. As His Grace's man of affairs, I would not ordinarily do so, and I prefer to keep my status as his adopted son in the background."

"Is that how the duke prefers it, as well?"

Immediately, she could have bitten her tongue at asking such a personal question, but Seth merely smiled. "Oh, no. He has never given the slightest indication that he cares one way or another." The words were uttered dispassionately and without a hint of self-pity. However, he apparently wished he had not uttered them. "As I believe I explained before, I think it would be very wrong of me to take advantage of the duke's good deed on behalf of a scruffy orphan boy."

"But, I promise you, Mr. Lindow, you are not even slightly scruffy now. It seems to me you have repaid His Grace a thousandfold for his kindness. Surely he is fortunate in having you not just for a skilled man of affairs, but as his son, as well."

Eden had spoken with a great deal more vehemence than she intended, and now she blushed. Seth's dark eyes lit with amusement.

"I thank you for your endorsement, Miss Beckett. However, the fact remains that I neither expect nor desire gratitude from His Grace. My service to him is of my own accord, and I consider it a private matter."

His tone was courteous, but Eden blushed yet again. Trying to ignore the pointed manner in which she had been put in her place, she turned the conversation to a more neutral subject matter, commenting on some of the dignitaries she had met that evening.

"The gentleman with the turban?" replied Seth to a question. "That is Randar Singh. He is a representative of the Maharajah of Gujarat. He is in London to negotiate with Parliament regarding the dispersion of certain property belonging to the maharajah. As I understand it, our government would like to build a road for the movement of troops in his dominion."

The two chatted in a similar vein for several more minutes before Eden was obliged to turn away to converse with the gentleman on her right, a Lord Wismouth from Exeter. She had been introduced to him earlier in the evening, and now discovered from his consequential dialogue that he rarely visited London, but preferred to remain among his gardens and books. When Eden professed a like sentiment, he became positively loquacious, describing his snug little property in Devon and the works of Sir Walter Scott, in which he was currently engrossed.

Eden was herself a devotee of Sir Walter and would have enjoyed her discussion with the gentleman from Devon, if she was not so conscious of the gentleman on her left, now conversing with the Countess of Silchester. At last, as part of the obligatory shift in conversational partners, she turned to Seth once more. There was a moment of silence before he spoke.

"Is Miss Zoë enjoying herself this evening?"

Eden's insides lurched unpleasantly. Seth had appeared fairly immune to Zoë's beguilements, but his question indicated more than a casual interest in her sister.

"I believe so," she replied cautiously. "Zoë enjoys any sort of social function, and one such as this must rank very high on her list of memorable occasions."

"Tell me about the rest of your family," said Seth abruptly. "I believe you have three married sisters."

"Yes," Eden replied, wondering at Seth's intent, for she was sure he had not posed his question out of idle curiosity. Why, she wondered distractedly, did she feel this familiarity with his thought processes? Nothing in his expression indicated that his query had been uttered from any other motive than idle courtesy. She knew, however, as surely as though Seth had hung out a sign, that he was after something. "Margaret," she continued, "or Meg, as we call her, is married to Joseph Mallow, a squire in Kent. Dorothy is next, and we don't see her very often as she lives in Northumberland. Her husband is Sir Arthur Beddoes and their estate is extensive. Eleanor's husband, as she is fond of telling us, is the nephew of the Earl of Waterston, and they reside in Bedfordshire."

"They all seemed to have married comfortably. Lord and Lady Beckett must be pleased."

Eden took a sip of wine. "Mm, yes. Although," she added with an engaging grin, "they would have preferred a trifle more rank somewhere in the mix. As with any parents, they desire to see their children marry well. Papa, especially—although I should not say this—especially enjoys Eleanor's connection with the earl."

"And your mother?"

Eden was beginning to grow uneasy at Seth's probing. "Yes, she, too, is pleased. She . . . she has taken pains, of course, to assure that all her daughters are creditably settled and secure."

"Of course." Seth paused meditatively. "Your sister, too, seems interested in making an advantageous marriage."

Lord, did he consider himself in the light of a suitable *parti* for Zoë? Was he using her merely as a sounding board?

"I would prefer," she answered stiffly, scooping up a forkful of croquembouche, "to say that Zoë knows her own worth and hopes to wed a man who will assure her of an amiable place in society."

Her manner so clearly indicated that she thought the whole subject none of his business that he smiled ruefully. "You must think me a regular Paul Pry, but I meant only that, since my visit to your charming home, I must confess myself interested in your equally charming family. I apologize if my curiosity has gone beyond what is proper."

Eden found herself at somewhat of a loss for a reply, and was grateful the next moment when a faint, startled cry issued from farther down the table. Darting a glance in the direction of the sound, Eden observed that Lady Dinsborough, whom she knew to be seated across the table from Zoë, held her napkin pressed to her mouth in obvious horror and distaste.

Eden's heard sank. Now what had Zoë done?

Chapter Nine

Eden was not obliged to contain her apprehension for very long. In a few minutes, Lady Shipstead rose to signify the retreat of the ladies to the drawing room. Eden hastened to Zoë's side, noting the dagger glances sent her sister's way by Miss Honora Paisley, who had been seated a place or two down from Zoë.

"What in the world happened?" she asked, grasping Zoë's arm.

Zoë laughed airily. "Nothing, really. I fear I put the divine Miss Paisley's nose out of joint. You know, of course, that she must weigh upwards of ten stone. Despite this, she considers herself an Incomparable. A Diamond of the First Water, no less. Really, Eden, she just infuriates me."

Eden bent a minatory stare on her. "What have you done, Zoë?"

"Nothing," the girl repeated. "Only, during dinner Lord Bascombe was seated next to me, and Miss God's Gift to the Males of London kept interrupting our conversation. Honestly, Eden, it was enough to make one sick the way she simpered and flapped her eyelashes and flopped her pudgy little hand on his arm every time he directed a comment at me. When the croquembouche was served—would you believe—she asked for a second helping! The footman asked if she'd like another after that, and she giggled and said that she mustn't, for she was obliged to watch her figure. Then she stared expectantly up at Lord Bascombe, just waiting for him to babble something complimentary. Well, the poor man was at a complete loss, and I said—oh, I know I shouldn't have, for I spoke directly across his lordship—but I said, 'Oh, but we're all watching your figure, Miss Paisley. How can one do otherwise?' "

Zoë ducked her head. "I must have spoken a trifle loudly, for

Lady Dinsborough, across the table from me, nearly choked, and Honora let out a squeal like a stricken rhinoceros."

"Oh, Zoë, how could you?" gasped Eden. "To so expose yourself to censure in the Duke of Derwent's home, of all places."

Zoë sighed. "I know it was wrong, but—oh, Eden, if you could have seen her. Tossing her curls and draping herself over Lord Bascomb's shoulder in the most *blatant* display. Besides, she's been quite horrid to me all evening, lifting that squashed-in little nose every time I approach, as though I'd just strolled in from the stables. After all, everyone knows her grandfather was in trade." She turned to Eden. "I heard her say something cutting about you, too, to Lord Wilburton. I almost gave her a setdown then. It's my belief that she can't abide the presence of anyone who might outshine her—which, of course, includes almost every female in the Home Counties." She sighed. "I wonder if this means we shan't be invited to Derwent House again."

Eden glanced at her, startled. "I should scarcely think we shall be invited back under any circumstances. Our being here tonight is only a courtesy due to Se—that is, Mr. Lindow's recent visit."

Zoë tossed her head. "Nonsense. I'm sure he will invite us back if I am nice to His Grace, and I intend to be ever so charming to him—and his sister."

By then, they had reached the drawing room, and Zoë drifted away to speak to one of the younger women to whom she had been introduced earlier. Eden frowned. She hoped Zoë was not pinning entirely unrealistic hopes on the possibility of gaining the Duke of Derwent's patronage. Certainly, if the duke were numbered among her friends, her social status would undergo a marked improvement, but surely Zoë did not believe that, even if such an unlikely event were to come to pass, a friendship with His Grace would lead to her highly desired union with a peer.

She moved to her mother, who had seated herself on a straw satin settee. She forbore mentioning Zoë's confrontation with Miss Paisley, seeing no good point in sending Mama into a spasm in the middle of a *ton* party. That lady was still very much in alt at their very presence here, and her conversation dealt entirely with the magnificence of the company, the elegance and cost of their dress, and the exalted gentlemen who she was sure were smitten to a man by their little Zoë.

She continued in this vein, unnoticing of the buzz that circulated as Miss Paisley made her way around the room, or the increasing number of hostile stares directed by the other ladies present at their little Zoë, until at last the gentlemen emerged from the dining room. Eden's gaze flew without volition to Seth, only to find herself staring straight into his dark eyes. She drew in a startled breath at the sharp, almost painful sensation that swept over her, as though she had been subjected to an electrical shock.

Seth's eyes widened as though acknowledging the same connection. The next moment, he smiled faintly and looked away. As the gentlemen entered the room, Eden observed Lady Dinsborough advancing on the duke. Her hands waved in the air as she whispered volubly in his ear, glancing several times in Zoë's direction. Good Lord, thought Eden, the woman was losing no time in reporting Zoë's hoydenish behavior to His Grace. Her ladyship was evidently describing the incident in great detail. At one point, Lady Dinsborough placed a hand on the prow of her bosom and gave an exaggerated tug to the bodice of her gown. She then inclined her body forward and at the same time twisted her mouth in an alarming grimace, meant apparently to imitate a seductive smile, all the while rolling her eyes wildly and fluttering her sparse eyelashes.

The duke listened attentively, his mouth twitching once or twice during the viscountess's narration. At the end, however, while he smiled courteously, his expression was grave.

Evidently, Zoë had also been watching the little drama, for scarcely had Lady Dinsborough left the duke's side, than she hurried to take her place. She opened negotiations with a winsome smile, apparently offering her own version of the contretemps with Miss Paisley. The winsome smile phased into one of charming contrition, followed by a flirt of her fan. It was difficult to ascertain the success of her efforts, for, although the ducal countenance wore a pleasant expression, it was quite unreadable. After a while, Zoë abandoned her efforts and turned away, her smile sagging a trifle.

Eden had no chance to interrogate Zoë on her conversation with the duke, for in a moment, the guests began to troop into the music room to listen to Madame Naldi, the Seasons's most popular singer, who entertained for some time with a pleasant range of selections from the classics to Italian folk tunes.

Eden, relishing the rare opportunity to hear one of the premier vocalists of the time, soon lost herself in the music, but jerked to attention at a light tap on her arm. She turned to behold Seth, who had come into the room moments before to seat himself next to her.

"Do you admire the Naldi?" he whispered, a warm twinkle in his eyes.

"Very much. I hope to see her at the opera sometime during our visit." Observing Seth's downturned mouth, she added, "You do not enjoy her performance?"

"Oh, of course, but I must admit I would rather listen to you and Miss Zoë. I prefer a fresh voice, one with unaffected sweetness, to one of such unrelenting culture. One could stir gravy with her vibrato."

Eden was surprised into a trill of laughter.

"Although," added Seth, "it could be just my commonplace origin speaking."

Eden shot him a startled glance. Had she detected a note of bitterness in his tone? He seemed to search out opportunities to insert his background into the conversation. She introduced a neutral topic, and the two chatted companionably until Madame Naldi had warbled her last. Then Seth left her again to attend his perceived duties. It was not until some of the guests made preparations to depart, the Becketts included, that she saw him again. The duke was on hand as well, Lady Shipstead at his side, to receive felicitations from his guests on a most pleasant evening. Seth moved to join them in the elegant entrance hall, as the duke smiled once more on Lord and Lady Beckett.

"I'm so pleased you could join us this evening. Did you enjoy yourselves?"

"Oh, yes," breathed Zoë. "It was lovely. I hope—"

But, what it was she hoped remained unspoken as a raucous bang sounded on the front door. Before the butler could approach, it was flung open to reveal a disheveled figure, swaying on the threshold.

"Bel!" exclaimed Seth in horrified accents, echoed by the duke and Lady Shipstead.

Lord Belhaven swept off his hat in a grandiloquent gesture

· and bowed, nearly toppling over in the effort. He tossed the hat
in the general direction of the butler and, removing his gloves
carefully, dropped them into the servant's outstretched hand.

"Thank you so much, Fosdick, isn't it?"

"No, my lord," returned the butler austerely. "Fosdick left
two years ago. I am Bentick."

Bel waved a dismissive hand. "O'course."

His gaze, red and unfocused, swept the entrance hall, coming
to rest on his father.

"But you did not tell me you're having a party, Papa," he said
sweetly. "By some oversight, you neglected to invite me. Although," he added with a loose smile. "I see that Seth is in attendance, as usual."

His speech was not slurred, but he spoke with the almost
painful precision of the very drunk. The other guests, lingering
in the hall, paused to stare in avid fascination.

"Bel!" said the duke again, hurrying toward him. "What the
devil are you doing here?"

"Just driving by, doncherknow," he drawled. "Saw the extra
flambeaux lit, the bustle of carriages, and all that. 'What ho?'
says I to m'self, and I realized at once that you would be devas-
tated were I not to participate in the festivities." He glanced
owlishly about the hall. "But, perhaps I am too late?"

At this, Lady Shipstead stepped forward. "Yes, you are, Bel,
and in your usual disgusting condition. Kindly oblige us by
leaving at once."

Bel swung to face the duke directly. His hand went to his
brow in a melodramatic gesture, and his eyes widened in an expression of wounded bewilderment. "But, Papa, you cannot
mean that my presence is unwanted?" He swept an arm about
the hall, again nearly throwing himself to the floor. "Surely, you
could not have planned to entertain the cream of society in our
home without your own son and heir at your side—the pride
and joy of your house?"

The duke spoke in a low tone. "Bel, certainly if we thought
there was the slightest chance that you would have come, of
course we—"

Seth stepped forward to grasp Bel's arm, gently interrupting
his father. "Bel, you must see this is not the time—"

"Ah, yes, my brother—good old reliable Seth, the sainted
cuckoo in our midst."

Seth, refusing to rise to the bait, said only, "Yes, yes, Bel, but right now . . ."

Aware of the eyes watching greedily for any tidbit of scandal, Seth attempted to propel his brother toward the door. Bel, however, had other ideas. Pulling himself from Seth's grip, he turned back to his father. His gaze encompassed the Becketts, who still stood nearby, rooted in stupefaction. On beholding Zoë, he first staggered backward, then lunged forward. Lurching to stand directly in front of her, he scrabbled untidily for his quizzing glass through which he surveyed her leisurely from head to toe.

Lord Beckett started forward. "Now see here, young sir!" he exclaimed with fists clenched.

But Seth was before him. Once more he grasped his brother's arm. "Bel, for God's sake! . . . You're insulting a lady!"

The lady, however, appeared in no way insulted. She blushed prettily and smiled, gazing up at the viscount through her forest of lashes.

Bel lifted her hand in his and brushed her fingertips with his lips. "But I think we have met before?" he whispered, an acquisitive gleam in his eyes.

"Oh, I don't think so," replied Zoë, meeting his gaze unabashedly. "I would have remembered."

The two stood, wrapped in mutual bemusement. Not another sound was heard in the hall except for the music, drifting down from the ballroom. Wordlessly, his hand still holding Zoë's, Bel moved to encircle her waist with his other arm. He drew her away from the group and began a slow waltz in the center of the hall floor.

Zoë at first stiffened in startlement, then with a self-conscious glance around her, joined Bel in his outrageous performance.

Eden gasped. Dear Lord, what did the man think he was about? For one of his reputation to approach a young girl in such a fashion! Zoë had not received permission to waltz from the patronesses of Almack's. Well, she wasn't even on speaking terms with those ladies, and her behavior so far this evening was not likely to promote such an eventuality.

Lord, what was she maundering on about? thought Eden wildly. She stared at the couple, performing a slow, sinuous dance, their eyes locked. The propriety of Zoë's waltzing was hardly the issue when what was taking place before her eyes seemed only slightly less than a full-blown seduction to music. Not a single one of the persons in the hall was making the slightest move to depart, but looked as though they intended to stay rooted to the floor until the little drama was fully played out.

Drawing a deep breath, Eden stepped forward. "This has been a lovely evening, Your Grace," she said in a clear, carrying voice. "We have so enjoyed meeting you, and . . . and your family. I do hope we shall meet again."

So saying, she took her mother's elbow and moved to where Zoë and the viscount swayed dreamily to the music.

"Zoë, dear, I am *so* sorry to interrupt your impromptu waltz, but the carriage has been brought about and the horses are standing."

She pinched her mother's arm, and that lady spoke in a shaking voice.

"Yes, indeed, my love. It is time to go."

For a moment, Eden feared her words had had no effect, and that Belhaven would not release her sister. However, she discovered with gratitude that Seth was right behind her. His features rigid with anger, he placed a hand on Bel's shoulder. Glancing up, the marquess smiled lazily at Seth, but stopped dancing and, bowing low, withdrew his arm from Zoë's waist.

Zoë tittered behind her fan and curtseyed.

Servants began to bustle into the hall at that point, carrying cloaks and hats and canes. The guests claimed their belongings and, their gazes lingering on Bel, somewhat regretfully bade farewell to the duke and drifted past the open door into the night.

Inside the house, the duke saw the last of the party-goers from the house and, white with anger, turned to his heir.

"Come upstairs, Bel. Bentick"—he gestured to the butler—"send someone up to the blue saloon with coffee." He laid a hand on his son's arm, but Bel shrugged it off.

"I ain't staying, Father. Only dropped in to see what I was missing, if anything. For God's sake don't try to turn it into a cozy family gathering."

"But, Bel—"

"On the other hand, for once I don't feel I wasted my time in coming here. Who was that charming little armful? And what the devil was she doing here among the pillars of society?"

"Her name is Zoë Beckett," interposed Seth. "Don't you recall Lady Saltram's ball? You saw her there, and were quite struck. We were talking about the current crop of marriageable young ladies," he added carefully.

Bel snorted. "Marriage? Li'l baggage is far more likely to end up in a Covent Garden nunnery. Where," he concluded with a crooked leer, "I shall take care to become her first paying customer."

What the dukc might have replied to this highly inflammatory statement was lost as Bel bade a peremptory farewell to his family and stumbled out the door. Thus, he was on hand as the Beckett carriage trundled away from Derwent House. He lifted a hand to Zoë in a sardonic salute.

"Well," declared Zoë in some satisfaction. "I *knew* a great deal of good would come of your association with Mr. Lindow, Papa. Only see, I have met a duke's son—and if I do say so, I can't help but believe he was taken with me." She twined a golden curl about her finger in satisfaction.

Lord Beckett twisted in his seat to stare at her. "Taken with you? *Taken* with you! It looked to me—and to everyone there with eyes in their heads—as though he was going to *take* you right there on the floor!"

Lady Beckett gasped, and she murmured incoherently between broken sobs.

"How the devil," Lord Beckett roared, "could you have let that . . . that thatchgallows maul you likc a common drab? *Dancing* with you—although that's not what I'd call it—in the duke's entry hall, and him drunk as a . . . well, as a lord. By God, I should have taken a horsewhip to the feller!"

"Oh, Papa," replied Zoë placidly. "He was a little well to go, as the gentlemen say, but *I* think he was being ever so romantic. I shouldn't wonder if hc wcre to call tomorrow."

"Well, if he does," Lord Beckett retorted with a snort, "I shall have something to say to him."

Eden spoke. "I think he was merely amusing himself, Papa. It's my belief he merely wished to do something outrageous enough to set the duke's teeth on edge. It appears to give him great satisfaction to embarrass his father. You would do well to remember that, Zoë."

"Oh, yes, I shall." To Eden's surprise, Zoë's voice was calm. "But the fact remains that I quite took his fancy. And," she added with a smile that Eden could only consider ominous, "he quite took mine, too."

Chapter Ten

Some time later, Seth and the duke conversed quietly in the library.

"You would not," said Seth, "want her parents running tame in Derwent House—or The Priory, for that matter. They're not bad sorts, actually, but . . . well, you saw how they were tonight, completely unhinged in the presence of exalted company."

"Except for the older girl," the duke mused aloud.

"Yes." Seth smiled warmly. "Except for Eden. She is a pearl beyond price, isn't she?"

The duke glanced up in surprise, and Seth rushed on. "That is, in comparison with her sister and her parents, she is a model of gentility."

"Mmm. Miss Zoë, on the other hand . . . She appears on the face of it to be an ideal candidate for Bel's bride—but in actuality, she is absolutely impossible. She has the deportment of a badly trained puppy. She's bumptious, ill-mannered, self-aggrandizing, and pursues her own whims with all the subtlety of a brass gong."

Seth sighed. "I had come to the same conclusion myself. It's my belief that she would very much fancy herself as a marchioness—and Mama and Papa Beckett would be ecstatic at the prospect. I was hoping that their aspirations would prove an incentive for her to fit herself into the proper mold. But, after seeing her tonight . . ."

"I do not believe that young woman would recognize the proper mold if it knocked on her front door and bit her on the hand. Nor can I see her sitting with her hands folded in submission for months on end on an estate in Northumberland, or wherever Bel should choose to tuck her away."

Seth sighed again. "No, she would probably be on the first

available coach to London—and she would no doubt create havoc once she got here." He lifted a hand in frustration. "I was so hopeful that Zoë Beckett would fill the bill. I shall just have to continue the search, although the choices—"

"However," interrupted the duke in a meditative tone, "I was very much taken with the older one. Eden, is it?"

For a moment, Seth felt as though his heart had stopped beating, a circumstance immediately proved false as that organ began banging against the walls of his chest like a prisoner attempting escape. "Eden Beckett?" he asked stupidly.

"Yes. She is everything that we discussed—everything that Zoë is not—quiet, reserved, well-bred and she likes living in the country."

"Yes, but . . ." Seth felt as though he were being plunged into a nightmare. "She has no desire—at least, it is my impression that she has no wish to become a peeress. Wealth and jewels and status and all that flummery mean nothing to her. She wants only to be left alone to garden and paint, and—"

"You seem to know a great deal about her," remarked the duke, his brows lifted.

Seth flushed. "Yes, well, I became rather well acquainted with her while I was at the Beckett estate, Clearsprings. Frankly, she was the only member of the family whose company I could tolerate for more than five minutes at a stretch. But surely—"

"I see." The duke tapped his finger thoughtfully on the arm of his chair before twisting to face Seth. "My boy, I believe she represents our salvation. You've already found her background to be suitable. She may not be impressed at the thought of an exalted title, but I should imagine she might be persuaded by the prospect of a life of comfort and ease in pleasant surroundings. She would be welcome at The Priory, but if she should wish to set up her own establishment at Broadbent, she can garden and paint to her heart's content. She may form friendships among the surrounding gentry and, should she wish to travel to London from time to time, I'm sure that can be arranged. I'm sure that once wed to Bel, she would not be a source of embarrassment for the family. In fact, if anyone might have a hope of persuading Bel to settle down, I feel it would be she. Horatia was much taken with her," he added, as though this fact convinced him of his wisdom in pursuing this plan.

Seth found that his hands were perspiring. He felt light-headed. Somehow, he had been able to salve his conscience at the idea of saddling young Zoë with his brother. The flighty young miss assuredly deserved better, but he had no doubt of Zoë's ability to reconcile herself to her circumstances in exchange for the position she craved. Eden was another matter. No, he *could* not subject this eminently likable young woman to a life of bondage to Bel's careless cruelty. He would have to make Father understand.

"I tell you, Seth, the more I think about it, the more I'm convinced that Miss Beckett's the gel we're after." The duke smiled thinly. "What I think you should do now is see a bit more of her—just to make sure our first assessment of her character is correct. While you're at it, you might make her aware of all the advantages of a union with Bel. There are quite a few, you know," he added reflectively, "particularly to one who craves only solitude and a comfortable life. Then, after a judicious interval, you can begin negotiations with Lord Beckett. When you've won him over, which shouldn't take more than five minutes by the look of things, we can hope that Miss Beckett will fall into line."

"Fall into line?" Seth spoke through a lump the size of Dorset that had settled in his throat. No! He could not do this. Eden must not marry Bel. The thought of Bel's hands on her, the demeaning insults—and worse—to which she would be subjected when Bel fell into one of his frequent rages, the abandonment through no fault of her own . . . He felt physically ill.

Seth looked at his father, absorbing the expression of relief that had replaced the strain so evident there in the past weeks. To his utter dismay, he also perceived determination in the duke's eyes. Seth went cold with the realization that the duke's wish in this matter would not be swayed lightly. Once the old man's desires had taken root, he would brook no opposition. Not that he wished to oppose his father in his desire to see Bel safely buckled. And, of course, there was no doubt that Eden would be the perfect wife for the marquess. Her affections, he believed, were not engaged with any other man of her acquaintance. Nor would she be likely to form a *tendre* for Bel, (and that was all to the good), for she did not seem the type to be taken in by his blandishments—even if he put himself to the trouble to trot them out for her. She could be content at Broadbent, Bel's far-flung estate, he felt sure, filling the place with books and her art work, and cultivating her roses.

Something, which he did not wish to examine closely, churned unpleasantly within him at the thought of Eden wed to his brother—or to anyone else, for that matter, but . . . His gaze turned again to the duke, who was watching him expectantly. It was obvious His Grace wanted this union very badly, and what the duke desired, of course . . .

Seth swallowed. "Yes, Father," he whispered through stiff lips.

"Very good, my boy." The duke frowned. "Spend some time with the gel, and we'll talk again, say, next week. I don't want to rush things, of course, but, as I believe I've said, it is essential that we get Bel safely leg-shackled, with an heir on the way, before he gets into some really serious difficulty."

He declined to specify what form that difficulty might take, but from his troubled expression, it was obvious that he still feared Bel's future iniquities might well cost him his life.

"I shall begin tomorrow, Father," said Seth in a colorless tone.

The duke then went on to chat inconsequentially about the success of his party. Seth found himself unable to contribute to the conversation and excused himself after a few moments. Making his way to his chambers, he moved in a fog of depression. The cloud grew heavier as he prepared for bed, assuming an almost physical weight that seemed to press in on him until he felt as though it were crushing him.

Once in bed, he stared sightlessly into the canopy overhead. Good God, what had he become? Was he so conditioned to pandering to the duke's needs that he could suppress the voice of his conscience without a second thought? Could he do this? he wondered. *How* could he do this? And why was it that, while he had had no difficulty in designating Zoë as the sacrificial lamb in his father's plans, it was almost more than he could bear to cast Eden in the same role? Was it simply because he knew of Zoë's relentless absorption in her own desires? Her driving ambition to marry a high-ranking peer and cut a dash in the *beau monde*? Did that make her deserving of a lifetime of misery with someone like the Marquess of Belhaven? Probably not, but the thing was, he told himself once again, that even were Zoë fully apprised of what she would be getting into, there was little doubt in Seth's mind that she would be willing to put up with almost any unpleasantness in order to gain the fulfillment of those desires.

Eden was as different from Zoë as night from day. She was an extraordinary young woman with an extraordinary talent. She might be willing to live in virtual isolation, might even thrive under such conditions, but no one deserved the emotional—and possible physical—abuse that would come from marriage with Bel. Of course, Seth would do his best to prevent Bel from harming his wife, no matter if it was Zoë or Eden, but he could not be on hand for every minute of their wedded life— particularly if Bel removed his bride to a distant estate.

Good God, he thought, self-contempt snaking through him, what was he doing in the midst of these machinations? Was nothing nothing but a toady, entrapping innocent young women for his father's purposes? He owed everything that he had become to the Duke of Derwent, but he had realized long ago that the duke regarded him as little more than a minor adjunct to his family. It had taken longer for Seth's blind boyhood love for the duke to wither, to be replaced by a mild, contemptuous affection. The strength of the vow remained, but was the task he had been set too much for any man of principles to attempt?

Seth had discovered early in himself a talent for the management of the Derwent interests. The duke's holdings had thrived under his care. In addition, he had carved a good life for himself. Careful investments on his own behalf with funds bequeathed to him by one of the duke's brothers had provided him with a more than comfortable independence. This was not the first time it had become necessary to implement an undertaking that was, perhaps, somewhat less than pure, but he had never been asked to compromise his standards so thoroughly. Could he now meet his first real test of what he perceived as his responsibility to the duke?

Of course, he would. For all these years, he'd done whatever it took to make the duke happy. Was this not his sworn duty?

These and similar reflections kept Seth awake for most of the night. However, despite having fallen into a restless sleep only as the clock struck five, he awoke just before seven. Groaning, he rose and, declining to ring for his valet, dressed in breeches and a comfortable coat. He stopped in the kitchen for a cup of coffee and a slice of bread before walking to the stable. In a few moments, he was mounted and clattering from Grosvenor Square into South Audley Street. From thence he turned into Curzon Street toward Green Park.

On this early April morning the park was still covered in patches of mist, slashed by slanting early rays of sunlight. No one was abroad, except for a few milkmaids come to tend the small herd of cows that ranged there. These ladies had just begun milking the cows for later dispensing of the milk at a nominal fee to strollers in the park.

Unheeding, Seth trotted toward the bridle path that ran from the basin to the Rangers' Lodge. When he had reached its head, he loosed the horse for a straight-out gallop, slowing only as he again reached the cows. Careful not to disturb these beasts, nor the young women engaged in their milking, he proceeded toward the west end of the park, only to be brought up short by the sight of a slight figure seated upon a bench nearby. She held a sketchbook in her lap and was apparently occupied in drawing the maids and their charges. Staring hard for a moment, Seth walked his horse toward the woman. She looked up at his approach.

"Mr. Lindow!" she exclaimed, seeming oddly flustered.

"You are out and about early, Miss Beckett." He dismounted and tied the reins lightly to a tree where the mare, Hyacinth, already stood tethered, in the care of a groom.

"It seems that I am no more able to lie abed of a morning in town than I am in the country," Eden said with a laugh.

"And, of course," added Seth gravely, "you were obliged to exercise Hyacinth."

"Indeed." Eden's eyes twinkled. "It is fortunate you did not come upon me a few minutes earlier, for I must admit to you that I let her have her head and enjoyed a glorious gallop, nearly stampeding the cows—of whose existence, I might say, I was heretofore unaware. They really ought to issue bulletins for strangers to Town to tell them of these things."

"But you are not a stranger. You have visited London before, for extended periods of time, have you not?"

"Yes, but it is only recently that I have asserted my independence so far as to ride out in the morning with only my groom for company. Before, I must needs wait for Zoë to rouse herself, and then we would only go to Hyde Park. I must tell you, I feel myself quite the pioneer, venturing into uncharted territory."

"And I must say to you, that pioneering agrees with you, for you are looking very fetching today, Miss Beckett."

Seth was surprised at the blush that spread from her cheeks down to the vee of her neck, where it disappeared into the collar of her riding habit. Was she so unaccustomed to receiving compliments? If she could just manage to stay out of the vicinity of her sister's showy beauty, she'd surely get more of them, for this morning she looked lovely. Her riding habit was conservative, but its tailored elegance suited her, outlining her supple curves. The polished mahogany of her hair peeped in an enchanting swirl from beneath a saucy hat whose wisp of a feather matched her habit. Her silken lashes swept over classically carved cheeks, still delicately flushed. The wings of her brows curved upward as she laughed, and Seth thought her altogether enchanting.

A sudden constriction in his throat made it difficult for him to speak, and he glanced instead at her sketchbook.

Following his gaze, Eden smiled. "Behold the milkmaids of Green Park."

Seth's brows lifted. The young women were accurately caught in their activity, but they were garbed in clothing that might have come from the previous century.

"I kept thinking of the Petit Trianon," she explained. "I could just see Marie Antoinette on her *faux* dairy farm, her ladies-in-waiting gathered about her, carrying shepherd's crooks and miniature yokes. I'm afraid I allowed myself to be carried away by the absurdity of it all."

Seth examined the sketch, his lips quirked in appreciation of the ladies' exaggerated posturing and the towering wigs with which each had been adorned. Eden laughed again, and tore the paper from its pad.

"Have you set up a studio in your aunt's town house?" asked Seth.

"Of a sort. I've commandeered a small room in the garret, amidst the maids' quarters. I believe they think I'm quite mad, but the light is good there, and I am content."

Seth mused angrily for a moment on Eden's family, who forced her to such measures in order that she might pursue the one thing in her life that seemed to give her true happiness.

Eden rose. "I believe I must return home. I did not leave word that I was leaving the house, and if Mama comes down to find me gone, she will be sure I have been abducted and sold into slavery." She moved toward Hyacinth and slipped the sketch pad into a saddlebag.

Accepting Seth's cupped hands, she swung into the saddle. Seth followed suit, and a moment later, the two, with Eden's groom following at a respectful distance, formed a sedate procession from the park. Emerging into Piccadilly, Seth urged both their mounts to the left in order to detour around a group of roisterers returning to their abodes after a night of carousing. They had progressed only a few paces toward Half Moon Street when Seth, to his consternation, heard his name called in slurred accents.

"Oy! Saint Seth! Aincher goin' to bid your favorite brother good mornin'?"

Seth suppressed a sinking in the pit of his stomach as he turned to face Bel.

Chapter Eleven

There were five of them, on foot. They were evidently returning from one of the unsavory sluiceries located just past Tattersall's near Hyde Park Corner. Three were relatively sober, apparently just entering into the throes of morning-after distress. The other two, including Bel, were still very much under the influence of their potations. The clothing of all was stained and disheveled.

Bel rocked back on his heels.

"I don' s'pose," he drawled, "that you, too, are returning home after a night on the tiles, brother mine, with this tasty dish in tow." He waved an unsteady arm at Eden.

Eden, under his unfocused leer, instinctively shrank closer to Seth. She felt unclean beneath that lickerish scrutiny.

As though relishing her distaste, Bel approached, leaving his companions murmuring among themselves on the pavement.

"Bel," said Seth, in a low, warning voice.

"Ah, staked out a claim, have you, Seth?" Blinking as though to clear his vision, he peered up at her. "Bu' wait, ain' I seen you before, my chick?"

Before Seth could speak again, Eden said in what she hoped was a voice of cool detachment, "I am Eden Beckett, Zoë's sister. I believe we met last evening."

Bel swayed. "Zoë Beckett. Now, I do remember her. What a cozy little armful! I wun' mind having her warm my bed for a night or two." He grinned loosely. "I'll have to pay a call on the pretty little pigeon."

Eden gasped, and Seth dismounted. He and Bel were approximately the same height, but to Eden it seemed as though Seth loomed over his brother by a good two feet.

"Bel," he snapped, "I'll thank you to remember you are in the presence of a lady—and so is her sister."

Bel chuckled muzzily. "No 'fense, ol' fella." He groped for his quizzing glass. "I mus' say, though, hard t'believe this one tricks out so nicely 'n dayli'." He paused and swung questioningly toward Seth. "Din't I think she was an an'idote when I saw 'er that night at La'y Watzername's ball? Aaugh!" he concluded, as at that point Seth knocked him to the pavement with a single blow to his jaw.

Bel's fellow inebriates watched in befuddled amazement as Bel scrabbled to raise himself on an elbow, one hand cradling his jaw. An ugly snarl formed on his features.

"Don't bother to get up," said Seth coldly. His eyes were like rain-washed slate, glittering with animosity. "I should only have to knock you down again, and I'd hate to take advantage of one so completely incapacitated."

So saying, he swung himself back into his saddle and, grasping Hyacinth's reins, led the mare away from the scene and into Half Moon Street. Bel called something unintelligible after him, but Seth did not so much as turn his head.

They proceeded up Half Moon Street in silence, and when they had turned up Curzon Street, Eden drew a long, shaking breath.

"I do not wish to speak ill of your relatives, Mr. Lindow, but your brother seems a most unpleasant young man."

Seth sighed. Lord, things were getting off to a rocky start indeed in his campaign to win Eden Beckett as a bride for his brother. Should he attempt to gloss over Bel's actions? No, he concluded. Let him be honest, if nothing else.

"Unpleasant hardly covers it, although," he added hastily, "he . . . he is not such a . . . a bad sort, really."

Eden's gaze flew to his, and she frowned doubtfully. He berated himself. For God's sake, that was no good either. Eden obviously realized that he did not believe what he was saying. Seth began again.

"Well, yes, he is . . . thoroughly impossible, at least since he reached adulthood. When he was younger, he could be pleasant. In fact, until he was seven or eight years of age, he seemed a perfectly normal little boy. Oh, he had his tantrums, but he laughed more than he cried, and he lavished loving attention on his puppies and even displayed a measure of affection for me.

"Then he began to change. He would fly into rages, and soon became completely unmanageable. He . . . he tortured the puppies. Now . . . Sometimes, he is not so bad as others, of course, but he always has an insult or a cutting remark, and if he knows you have a tender spot, that is where he will prod." Seth shook his head. "The transformation took place so abruptly, it was almost as though an evil spirit had laid a curse on him. He began to complain of terrible headaches. His moods would swing from an almost feverish gaiety to the depths of despairing gloom, and he became violent.

"He took delight in setting up the backs of the neighbors and driving the duke and duchess to distraction. He tormented his sisters almost beyond endurance. As for me, he did his best to make my life a living hell, particularly at Eton, where he lost no opportunity to inform the student body at large of my common background. He and his friends made it their mission in life to humiliate me."

"Dear heaven!" breathed Eden. "Did your father do nothing to stop him?"

"Father made it clear early on in my life that I must fight my own battles, for he would or could not be bothered." Seth brought himself up sharply. "Good God, please forgive me. I must sound like a sniveling shag bag. Indeed, I felt abominably sorry for myself at the time, but, having survived, I emerged the stronger for Bel's tender mercies."

Seth discovered he was perspiring. What had possessed him to maunder on about the bad old days to this woman who, for all the connection he felt with her, was still a virtual stranger. What was it about her that seemed to compel him to reveal matters he hadn't discussed with another living soul? He drew a deep breath.

"At any rate, these days, even when he's calm, he seems to take pleasure in inflicting pain on others, both physical and emotional—even those he loves. At first, he would be thrown into an agony of remorse over his offenses, but as he grew into manhood, he began to flaunt them—to boast of them—to sink himself deeper into iniquity with each escapade."

"What about their other children?"

"The girls? There are three of them, all married now, and they are all of a sunny disposition. They have . . . treated me with forbearance."

"And affection?"

Seth did not reply, but shrugged uncomfortably.

"And yet," said Eden tentatively, "you remain with the family."

Seth raised his brows discouragingly, but Eden would not be halted.

"Despite your being swept up and out of a life of poverty, it seems to me the family has treated you very badly. Why have you squandered all of your energy since you reached adulthood in making the duke even richer than he already is? Your devotion, while perhaps praiseworthy, seems unwarranted."

Seth drew his horse up in the middle of the crowded street. Oblivious to the traffic that surged around them, he knew an urge to give Miss Beckett the set-down of her life. How dare she question his motives? One glance into her eyes, however, told him that the remark had been made solely from concern. Moreover, he was appalled to discover that he welcomed her interest. He listened in astonishment to his next words.

"You may be surprised to discover I've given that matter some thought myself. As you say, I certainly owe His Grace a debt of gratitude, and that is one reason I have worked so assiduously on his behalf. I must repay that debt to the best of my ability. In addition," Seth continued slowly, "serving the duke gives my life purpose."

"I think I see," Eden mused aloud. "If your existence is useful to the duke, then you, as a person, must be of some value. You have a reason for taking up space on the planet and breathing God's good air."

"Yes!" exclaimed Seth. "You do understand!"

"Yes," replied Eden angrily. "And I must say it's the greatest piece of nonsense I've ever heard in my life."

"What?" asked Seth blankly.

"Has your brother been so successful in his campaign to destroy your sense of self-worth that you believe the only reason you have for existing is to serve the Duke of Derwent? It seems to me you have repaid that gentleman a hundred times over for his momentary whim. A good deed that he knew would cost him nothing."

Seth stared at her, white-faced. No one had ever spoken to him like that! He had carefully cultivated a distant, forbidding mien to discourage such encroachments as Eden Beckett had just perpetrated. He had known this female for less than a month and, while a certain intimacy had grown between them, she had no right to pick him apart like a laboratory specimen for her own amusement.

Watching him, Eden wished the ground would open and swallow her up. How could she have spoken so? To a man with whom, for all intents and purposes, she was barely acquainted. She had asked her questions out of interest in his background, but when she heard the injustices he had suffered—when she heard the anguish borne by a young boy reflected in the voice of the grown man—she had lost all sense of propriety. She was overwhelmed by a desire to make everything right for him somehow.

Now, just look at him. He no doubt wished her to the very devil, and in an instant would tell her so.

To her surprise, after an instant, his expression softened.

"It is kind of you to take an interest, Miss Beckett," he said awkwardly, if somewhat forbiddingly. He touched her hand in the lightest of caresses. "And you have given me something to think about." He urged his mount forward once again, and after a moment's hesitation, Eden followed suit.

They were by now approaching Grosvenor Square. Instead of turning his mount to the east, however, Seth maintained a course into North Audley Street.

"Mr. Lindow!" exclaimed Eden. "You are going in the wrong direction."

Seth's eyes smiled into hers. "Are you not going home?"

"Yes, but—"

"Then you must permit me to escort you, Miss Beckett."

Eden felt unaccountably flustered. "But I have an escort." She gestured to the groom, following at a respectful distance.

"Nonetheless, I hope you will grant me the pleasure of a few more moments of your company." He hesitated for the barest moment. "In addition, I wonder if we might dispense with Miss Beckett and Mr. Lindow. I am becoming heartily bored with both of them." Seth moved closer to lay a hand lightly on Eden's arm. "I am perhaps being forward, but the first time we met, I had the oddest feeling that we were already known to one another."

Eden's eyes widened. So he had felt it, too. That strange sense of recognition—of connection. Her gaze fell to where his fingers had begun a slight caressing motion on her sleeve, and a trembling began deep within her. Following her gaze, he dropped his hand abruptly, but his lips still quirked in a smile that warmed her to her toes.

She opened her mouth to issue a prim rejoinder, but to her astonishment, what emerged was a weak, "That would be very nice . . . Seth."

He grinned, completing her disintegration. "Good." He reached to grasp her bridle for the crossing of Oxford Street, already, despite the early hour, crowded with wagons, drays, and the carts of hundreds of vendors.

"I have been remiss, Mr.—Seth," Eden said abruptly. Seth's brows lifted.

"I have not told you what a marvelous time we had last night at Derwent House."

"Despite the advent of my brother on the scene?"

"A mere trifle. My mother and Zoë were in alt afterward."

"And you?"

"I, too, enjoyed myself immensely. After all, how often is a country mouse presented with the opportunity to rub elbows with such luminaries as the patronesses of Almack's, to say nothing of the prime minister and my lord Castlereagh. Quite dizzying, I assure you."

"But were you not struck by the melancholy truth that these high-flown personages were like unto you and me—that is, extraordinarily commonplace?"

Eden chuckled. "A lowering reflection, sir, but quite true."

"By the by," said Seth, deriving no little enjoyment from the sound of her laughter. "I hope you will allow me to show you whatever sights that may have escaped you in your previous visits. I understand a new exhibit is opening up at the Royal Gallery."

"Oh," breathed Eden, "I would like that above all things. The gallery is always my first priority when I come to town, and I've been looking forward with particular interest to the new exhibition. However, I have such a time persuading Mama or Zoë to accompany me there, for it takes me hours to view all the paintings." Her eyes widened with a twinkle, and she pressed her fingers to her lips. "There, I am undone. Now you will retract your offer like a baker pulling loaves from the fire."

"You wrong me. I shall merely pack a lunch and bring a camp stool with me, thus ensuring myself a reasonable degree of comfort while you browse to your heart's content."

How pleasant this was, reflected Eden, as she laughed at this absurdity. She had many acquaintances in the neighborhood of her father's estate, and she was on excellent terms with most of them. However, there were few whom she could call friend— and with none of them did she feel this warm rapport. Here was a man to whom she felt she could say anything and he would understand. She had already confided in him more of her dreams and hopes than she had to any other human being.

She glanced once more into the eyes that smiled so warmly into hers. If there was a light in the back of those eyes that caused her breath to quicken, she thought it must be merely a trick of the sun—which was, to be sure, shining with unusual brilliance this morning.

On drawing up before Aunt Nassington's town house, Seth dismounted and helped Eden from her saddle. He refused her polite invitation to join her for coffee in the breakfast room, saying with a grin, "No, indeed. Your Mama would be justifiably incensed at the prospect of receiving a visitor at such an ungodly hour. Perhaps later this week, however, we might venture to the Royal Gallery."

"That would be lovely."

They set a time for two days hence, and Seth with a tip of his hat mounted his horse once again and trotted away toward Grosvenor Square. Eden gazed after him for a moment before entering the house.

"Who was that?" a voice called from the head of the stairs. Zoë was just descending, applying a last-minute adjustment to her curls. "Seth Lindow?" Her brows rose in response to Eden's reply. "What could he be doing here at this hour of the morning? Did he come to see me? Oh, dear, why didn't you tell me? I know it's early, but since I am downstairs, I would have received him."

Eden smiled broadly. "No, Miss Beau-catcher. The gentleman was here on my behalf. He escorted me home from the park."

Zoë's eyes widened. "You?"

Eden described her encounter with Seth, omitting the confrontation with Bel.

"Well!" exclaimed Zoë. "And he brought you all the way back to Portman Square? Humph!" she declared with saucy grin, "I can't imagine that he could have hoped to see me at

what is little more than the crack of dawn, so I can only conclude he is smitten with you."

"I think not," replied Eden, laughing. "He was merely acting
out of . . . of friendship."

Zoë's delicate brows rose. "Really?" Her rosebud mouth
opened in a yawn. "Well, I have no objection to your having
him. As far as I'm concerned, he fulfilled his purpose. He
arranged to have us invited to Derwent House, where I met the
duke's son."

Eden glanced sharply at her sister. "For heaven's sake, Zoë, I
trust you do not plan to pursue that venue. The Marquess of
Belhaven is the last man in London with whom you should consider starting up a flirt."

"Oh, no, m'dear. Never fear, I do not intend to flirt with the
man."

So far from being assured by Zoë's words, Eden was made
extremely uneasy by the wickedly sparkling expression that accompanied them. Her foreboding was further increased when,
that afternoon, she and Zoë took the air in Hyde Park at the
fashionable hour of five o'clock. The attention paid to the two
sisters on this occasion as they proceeded in an open carriage
was more than satisfactory. Eden was at once relegated to her
position of foil to Zoë's beauty, as first one gentleman then another stopped their carriage for what passed as conversation in
the Polite World.

They had met some of these tulips of fashion at Derwent
House the previous night. They received the full treatment of
Zoë's fluttering lashes and flashing dimples. Others were acquaintances from previous visits to town and were accorded a
slightly less enthusiastic response.

Eden found her attention wandering during these inter-
changes, and she allowed her thoughts to drift to the events of
the morning. Had she imagined the warmth in Seth Lindow's
dark eyes? Surely he had been pleased to see her in Green Park.
He could have, with perfect propriety, bid her farewell at the
Piccadilly Gate and left her in the care of her groom. Instead, he
had consumed a good bit of his no doubt valuable time to return
her to her home himself. In the process, he had arranged to see
her again in two days. Surely, that meant . . .

Meant what? Merely that he enjoyed her company. Was that
not enough? Before Seth Lindow's advent into her life, she

would have thought having a friend in London—a male friend—a very pleasant circumstance. What else could she want from Seth Lindow besides friendship? A vision of the devil-glow she had imagined earlier flashed before her.

Really, she thought, aware that her pulse had quickened, she was being the veriest—

"Why, it is you, my lord," Zoë's voice trilled at her side. Eden's head jerked up at the tone in her sister's voice. Good Lord, the girl was virtually purring. The next moment, Eden's heart sank, for the gentleman who had drawn up to the carriage and was now bent caressingly over Zoë's fingertips, was the Marquess of Belhaven.

Chapter Twelve

The difference in the marquess's appearance since their encounter earlier in the day was marked. For one thing, he seemed to be sober. He was still dressed carelessly, but this, Eden knew, was a studied effect. He rose astride a showy bay, and his buckskin riding breeches clung to muscular thighs. His coat of dark blue superfine bore several whip thongs thrust through the buttonhole, and his cravat was tied in a semblance of neatness. Golden curls, tossed in an untidy Brutus, glinted in the late afternoon sun as he swept his hat off in an exaggerated gesture.

"Miss Zoë," he murmured, his tone indicative of stolen kisses in secluded bowers. "I was hoping I might see you today." He glanced cursorily over Eden. "Miss Beckett," he said coolly.

"Good afternoon, my lord." Eden's nod was insultingly brief, but the marquess, whose milky blue gaze had swung immediately back to Zoë, apparently did not notice.

"Now I know it is truly spring," the marquess said with an intimate smile. "For all the sunlight and birdsong seem collected right here in the park."

"Really?" replied Zoë, glancing about ingeniously. "I hadn't noticed. In fact, I was just saying to my sister that we should be going, for the breeze is turning chill." She bestowed a coquettish smile on the marquess.

"That's odd," he responded instantly. "I think it's uncommonly warm today. Indeed, I feel flushed—all over."

Zoë twirled her parasol and lowered her lashes.

"Sir!" interposed Eden. "You go beyond what is proper."

Bel's glance slid from Zoë to herself, putting Eden in mind of a lizard considering its next consignment of flies. "Apparently, Miss Beckett, our opinions of what is proper and what is not are eons apart." He turned again to Zoë. "Have I insulted you, my dear?" he asked, smirking.

Zoë, apparently feeling somewhat out of her depth at this exchange, contented herself with another smile and a flutter of her eyelashes. "If none was meant, sir, none was taken, although"—she giggled—"I do not believe I am your dear."

"Do you not?" Bel did not elaborate further, but fell silent. He continued at Zoë's side for a few moments before asking meditatively, "Do you go to the masquerade at Covent Garden this evening?"

Zoë leaned forward. "A masquerade? I did not know there was to be a masquerade!" She turned to her sister. "Oh, Eden! Do you think—?" she asked, her eyes sparkling.

"No, I do not think," was Eden's curt reply. "Those masquerades are not at all the thing, Zoë, particularly for a young girl. You know Papa will not—"

"Oh, what fustian!" cried Zoë gaily. "We will get Mama to go with us, and we can dragoon a footman or two to satisfy Papa." She swung to face Bel once more. "Of course, we shall be there. I wouldn't miss it for all the world!"

Bel's mouth curved in a pleased smile. "Then I shall no doubt see you there." Raising his hand to his hat, he murmured, "Ladies," and cantered off to greet a party of horsemen just approaching.

Zoë leaned back in the carriage and sighed beatifically. "Is he not the handsomest creature you've ever seen?"

"Oh, Good Lord, Zoë," replied her loving sister impatiently, "you are not seriously proposing to set up a flirt with that odious man?"

"Odious?" Zoë sat up very straight. "Why, he is nothing of the sort. He may not dress in quite the first stare of fashion—I believe he sets his own—but do you not think him very dashing?"

"No, I do not. Heavens, you sound the veriest feather-wit. The man is a complete degenerate, and I cannot believe you think him an appropriate target for your wiles."

Zoë could not fail to perceive the disdain in Eden's voice, and she bounced indignantly against the carriage squabs. "Eden Beckett, I believe you are jealous!"

"Jealous!"

"Yes, I think you're so set up in your own estimation, having captured Mr. Lindow's attention for a few minutes, that now you're spitting like a cat just because a duke's son has taken a fancy to me."

Eden sat in affronted silence for a moment, several spirited rejoinders churning on her lips. In the end, she decided on a dignified silence. No good could come of setting Zoë's back up any further. Another word against the Marquess of Belhaven would have the silly chit flinging herself into the reprobate's arms—with disastrous results. For if ever she perceived a certified viper, bent on seduction, the Marquess of Belhaven filled the bill.

"No, Zoë," she said at last in a quiet tone, "I am not jealous. I know it does no good to warn you against a man whose intentions are so obviously, er, improper, for you always go your own way, but I beg you will consider carefully before you give him any encouragement."

Zoë's perfect lips curved in a repentant smile. "I'm sorry, dearest. That was a horrid thing to say. You haven't a jealous bone in your body, after all. As for the marquess, I assure you I have taken his measure. He shan't persuade me to do anything against my will. Believe me, it is not in my plans to find myself ruined by the likes of the Marquess of Belhaven."

With that, Eden had to be content, and she turned her thoughts to the evening ahead. For there was not the slightest doubt in her mind that she and Mama would be attending the masquerade at Covent Garden with Zoë.

Events proved her entirely correct. Upon being apprised of the plan, Lord Beckett issued his usual veto. This was followed by Zoë's usual blandishments, concluding with her customary tantrum when the blandishments failed to produce their desired results. The fashionable hour of eleven of the clock that evening saw the Beckett ladies disembarking from their carriage, with the assistance of two footmen, at the steps of the Opera House in Covent Garden. All three wore voluminous dominoes.

"Ooh, isn't this exciting?" exclaimed Zoë, her eyes sparkling through the slits of her mask. She arranged her domino about her shoulders. "I do wish we had a gentleman with us."

"So do I," remarked Eden. "We present a decidedly odd appearance, if you want my opinion."

"Well, I don't," snapped Zoë. "Want your opinion, that is,

Miss Sobersides. For heaven's sake, Eden, we are here to enjoy ourselves."

Eden smiled grimly. She doubted that she would be deriving any enjoyment from this evening's adventure. She had never felt so uncomfortable in her life. Three women on their own would be the cynosure of at least a few pairs of eyes—probably those by whom she would least prefer to be seen. From what she had heard, the prospect of encountering any ladies of quality at the masquerade was remote. However, the gentlemen of the *ton* were not so nice in their tastes, and it was highly likely one or more of them would discern the presence of Miss Zoë Beckett at this far-from-genteel function. Word would inevitably drift back to wives, sisters, and daughters. Any hopes Zoë might cherish of procuring vouchers for Almack's would go a-glimmering. In addition, the masquerade would most likely turn into a romp in a few hours. The footmen would afford protection against unwanted advances, no doubt, but they could provide little respectability to the Beckett entourage. Eden could only hope their dominoes and masks would guarantee anonymity.

She stared about her as they made their way to the box procured for them earlier by one of the footmen now striding behind them in attendance. At least, thought Eden, the box was on an upper tier. The ground floor boxes were altogether too accessible to the young men strolling about the pit, quizzing glasses at the ready, ogling the ladies seated there in costumes that displayed alarming décolletages. These damsels received the lavish masculine attention with unladylike squeals of mirth, accompanied by much slapping of fingers with fans and the masks they had removed at the outset of the fun.

Not, Eden mused, that the setting was less than elegant. Huge crystal chandeliers illuminated a painted ceiling and four tiers of boxes draped in crimson. The stage, upon which the dancers disported themselves, was huge, extending past the first several boxes, and backed by an idyllic rural scene. The whirling couples glittered, and the music was lively. She might have enjoyed herself, she reflected, were she with someone whose company she relished and upon whom she could rely to protect her from either unwanted advances or social censure. A sober figure with night-colored eyes rose in her mind, to be firmly banished.

Eden's uneasiness grew as the evening progressed. She did not perceive any of their acquaintances, but she was hard put to quash Zoë's ebullience. From the moment they arrived, the males present, as though the girl sent some sort of aphrodisiacal fragrance into the air, began to flock around her like wolves scenting a female in heat. Zoë, as Eden has feared, encouraged their advances in a scandalous manner, tossing her head and flirting with abandon. All the while, she searched the crowd expectantly.

Neither of the ladies, to Eden's surprise, lacked for dance partners, and Eden found herself enjoying the music and the glitter despite herself. Mama remained in the box, keeping a sharp eye on her daughters, and waving discreetly when the dance brought them into proximity.

It was, however, not long before the festivities began to lose whatever propriety had been maintained earlier. The noise level increased in pitch and intensity as the gentlemen began pursuing the ladies in earnest. Screams and piercing giggles issued from these females as they capered about the pit, skirts raised to their knees. After repulsing a particularly inventive fellow in pirate's garb, Eden took refuge in the second-tier box beside her mother.

Accepting a glass of punch from a passing servant, she sipped quietly for several moments, regaining her breath and searching the seething crowd below for Zoë. Her gaze finally fell upon the girl on the far side of the room. She was still masked, but the hood of her domino had fallen back, exposing golden curls that hung down over her shoulders in disarray. She was dancing with an obviously inebriated Romeo. With each turn, her eyes scanned the crowd, and an ecstatic smile sprang to her lips when a man in a black domino suddenly approached the couple. With a touch of his hand, he dispatched Zoë's partner, and placing an arm around her waist, he whirled her into a scandalously intimate waltz. Zoë's entire demeanor was transformed. Where before she had sparkled, she now glowed with an almost febrile incandescence. As Eden watched, the girl's body seemed to mold itself to fit every curve of the stranger's body.

"Oh, dear God," murmured Eden, for despite his mask, she had no difficulty in discerning the identity of Zoë's mysterious partner. To no one other than the Marquess of Belhaven, Eden felt, would her sister express such an unspoken adoration. Pale curls glimpsed below the rim of the domino's hood dispelled any doubts she might have had.

Eden rose. This must be stopped! Before she could move from the box, however, Zoë and the marquess disappeared. Wildly, Eden's glance swept the stage and the pit below it. She hurried from the box, pausing only to summon one of the footmen standing in somewhat careless attention at the box's entrance.

She was accosted at almost every step as she descended to the ground floor, only the presence of the burly footman saving her from several unpleasant encounters. The pit was crowded with milling party-goers, all in mindless pursuit of their varied pleasures. She did not attempt to seek Zoë on the stage, for she was sure her sister and her partner were no longer interested in dancing. She remained in the pit, searching the perimeter for exit doors. As it happened, there were several of these, and Eden, summoning up all the fortitude she possessed, began on the first and proceeded around the room. Most of them exited onto the street, but several led into secluded alcoves, each of which was populated by a shadowed couple in some stage of undress. Eden was shaking with humiliation and disgust as she murmured disjointed apologies in the doorways of one chamber after another before slamming the doors shut again. She did not know how many times she had repeated this embarrassing procedure before she at least discovered her quarry.

In one of the smaller nooks, illuminated by a single candle, stood Zoë, locked in Belhaven's embrace. He had drawn her to him so tightly that Eden wondered if the girl was still breathing. His mouth was fastened on hers in a kiss that seemed as though it would pull her soul from her. Zoë moaned in response to the movement of Bel's hands on her back and reached up to clasp his hair with both hands, pulling him to her as though to absorb his straining passion into her very bones.

"Zoë!" cried Eden in horror. She was forced to repeat herself not once but twice before Zoë, with great reluctance, began to free herself. Belhaven, his breath coming in gasps, gazed at her, dazed and almost unbelieving.

"Sir!" Eden exclaimed. "You will have the goodness to unhand my sister."

Belhaven, however, did not release Zoë. He dropped one

hand, but kept the other about her waist, his expression still one of bemusement.

"Sir!" Eden said again. She turned to gesture to the footman, who was still in tow, but that young man had remained outside the door, apparently unwilling to enter into such an awkward situation. He was now gazing studiously at the revelers about him. Swinging back to Belhaven, she attempted to infuse her voice with menace. "You will cease molesting Zoë, or I shall be forced to call the . . . the proprietors."

Belhaven, whose thin mouth had curved into a lazy smile, merely sneered. "And what do you think the proprietors will do to a duke's son? In addition, if we are to talk of molesting, it seems to me your sister was participating most willingly in our little interlude."

Zoë, by now had apparently been brought to the realization that this time she had gone too far, and that her *beau ideal* was displaying feet of mud. She tried to speak, but Eden silenced her with a sweep of her arm. "Willing!" she cried, aware that she was on the verge of hysteria. "Zoë is an innocent, you vile—"

"Innocent?" Bel's slurred laughter was an assault. "Good God, you insufferable prude, she's hot as a harlot and as ripe for plucking as a Christmas goose. I could have lifted her skirts and taken her right here on the floor." He dropped his arm to squeeze Zoë's derriere. "Couldn't I, my sweet?"

Zoë's mouth dropped open, and she wrenched away from him with a sob. Eden, a red mist rising before her eyes, stepped up to him and without thinking she delivered a stinging slap across Belhaven's mouth.

The next moment, with an enraged snarl, Belhaven raised his own hand and slammed it against Eden's cheek, sending her reeling backward, almost tumbling to the floor.

At this, the footman, at last recalled to his duty, ran into the little chamber. " 'Ere!" he exclaimed. "What's all this?"

His eyes bulged in horror as he observed Eden struggling to maintain her balance, her hand pressed to her cheek.

The footman raised both fists, prepared to administer retaliation, but it was not he who surged forward in a cold rage. For the second time that day, Seth Lindow felled his brother, first with a smashing right to the center of Belhaven's face and then a left into his stomach.

Chapter Thirteen

"**O**h, Seth!" sobbed Eden, so grateful to behold him at that moment that she did not pause to wonder at his sudden appearance. Seth bent over Bel, his face white with a primal fury. He delivered another blow before grasping Bel by the throat, throttling him with both hands. He lifted his brother from the floor and slammed him back again until the footman, galvanized to action, restrained him with some effort. Seth rose, his breath coming in harsh gasps. After contemplating his brother's supine form for a moment, he swung to Eden. Placing an arm about her shoulders, he drew her toward him, cupping her head in one hand.

"My God, Eden, are you all right?" He bent to examine the bruise that was already forming on her cheek.

"Yes, but Zoë . . ."

Seth glanced indifferently at Zoë, still standing in frozen silence. "She seems to have suffered no harm," he said, his eyes again on Eden.

On the floor, Bel stirred. Blood was streaming from his nose, and he groped in his pocket for a handkerchief. Pressing it to his face, he struggled to a sitting position. Somewhat to Eden's surprise, he did not evince any desire to get to his feet, nor did he display an intent to retaliate. In fact, a muffled snort of laughter emerged from behind the handkerchief.

"Did you leave your snow-white palfrey parked outside, Seth? Lord, if you make it a habit to rescue any more maidens in distress, they'll be putting up a stained glass window in your honor at Westminster Abbey."

He held out a hand to the footman standing by in some bemusement, and after a questioning glance at Seth, from whom he received a permissive nod, the servant assisted Bel to his feet.

Seth raised his fists as though he would strike Bel again, but at a gasp from Eden, he halted.

"I would very much like to kill you." Seth's words were spoken in the softest of tones, but the ice in them chilled Eden to the bone. Zoë, too, shivered. "Repeat the offense," Seth continued, "and I certainly shall."

Bel's response was another brief gust of laughter—albeit shaken, noted Eden. After one look at Seth's face, white and set and undoubtedly murderous, Bel pushed past the footman, and, the handkerchief still pressed to his face, lurched from the little alcove.

Eden glanced at Seth, and once more a moment of communion passed between them. Eden felt as privy to the turmoil raging within him as though she could read through his eyes into his soul. She knew, moreover, that Seth was aware of the emotions that were tumbling about in her own mind—even though she was unable to sort them out herself. Uppermost was gratitude, certainly, and outrage at Bel's behavior, but beneath them lay a deep acknowledgment of the urge that had prompted Seth to react so unthinkingly and so violently on her behalf.

His fingers traced the burgeoning mark on her cheek, and hers went up to caress them in a feather-light touch. Abruptly, she swung away to go to Zoë, who had begun to cry.

Eden smiled grimly as she grasped her sister by the shoulders. "I don't know whether to shake you or hug you. Are you all right? What in God's name possessed you to creep off with that slimy libertine?"

"He's *not* slimy!" exclaimed Zoë, then smiled sheepishly as she realized the implication of her words. "I'm so sorry for what he did to you, Eden. I had no idea . . ."

If Eden thought it odd that Zoë should apologize for Belhaven's actions, she said nothing, merely remarking, "I think there is nothing beneath him. At least now your eyes are opened."

"Yes," replied Zoë in a voice that to Eden's critical ear sounded unconvinced.

Eden prepared to lead her sister from the little chamber, but was stayed by Seth's hand. The rage had died from his eyes, but his features still bore traces of a cold fury.

"What the devil are the two of you doing in a place like this?"

"Oh," said Eden. "Zoë—that is, we have never been to a masquerade, and we thought it might be . . . enjoyable. Mama is with us," she added hastily. "We hired a box so that we would not have to mingle if we didn't choose, and we brought two footmen."

"Indeed," Seth retorted scathingly. "I can see what wonderful protection they have been." He swung to Zoë. "Have you no better sense than to go off with a man possessing the worst reputation in London? As for you!" He turned on the hapless footman. "How could you allow your mistress to be assaulted in that manner? If you were in my employ, you'd be turned off without a character."

The footman reddened, and Zoë began to cry again—angry, unrepentant tears that threatened to blow into a full-fledged storm.

"Not now, Seth," pleaded Eden. "I must get her back to Mama, and thence home. Heavens, I only hope Papa does not hear of this contretemps."

Seth stepped back to allow the sisters through the door, then followed them, with the chastened footman following. Before they re-entered the theater proper, Eden turned once again to Seth.

"Thank you again," she said, lowering her gaze almost immediately at the expression she encountered in his. "I . . . I do not know what we would have done if—" She stopped abruptly. "How did you know we were here?"

Seth's lips quirked in an unwilling smile.

"During my visit to Clearsprings," he said, "my man—Moppe—made the acquaintance of your maid—Makepeace, I believe her name is. The two have been walking out since our return to London. This afternoon, she mentioned to him your proposed, er, outing. Moppe, correctly assuming I would be interested in this information, relayed it to me upon his return home."

"Makepeace?" Eden gasped. "But, how—what—?"

Seth's voice harshened once more.

"I shall accompany you home," he interrupted curtly.

"Oh, but—"

"Come," said Seth peremptorily. "Your mother must be wondering where you've got to."

Indeed, Lady Beckett was in something of a taking when

they returned to the box. "Where have you *been*?" she cried, almost in tears. "I was about to send Watkins to look for you—" She pointed a wildly shaking finger at the remaining footman, stolidly retaining his post at the door to the box. "But, I was fearful of his leaving me alone in this . . . this . . ." Her gesture swung to encompass the melee that was taking place in the pit. The masquerade had degenerated into a complete romp, most of the dancers having left the stage to disport themselves in the pit. Couples embraced openly. Others, displaying more restraint, slapped away the exploring hands of their beaux, all the while laughing uproariously and otherwise displaying no discouragement. In one corner, a noisy mock battle took place among several damsels riding the shoulders of swains so drunk they could barely maintain their equilibrium. In another, an impromptu jig was taking place, regardless of the waltz being played by the orchestra. The dancers whisked coattails in abandon or raised skirts to their hips, depending on their sex.

Seth took one look at the proceedings and ordered the entire group, footmen included, out of the box and out of the theater. Once outside, he bundled his charges toward his carriage, which he had ordered to remain standing nearby.

"It will take an eternity to have yours brought around," he said brusquely to Eden. "Here, you," he barked at the footman. "Order up her ladyship's carriage, and when it arrives, take it home." The young men, without so much as a glance at Lady Beckett, scurried to do his bidding.

"Now then," began Seth again in a slightly milder tone, when the ladies were ensconced in his carriage and the vehicle was moving down Bow Street away from the unsavory confines of Covent Garden. "What were you—?"

Eden, however, interrupted him. While she was grateful for his timely arrival on the scene in the theater, she experienced a spurt of irritation at his high-handed disposal of their carriage and his peremptory manner in taking charge of the situation. "For heaven's sake, Seth. I know it was not at all the thing for the three of us to attend the masquerade, particularly with no gentleman in attendance, but we . . . we thought it would be a lark."

At this, Zoë spoke up. She had stopped crying. Indeed, she looked remarkably composed for a gently bred maiden who had, only moments before, been the target of a gentleman's most sinister intentions. "There's no need to wrap it in clean linen, Eden. It was all my fault," she said to Seth. "I've never attended a masquerade, and I thought this would be great fun. I knew it wouldn't be the sort of thing a lady would attend unaccompanied, but I thought that merely meant that we wouldn't meet anyone . . . well, important."

Eden glared meaningfully at her sister, for she knew full well Zoë's purpose in coming to the Opera House. It had been obvious from the moment she set foot there that the little minx had been looking for Belhaven. It was equally obvious that, in addition, Belhaven had been perfectly correct in his odious remarks about Zoë's acquiescence in her own ruination. What in the world had Zoë been about? The girl was a natural flirt, but up until now she had always remained firmly in control of the flirtee. She had never been known to allow a situation to proceed any farther than she wished. What had made her all but toss her bonnet over the windmill this evening? Dear God, could she have formed a serious *tendre* for the black-hearted Marquess of Belhaven?

She wrenched her attention to the conversation taking place between Zoë and Seth, punctuated by self-exculpatory, albeit nearly incoherent explanations by Lady Beckett. Zoë was all pretty contrition, which obviously made no dent in Seth's disapproval. It was not long before Zoë's eyes began to glitter ominously, and Eden felt obliged to step in before open war erupted.

"Yes," she said prosaically, "it was an unpleasant experience all around, but it's over, and none of us the worse for it. Zoë, I'm sure, learned a lesson tonight, and, thanks to you, Seth, no real harm came to any of us. I think we can safely say that we were not seen by anyone whose opinion counts for anything in the Polite World. Our reputation," she concluded rather grandly, "remains unblemished."

Seth snorted, but by now the carriage had rolled into Portman Square. As luck would have it, the vehicle drew to a stop before Mrs. Nassington's home just as Lord Beckett was disembarking from his own carriage, having spent an agreeable evening at his club. His expression, as he beheld the arrival of his wife and daughters, garbed in dominoes, was anything but agreeable.

"*Where* have you been?" he demanded explosively. "No,

never mind, you don't have to tell me. You've been to that cursed masquerade, haven't you? After I expressly forbade—"

Here Seth stepped forward, and Lord Beckett's expression underwent a marked change. "You? Here?" he blurted in puzzlement.

"Indeed, Lord Beckett," proclaimed Seth smoothly. "I fear I am at fault in your ladies' disobedience. I chanced to visit Miss Zoë earlier this evening, and she told me of her desire to participate in the masquerade. Knowing that it is not uncommon for the most respectable ladies to visit the Opera House masquerades in the company of a gentleman—at least during the earlier portion of the evening," he interposed austerely, "I volunteered to escort them there. Pray believe me, sir, when I tell you the expedition was entirely unexceptionable."

He became the focus of three worshipful gazes as the Beckett ladies breathed a sigh of relief. Eden breathed a prayer of gratitude for the night that covered the bruise she was sure must be burgeoning on her cheek.

Lord Beckett harrumphed for another moment or two, but at length barked a jovial, "Hah!" and invited Seth to join him in his study to imbibe a late evening potation. This Seth declined courteously and took himself off in a cloud of good wishes and heartfelt, if silent, gratitude.

In the house, Eden followed Zoë purposefully to the girl's bedchamber, but at the door, Zoë turned.

"I really don't feel like a lecture tonight, Eden," she said, the tearstains on her cheeks reinforcing her expression of strain. "I know everything you are going to say, so you might as well save yourself the trouble. I have some thinking to do, and we'll talk tomorrow."

Brushing Eden's cheek with her lips, she slipped into the chamber and closed the door firmly behind her, leaving Eden standing in the corridor, feeling remarkably foolish. Promising herself a confrontation with Zoë first thing in the morning, she sought her own chamber.

Her quarry proved elusive, however. Zoë elected to breakfast in her room the next day, and was not seen until well after noon when she appeared in the drawing room to receive morning callers, in company with her mother and her aunt. Eden, too, made herself available to receive visitors, and by the time the ritual was concluded, it was time for a light nuncheon. After-

ward, Zoë bustled upstairs to make herself ready for the promenade in Hyde Park, in which, she averred, she was to be accompanied by the Honorable Algernon Kipp, son of the Viscount
Stebbington, known to his friends, incomprehensibly, as Pinkie.

That night, the whole family was bespoken for a soiree at the
home of Constance, Lady Felch, which lasted into the small
hours of the next morning. Zoë made herself equally scarce
over the course of the following day, as well, but Eden noted
that on the rare occasions when she was in view, her sister wore
a pensive expression and, when not actively engaged in some
task, tended to gaze unseeing out the window.

The following day, Thursday, was the day appointed for
Eden's visit to Somerset House with Seth, which effectively
banished the problem of Zoë from her mind. Seth had been
much in her thoughts since the incident at the Opera House.
Bel's words had struck an unwilling chord, for it seemed to her
that Seth had behaved very much like a hero out of an old tale.
She would never forget his outrage on her behalf. She had been
almost overwhelmed by the sheer masculine power he had
fairly exuded. It was, she concluded, almost fearing to put the
thought into words, as though he cared about her—that he felt
something for her beyond friendship. Perhaps the kiss in her
studio had meant something to him, after all.

Contemplation of this notion led to an examination of her
own feelings about Seth. She liked him very much, of course,
much more than she would have thought possible on their first
meeting. She was not of his milieu, but perhaps this did not
weigh with him, if his affections were truly engaged.

Thus, she awaited Seth with some degree of discomposure. A
judicious application of white lead paste and a slight rearrange-
ment of her hair had hidden the bruise, which in any case had
not proved as unsightly as she feared. In preparation for this
visit to London, she had paid stricter attention to her wardrobe
than on previous sojourns. With her mother and sister, she had
traveled to Guildford to procure silks and muslins in colors she
knew would become her. The village seamstress, declaring she
was glad that at long last Miss Beckett had decided to garb herself in something that did not make her look like somebody's
poor cousin, had created several gowns in which Eden felt herself all but transformed.

On this particular day, she wore a jaconet walking dress over a pale peach-colored sarcenet slip. It was trimmed with a triple fall of lace at the throat, and the skirt was flounced with rich French work. Over all, she wore a spencer made of lutestring, ornamented with braiding. A high-crowned bonnet trimmed with a taffety ribbon was tied in a rakish bow just under her left ear. She wondered if the entire ensemble might not be considered a trifle too dashing for a spinster of her advanced years, but the expression in Seth's eyes when he beheld her in the Beckett drawing room laid her fears to rest.

"I wish," he said, smiling, "that I were more adept at offering a compliment to a lady. If I were, I'd say something about all the attention at Somerset House this afternoon centering on you rather than the other works of art."

She glanced up at him, startled, and willed away the treacherous flood of heat that stained her cheeks. She murmured something completely inane, cursing herself for magnifying a compliment that any gentleman might have paid to any lady out of sheer courtesy.

She was unable to convince herself, however, that the warmth in his gaze was no more than that to be found in any gentleman tossing off a pretty phrase. Taking up the parasol that matched the peach slip, she allowed Seth to usher her from the house to his waiting curricle. Seth, perhaps aware of the unwonted extravagance of his greeting to her, maintained a comfortable flow of conversation, and soon Eden was at her usual ease with him.

They had traveled only a few blocks when Eden laid her hand on his arm, and the seriousness of her expression caused Seth's brows to lift.

"I . . . I haven't properly thanked you for the . . . incident two nights ago," she said in a low voice. "I know I tried to make light of our presence there, but I am fully aware that we should not—"

"And *I* am fully aware of the reason you had come. Devil take it, Eden, why do you and your parents allow Zoë her way in every whim, no matter how disastrous. She has no more idea of how to comport herself in society than a spoiled baby— which she is, of course—and to see her making your life miserable— Frankly, I don't know what your father can be thinking."

Eden stiffened for a moment, her hackles rising at this unvarnished assessment of her sister's behavior. What right had he to make such a judgment on a member of her family? Or to express that judgment so forthrightly? A moment later, she shrugged uncomfortably. She knew he spoke out of concern for her, and she was warmed, despite herself, that he viewed their relationship as one that permitted—nay, compelled—such honesty.

"Zoë can be . . . difficult," she said in a low tone.

"I'm sorry," Seth said instantly. "I have been unforgivably forward."

"No, you are right. Zoë is the baby of the family, and, as in so many similar cases, she has been given her own way since birth. I love her dearly, for she is open and giving and many other good things, but there is no denying she can be a perfect hellion—and usually is. She's headstrong beyond permission, and frankly, has grown beyond either Mother's or Father's ability to contain her outrageous starts." She sighed. "Frankly, I don't know what will become of her."

Seth smiled wryly. "I know the feeling. I am closely related to one who makes your sister look like a plaster saint."

They laughed companionably, and Seth tucked Eden's hand in his arm.

On arriving at Somerset House, Eden's attention was almost immediately riveted on the paintings that covered the walls all the way up to the high ceilings.

Seth watched her, bemused. She looked quite lovely today, he thought. She had evidently decided to come out from behind her drab, protective attire—and it was high time. She seemed to have permanently dispensed with the cap, and her hair, dressed in a knot atop her head with escaping tendrils framing her face in a dark witchery, glowed in the intermittent shafts of light beaming through the windows of Somerset House. If the other patrons were not distracted from their perusal of the hanging artworks, he certainly was.

In fact, Eden Beckett had been on his mind for most of the night, interfering with his customary repose. He was still in considerable astonishment at the maelstrom of emotions that had surged through him at the sight of Eden sustaining a blow from Bel that had nearly knocked her to the ground. He had been sickened at Bel's actions, for he had never known his brother to hit a woman before, although God knew there was nothing in Bel's character to indicate that he would hesitate to do so. Uppermost in Seth's breast, however, had been a murderous rage, coupled with anger at Eden for having put herself in such close juxtaposition with one whom she knew to be wholly the villain. What the devil was she doing in a secluded chamber with him at a social function notorious for its impropriety? It was not until he noticed Zoë standing nearby that the situation became self-explanatory. By that time, he had already dispatched Bel, and such was his temper that he was ready to wreak a similar punishment on Zoë. Only the fact that he was wholly focused on Eden at the moment prevented him from grasping the little twit and shaking her until her bones rattled.

The expression in Eden's eyes had shaken him to his core. No one had ever looked at him with such luminous warmth—and gratitude—and perhaps something more. He had truly felt like St. George at that moment, and his most burning desire was to throw Eden over his figurative saddle and ride off with her to pledge his eternal devotion in a secluded glen.

Good God, had he really entertained such mawkish maunderings over a female for whom he felt nothing but the mildest friendship? If so, he reflected dryly, in the best Gothic tradition, he was doomed to remain at a respectful distance. For surely, the maiden fair was aware that she must look higher than the son of an army sergeant for her *beau ideal*.

Particularly, since it was his task to persuade said maiden to wed the very man from whom he had rescued her earlier in the evening. The episode was bound to have given her a permanent and irrevocable aversion to Bel. He doubted that a promise of wealth, position, security, a place to paint, and garden to her heart's content, or even a guaranteed position as President of the Royal Academy of Art would convince her to actually marry Bel.

Besides, dammit, he didn't want her to marry Bel. On reflection, of course, he didn't want to see any female married to Bel. He thought of Zoë again. He had not witnessed whatever had taken place in the little alcove before his entrance on the scene, but it struck him in retrospect that Zoë had borne the aspect of a girl recently kissed with great thoroughness. One, moreover, who had participated in the proceedings with some enthusiasm.

Was she simply susceptible to attention from anything in a shirt and trousers? Or were her expressions of affection reserved for peers of the realm, with riches to go with their titles?

Or—and he thought of her rapt expression in Bel's arms the night of their disgraceful waltz at his father's dinner party— was she smitten with Bel in particular? How unfortunate that Father had deemed her unacceptable!

No, it was not. Zoë deserved better than Bel. Good God, for that matter, Lucrezia Borgia deserved better than Bel. He sighed, a breath that seemed to come from the depth of his being. He had never defied the duke before. All through his life he'd accomplished every task the old man had set before him. He had devoted every waking second of his adult life to husbanding the Lindow holdings, and had increased them tenfold. In the process, he had sometimes entered into dealings that shamed him. Was that not enough? Was it necessary that he sacrifice the last of his principles to the Derwent interests? No. This time the old man asked too much.

To be sure, the belles of the *ton* were willing to go to any lengths to make an advantageous marriage, but he simply could not bring himself to assist in shackling one of them to Bel. If Bel came to a sticky end, so be it. He grieved for the boy his brother had been, and the man he might have grown into, but Seth was not responsible for the failure he had become.

He started, aware that Eden was looking at him quizzically.

"What?" he asked, returning her expression.

"What was in that sigh? You sounded as though the weight of the sins of mankind were settling on your shoulders."

He smiled painfully. "Perhaps they have." He took her hand. "Tell me, what do you think of that painting up there?" He pointed to a depiction of Boadicea, the Warrior Queen.

"Oh, yes! It's by Rebecca Seaton! I do so admire her work. Her technique is marvelously distinct, and her composition is always compelling. I like her use of color, too."

"Mm, yes. She is married to the artist Kenneth Wilding, you know. He is famous for his battle scenes. Let's see—oh, yes— over there." He indicated a large painting on which was portrayed a moment from the Battle of Badajoz. It was wrenching, thought Eden, evoking all the horror and glory of war.

"It's magnificent," she murmured. Turning, she faced Boadicea once more. "I think I prefer Madame Seaton's work, however."

"Ah, you feel a kinship to the warrior queen, then?"

Eden laughed. "Hardly. But I find myself responding to the power of the figure and the atmosphere the artist has created."

As they moved on to a discussion of some of the other artists displayed, Eden was intensely aware of his presence at her side. He seemed to be in a strange mood. Reflective and distant, yet seeming to relish her company. Indeed, she almost gained the impression that he needed her beside him right now. Again, she experienced the now-familiar sense of oneness with him. He was troubled, she knew, without knowing how. She glanced at him from beneath her lashes. What was it that brought such a heaviness of spirit into his eyes?

Sometime later, having finished their perusal of the paintings, the two walked along the river embankment. They chatted amiably, and it seemed to Eden that whatever thoughts had darkened Seth's demeanor earlier had vanished. As they approached a tea shop with tables set up on the pavement to catch the early spring sunshine, he turned to look down at her, and his gaze warmed. It was at this point that she decided to broach a subject upon which she had been giving much thought since her arrival in London.

"Seth," she began tentatively, "I would like to ask your advice."

"Certainly, my dear."

Pretending she had not heard that last, she continued in a rush. "I must ask you to keep this confidential."

Mystified, he smiled. "Of course."

"You asked once before if I had thought of selling any of my paintings. Well," she continued at his nod, "when I said no, I was not being altogether truthful. I have indeed tried to sell a few, with a notable lack of success. When we were in Town before, I went to a Mr. Rellihan. He owns a gallery in Oxford Street. I had visited his place of business on several occasions, and it seemed to me that he favored artists whose work was, um, avant-garde. Not precisely the kind of thing I do, but different from the established mode. I showed him some of my paintings, and he said he liked them very much, but that he did not think they would sell."

"I know Rellihan's gallery," commented Seth. "My father has acquired a couple of pieces from him. He has a rather exclusive—and discerning—clientele, the sort who want to be beforehand on the latest trends in art."

"Yes. Well, this time I brought some of my portraits to show him. As you noted, they are in a more traditional vein than my still lifes, but I believe they are something a little out of the ordinary. I've been told by one or two people," she added shyly, "people whose opinion I trust, that I have a certain gift for portraiture."

Recalling the stunning study of Zoë he had examined in her studio, Seth vouchsafed a heartfelt agreement.

"I have an appointment with Mr. Rellihan next week. I don't anticipate any more success with him this time than the last, but if he should agree to take some of my work, I shall need some advice. I do feel," she concluded solemnly, but with that glint in her eye that Seth had come to cherish, "that I can do no better than to go to the Duke of Derwent's counselor in business affairs."

Offering a punctilious bow, Seth took her arm. "I am at your service, Miss Beckett." He turned into the tea shop. "Do step into my office, and we shall see what is to be done with your soon-to-be acquired wealth."

Chapter Fourteen

"You see," confided Eden over a steaming cup, "my aim is to become independent of my family."

"Independent?" asked Seth cautiously, his brows lifting.

Eden flushed. "I know it is almost unheard of—and truly I'm not one of those female firebrands who wish to burn down the establishment, but I would like to . . . to live by myself," she finished in a rush.

"What?" exclaimed Seth, a note of disapproval in his voice.

"It's all very well for you to say, 'What!' " Eden exclaimed with some asperity. "You have no idea what it is like to be the oldest daughter of the house—and still unmarried, to boot. It's not so bad right now, but my sisters are already making demands on my time and energy. I don't mind helping out in their various crises, but they, as well as my parents, seem to think there is nothing I would rather do with my life than run to Kent when Meg's youngest contracts the measles, or down to Bedfordshire to help Dorothy plan her annual spring house party. Mama volunteers my services for everything from the church fete to taking the neighbor's children on a picnic when their parents wish to get them out of the way, and she relies on me to keep Zoë in line. Which," she added with a grimace, "I think you will agree is a well-nigh impossible task."

Seth could only nod a heartfelt agreement, but he was startled at this sudden outpouring of grievance. Catching his expression, Eden halted abruptly.

"I must sound like the greatest whiner in nature," she said in some mortification.

"Not at all," Seth responded hastily. "I was only reflecting that we males have little comprehension of the woes of the opposite sex. I always considered it unfair in the extreme that when a woman marries, she is forced to place her well-being in the hands of her husband. However, now I see that a woman who, er, forswears that state is no better off. She is doomed to a life of sufferance on the good will of not just one man, but all the members of her family."

"Precisely." Eden experienced a surge of irritation that, though Seth seemed reasonably enlightened for a man, this concept had not previously occurred to him. On the other hand, she concluded philosophically, like every other man of her acquaintance, nothing he had experienced in his entire male-oriented span of years would have caused him to so much as consider the plight of women.

"So," continued Seth, steepling his fingers before him, "you are wondering what to do with the profits from your artistic endeavors."

"Yes, if I should persuade Mr. Rellihan to accept my work. And, of course, provided he might actually sell one or two paintings."

Seth had some private thoughts on that matter, but forbore to discuss them with Eden until he had had a chance to bring them to fruition.

"Um," he said instead, "you could just keep your earnings in a sock beneath your mattress, but that would, in my opinion, be extremely imprudent. What you want to do is open your own account at the bank of your choice. That way you will earn some interest on your savings. Then, when you have accumulated a little, you can consider investing the money in the consols, or in some other, perhaps more profitable venture."

He glanced up to note that Eden's eyes had glazed over. Even in a state of blank incomprehension, he noted, they reminded him of a summer mist. "Am I making sense?" he asked, his voice husky.

"I suppose so, yes. At least you would be if I had the slightest notion of how to open a bank account or to make investments." Her gaze fixed on him hopefully. "I cannot go to my father, of course, for I must keep my dealings secret from him. I hate to behave in such an undutiful manner, but if he were to get wind of my plans, he would quash them immediately. Even if he were to allow me to enter into an agreement with Rellihan, which I consider highly unlikely, he would lose no time in appropriating my earnings for the family coffers. I plan to exhibit my work under a pseudonym," she added, her eyes lifted anxiously to his.

"I will, of course, honor your confidence, my dear, and I would deem it an honor if you would allow me to be your guide in the matter," he said, following his cue with gratifying promptness.

Impulsively, Eden laid her hand on his arm. "Oh, my, I was hoping you would say that." Seth covered her fingers with his own.

They sat thus for some moments, lost in each other's gaze, before Eden removed her hand and said, briskly, "Very well, then. I shall speak to you when I have seen Mr. Rellihan—if I have good news, that is."

"Please—send round to me either way. I'd like to know what he says."

Seth congratulated himself silently in a fair surety of Rellihan's reaction. The gentleman had made several profitable sales to the Duke of Derwent through the duke's efficient man of affairs, and if Seth was not very much mistaken, Mr. Rellihan would be quick to encourage one who was represented to him as a protégé of both the duke and himself.

This proved to be the case, for when Seth visited Rellihan's gallery later that same day, the gentleman professed his eagerness to take up the young artist's cause, particularly when Seth declared his intention of purchasing at least one of the paintings. In addition, His Grace, of course, would wish one himself. A floral work, perhaps, suitable for one of His Grace's reception rooms.

Seamus Rellihan, a rotund personage of some fifty summers, rubbed his hands gleefully. The late afternoon sun glinted off the surface of his polished bald pate and created little halos around his gold-rimmed spectacles.

"Yes, indeed, Mr. Lindow, I am not surprised to hear that His Grace was taken with Miss Beckett's work. I found it remarkably expressive—evocative, as it were. I'm pleased that she found favor with him, for, while I must admit I had my doubts about her marketability, I very much like her style, myself. I shouldn't wonder, with His Grace to bring her into fashion, she might become all the rage."

Seth left the little man lost in his beatific vision and repaired to Derwent House, where he spent the rest of the afternoon in his study, staring at the wall.

What was he to do about Eden? The question buzzed about in his mind like a bothersome insect. It had always been his policy to avoid the maidens of the *ton*. On the rare occasion when he had been attracted to one of them, he lost no time in distancing himself. He was a burnt child who had learned his lesson well, he reflected, his thoughts hurtling back to the Lady Melissa Frumenty, whose path had crossed his not long after he had come down from Oxford. The daughter of an earl, endowed with beauty, wit, and warmth, she had responded to his attentions with a flattering enthusiasm. Matters progressed, but just as he had begun working up to a proposal of marriage, her father had got wind of their *affaire de coeur*. He had threatened to horsewhip Seth and had gone to the duke, full of a fine outrage. Father had read him an abrupt lecture on his station in life. The earl, apparently, discoursed to his daughter on the same subject. The next time he and Melissa met, she favored him with two fingertips and an anguished glance. After that, he rarely saw her at all. A few months later, he read of her betrothal to the Marquess of Milverhampton's son and heir. For some months, he felt his life blighted and not worth living, but in an astonishingly short time, he had made a full recovery. Thereafter, however, he had confined his amours to brief, meaningless flirtations. From time to time he kept a mistress in a discreet town house in St. John's Wood, leased for this purpose, but of late years, even this pleasure had palled. The house had stood empty for some months.

And now, into his life, had blown Eden Beckett, like a delicate leaf borne on a gust of brisk March wind. Was he attracted to the unusual Miss Beckett? Oh, yes. For all his protestations of mere friendship, he could not spend five minutes in her presence without falling into the moonlit pools of her gaze. He thought often of the kiss they had shared in her studio at Clearsprings and very much wished to repeat the experience. He felt he had known her always, and that there was nothing he could not talk about to her.

He almost groaned aloud at the sheer folly of his musings. It was unlikely that Lord Beckett would accept an offer for his daughter's hand from the offspring of an army sergeant, adopted son of the Duke of Derwent or no. Beckett wanted money very badly, and Seth was wealthy in his own right, but would that be enough to sway the status-hungry lord? Seth doubted it.

As for Eden, how would she feel about marrying one of such low birth? He felt she would not be much swayed by his wealth, even if she were aware of its full extent. He thought she might have some feeling toward him—again the memory of that stolen kiss washed over him. She had responded with an ardor that astonished and delighted him. However, one might chalk the experience to the circumstances—the isolated intimacy of the dimly lit studio, and perhaps too much wine earlier at the Becketts' party.

In any event, it was apparent she thought of him as a friend, one who could help her in her present endeavors. Was that all she saw when she looked at him? It was impossible to say, but he felt sure that if a more likely suitor were to appear on the horizon, Eden would not hesitate to accept his attentions, forgetting she had ever known Seth Lindow.

He shrugged and turned his attention to the papers that lay scattered on his desk, reminders that he was paid handsomely to manage the Duke of Derwent's affairs and he had better not forget that fact.

The next day, Eden turned her attention to Zoë. This time Zoë's efforts to play least-in-sight were to no avail. When the girl's maid entered her bedchamber with a breakfast tray, Eden was right behind her. She ignored Zoë's expression of displeasure on beholding her sister.

"Good morning, dearest," Eden said brightly. "It promises to be fine today. Would you like to go for a stroll in the Park? Or perhaps some shopping in Bond Street? I declare, after some consideration, I believe you should purchase the shoes you saw in Megrieve's window. They would admirably complement your new ball gown."

She plumped herself down on Zoë's bed and helped herself to a slice of toast as the maid busied herself about the room, flinging open the curtains and pouring water in the washbasin. When the servant had taken herself from the room, Zoë favored her sister with a grimace.

"What is it you want, Eden? And do stop burbling about the weather."

"You know very well what I want. You've been avoiding me for two days, and it's time for a cozy chat."

"Very well. I will admit that it was singularly ill-advised to participate in a tête à tête with B—that is, the Marquess of Belhaven."

"You must surely have known that before you ever swept off with him to that scrubby little alcove. Zoë, you intended to meet him at the masquerade—that's why you whined and wheedled your way into going!"

"Yes," replied Zoë unrepentantly.

"Then, why—?"

"I'm very attracted to Bel," said Zoë sulkily. "You have to admit there's a lot to be attracted to. All those muscles, the masses of golden hair, and his eyes—such a compelling shade of blue, don't you think?"

"And his habit of seducing anything with a bosom—to say nothing of his fondness for striking women."

A frown creased Zoë's forehead. "Mm. That did come as an unpleasant surprise. I . . . I'm sorry that you should have been the victim of my poor judgment in meeting him alone."

"Does this mean you do not plan to do so again?"

Again Zoë's forehead wrinkled. "I'm not sure."

"Zoë! Good God, how can you even think of seeing him again? Even the thought of encountering him in a roomful of people is enough to give me the shudders."

"I know, but, Eden, there's something about him. I don't know . . . when I'm with him, I feel . . . alive. I know he has a perfectly dreadful reputation, and I'm sure it's well earned, but I can't help feeling that underneath, he's . . . I don't know . . ."

"Just waiting for the love of a good woman?" asked Eden caustically. A flush rose to Zoë's cheeks.

"Yes, something like that," she returned defiantly. "And I'm sure I could make him love me."

"I can only say, I think you've taken leave of your senses."

"That may be," Zoë retorted, "but I've heard it said that love is a fine madness."

"Lord, are you in love with him?"

"I . . . I'm not sure, but I think I could be. And I'd like to find out."

Eden felt chilled to her marrow. "Zoë! You'd be walking into a . . . Gothic novel! You can't . . . you *surely* can't be thinking of marrying him."

Zoë took a thoughtful sip of coffee. "I don't know," she said slowly, and Eden felt the blood congeal in her veins. "I would like to be married to a marquess—and even better I'd like to be a duchess later on. Even if he were a failure as a husband, I would still be a duchess. Perhaps I could be like the Duchess of York, who rarely sees her husband at all." Eden stared as she laughed airily. "I could breed dogs at—where is it? The Priory, I think—and invite interesting people to come see me. I could give parties and sweep into London now and then to set the town on its ear."

Her vivid little face suddenly grew serious. "But I would try very hard to make Bel become a good husband. There is—I don't know how to explain it—something between us, I think— and I believe he felt it, too—from the moment he took me in his arms for that disgraceful waltz. Something he has not experienced with many women—if any at all."

She glanced up from beneath her lashes. "I suppose I am not making a particle of sense, but I very much fear that, having met the Marquess of Belhaven, no other man will do for me."

"Oh, dear God," murmured Eden. What was there about the Derwent men, she wondered dazedly, that seemed to attract the Beckett women like lemmings to the nearest cliff? For she could not help but recall yet again the sense of contact she felt every time she was with Seth. Not that she felt Seth was the only man for her, of course. She was shaken by a swift, sudden inner turmoil. Good Lord, she didn't, did she?

Unwilling to pursue this line of thought, she rose from Zoë's bed.

"You're right, dear sister. You are talking arrant nonsense. I suppose there is nothing I can do to prevent you from making a mess of your life—beyond going to Father, of course and—"

"Eden!" Zoë's face whitened. "You would not! You've *never* done that! If you . . . I'd never forgive you!"

"No, of course I won't. But, believe me, I'll do anything else in my power to keep you from making the biggest mistake of your life—up to and possibly including slipping something lethal into his lordship's soup."

Zoë giggled—a girlish, carefree sound that saddened Eden inutterably. "Oh, Eden, you are so absurd. I think that's why I love you, even when you are your most spinsterly disapproving self."

For the next week, Eden did not let her sister out of her sight. During the day, she accompanied Zoë on shopping expeditions, a picnic to Richmond Park with friends, a visit to Bullock's Egyptian Hall to see the latest in that establishment's collection of rarities from the ancient world, and even to tea with their mother at Grillon's Hotel, taken in company with an elderly relative up from the country. In the evenings, there was the usual round of balls, soirees, and dinner parties, at which she enacted her role of foil for Zoë's beauty. On these occasions, the girl did not so much retire to the ladies' withdrawing room without her sister close on her heels. Belhaven appeared at one or two of these functions, but appeared to pay little attention to Zoë beyond the exchange of a few innocuous pleasantries. After some days, Eden began to think that she had not so very much to fear in that direction after all.

Thus, she set off on her appointment with Mr. Rellihan with an untroubled mind. Surreptitiously bundling a small collection of her paintings into her father's carriage, she set off with her maid, her heart high with what she realized were perfectly absurd hopes. At their last meeting, the gallery owner's attitude had been anything but promising.

To her astonishment and great pleasure, however, Mr. Rellihan displayed a most flattering degree of attention toward her work. He examined each one carefully and set them against the walls of his shop, positioning them for effect among the works of other artists. At last, when Eden felt she had been holding her breath for hours, Mr. Rellihan expelled one of his own.

"Yes, yes, I believe we can find a buyer or two, Miss Beckett." Eden exhaled with an unladylike burst of gratification and surprise. "I particularly like your portraits. I realize that commissions for those will be contracted with individual patrons, but you must understand that if I display your other works, I shall naturally expect a commission on any such agreements."

Eden nodded wordlessly.

"Fortunately, the two endeavors will go hand in hand," continued Mr. Rellihan, rubbing his hands. "The more of your nature studies we sell, the more portraits will come your way, in all likelihood—and vice versa."

"Oh, yes," breathed Eden.

Mr. Rellihan went on to speak of the contract that he would have drawn up, the method of payment, and other mundane concerns, to which Eden, floating in a rosy cloud of disbelieving bliss, scarcely listened. When the gallery owner had finished enumerating the conditions under which they would operate in the future, she bade him a cordial good-bye. Emerging onto the street, she blinked, dazzled as much by the vision of the future upon which she had just embarked as by the blaze of morning sunlight that flooded Oxford Street.

Her first act upon arriving home was to pen a note to Seth, informing him of her good fortune. Afterward, she repaired to her studio to finish up a work in progress—another scene from the park, this time children at play, and to think about her next project. She was surprised, upon her descent to the breakfast room to join her mother and sister for a small nuncheon, to receive a missive from Seth, expressing his felicitations and his intention of calling on her that day to discuss the ramifications of the business end of her new career.

"For, if you don't mind," said Seth on his arrival at the Beckett home later that afternoon, "I would like to go over the Rellihan's proposed contract. I believe him to be an honest merchant, but I should not want to see you taken advantage of due to an ignorance of common business practice."

"Indeed, I would be most grateful. Of course—" She halted abruptly as her mother bustled into the room. Upon being apprised of the highly improper circumstance of her daughter's entertaining a gentleman in the drawing room sans chaperon, Lady Beckett had at once abandoned the laundry inventory she had been contemplating with the housekeeper and hurried to the drawing room to provide suitable chaperonage. If she felt any surprise that the gentleman had apparently come to see Eden rather than Zoë, she concealed the emotion admirably. When Mr. Lindow suggested that Miss Beckett might enjoy a ride to the gardens near Kensington Palace to enjoy the fruit trees blooming there, she made no demure, merely adjuring her daughter to don a warm pelisse, or at least a shawl, for if she was not mistaken, the wind would rise sharply later in the day.

Seth had hardly turned from Portman Square into Seymour Street when Eden began in a breathless rush. "Seth, he actually wants my paintings! He said one or two other artists are experimenting with what he calls stylistic impressions and they have proved highly popular. He says that the thing he likes about this style is that each artist is allowed such individual freedom of expression, and Mr. Rellihan says . . ."

Seth's mouth curved in a smile of infinite tenderness. Her happiness filled him and made him want to enfold her—to keep the world at bay—to keep the glow that radiated from every fibre of her forever safe and secure.

It was not until they had reached the environs of the palace that Seth drew his curricle up near the Round Pond and, bidding his tiger to walk the horses, drew Eden along a path bordered by blooming apple and plum trees. Since the spot was nearly unknown to those wishing for a fashionable promenade, the two found themselves virtually alone in the shade cast by the low-hanging branches.

"Now, then, about this contract Mr. Rellihan wishes to form with you . . ." he began.

"I have no compunction about such an arrangement," said Eden earnestly, "for any portrait commissions I receive will be due to his sponsorship. Actually," she mused, "I don't think I have the makings of a 'society portrait painter.'"

"I agree," commented Seth. "Your portraits are studies of the inner person. They are honest and seeking. Those with the means to have their likenesses painted are interested mainly in the outer person. They wish to be flattered, in the style of Gainsborough. They want the viewer to see their prosperity in the richness of their garb, and their material possessions in the background."

"That's very true," agree Eden thoughtfully. "I do like to get under my subjects' skin. In any event, it will be difficult to maintain my anonymity if I waltz into someone's home, paint pots and brushes in hand, one day and encounter them at my lady Highnose's ball the next evening."

"Quite," said Seth, laughing. "Of course, you could wear a disguise. Appearing in their drawing rooms, wearing a false nose and a wig would certainly provide a piquant air of mystery."

"Oh, yes," Eden cried delightedly. "And I could wear a voluminous cap and perhaps affect a limp."

"No one would know you in a hundred years," Seth assured her gravely. He paused and lifted his hand to brush a few stray blossom petals that had drifted into the cloud of her dark hair.

Eden stood still under his ministrations, and when his fingers remained to trail along her cheek, she lifted her eyes to his.

Immediately, Seth felt a renewal of the sensation that he was sinking into the warm, soft, misty depths of her gaze. Slowly, almost wonderingly, his head bent to hers until at last his lips covered hers in a kiss that was warm and searching. The feel of her in his arms was unlike anything he had experienced before—except for the last time he had kissed her. Her supple womanly curves pressed against his body, making him wild with desire. No, not just desire. He recognized dimly through the maelstrom of wanting that coursed through him that what he felt for Eden Beckett went far beyond lust. He wanted to hold her, to protect her, to somehow draw her within himself, to keep her safe forever.

He had never felt more frightened in his life.

Chapter Fifteen

The sound of approaching voices brought Seth back to reality. He stepped back abruptly, steadying Eden, whose arms dropped with equal suddenness from around his neck.

"Good God," whispered Seth. "I must apologize, Eden. I don't know what . . . That is, I must have been . . ." In any event, he concluded, "I . . . I apologize."

"Yes," said Eden when she had recovered enough breath to speak. She cursed herself for the inanity of her reply, but she felt as though all her strength had drained out of the bottoms of her jean boots, to be replaced by a tremulous weakness that tended to make her knees give way and her heart pound like a child's drum.

She turned and walked back toward the curricle. Seth hurried to catch up with her, and cupped a hand under her elbow.

"I did not mean to distress you, my dear," he said softly.

Eden swung about to face him directly.

"I am not distressed . . . precisely. I have to admit that I like kissing you, Seth. You are very accomplished in the art. However, it is not my practice to fall into a man's arms as I seem to do with you, and I am more overset by my own actions than I am with you. After all, men are predatory by nature, and one must not be surprised when they, er, seize the initiative. I wish us to remain friends, however, and I hope you feel the same. So . . . again, let us just forget this happened."

Seth studied her face for so long that Eden felt the heat rise to her cheeks once more. "I agree with you, my dear," he said at last, "except for the part about forgetting it happened. I'm afraid I can't do that. Indeed, the moment will remain one of my happiest memories."

At this, Eden found herself blushing and speechless. Silently, she accepted his arm once more and proceeded sedately down the path at his side.

Their conversation on the way home dwelled on trivialities. Eden constructed elaborate castles in the air, describing her upcoming success as a painter of fashionable portraits. Seth tried to initiate her into the arcane world of contracts and investments, with little success. They were both laughing companionably as the curricle drew up before Mrs. Nassington's home. Seth declined to recoup his strength with a cup of tea, and deposited her inside the house with due ceremony and a promise to visit again in a few days.

It was not until Eden had removed her bonnet, pelisse, and gloves and ascended the stairs to her bedchamber that she allowed her thoughts to return to that shattering experience under the apple trees at Kensington Palace. She flung herself facedown on her bed, giving herself up to the memory.

Despite what she hoped was her poised discourse on the subject to Seth, she had been shaken to her core by the heat of his kiss. The fire ignited by his lips on hers had surged through her like a lightning strike, and the feel of his hands moving along her back had nearly undone her. All she had wanted to do was curl into him, never to be separated again. She wanted the kiss to go on forever. And she wanted more. She wanted his hands on her, those wonderful, strong hands. She wanted . . .

She drew a deep, shuddering breath. She turned over and gazed at the ceiling. She very much feared she was falling in love with Seth Lindow. For the first time she thought seriously of marriage—marriage to a man with whom she could join in a true union of spirit and body. Her thoughts drifted off into rosy visions of long walks down secluded lanes, of evenings spent with her head close to his before a cozy fire, of waking to find him next to her, his long body curved about hers . . .

Humph, my girl, she thought abruptly. This nonsense is all well and good, but what about Seth? It was obvious to the meanest intelligence that he had enjoyed the kiss he had instigated. He had no doubt enjoyed the embrace in her studio a few weeks earlier. A few moments of pleasure, however, was not enough to drive a man to the brink of matrimony. But, was that all Seth had found? A few moments of pleasure? She had sensed more in his touch. In truth, she had believed him as stirred by the episode as she.

"You're being a fool," she said aloud. "You are counting eggs and crossing bridges. Seth Lindow is your friend, and a couple of kisses do not a commitment make. You'd best be content with his friendship."

The next few weeks seemed to Eden the happiest she had ever known. To her delight, Mr. Rellihan sold three of her paintings. To be sure, one had gone to the Duke of Derwent, and one to his man of affairs, but a third had been purchased by a wealthy merchant. This gentleman, though he might smell of the shop, had a genuine eye for fine art, and was in the habit of acquiring paintings simply because he liked them. In addition, the Countess of Weirhaven, having seen the portrait of the Simms twins, declared that she must have just such a study of her two darling little daughters.

When Eden appeared at Weirhaven House to begin work on the project, she was accompanied by her maid, whom she had taken into her confidence. Makepeace had been in her service since her come-out and was completely devoted to her mistress, thus Eden had no hesitation in entrusting the woman with her plans for her future. For this first sitting by the Weirhaven offspring, she wore an austere gray linen round gown, and tucked her hair firmly under a matching, unadorned cap. Since she had never met the countess and thought it unlikely that they would encounter each other at any social function, Eden felt fairly secure in the hope that, so far, the secret of her career was safe.

She saw Seth frequently. On receiving from Mr. Rellihan the contract he wished her to sign, she had delayed doing so until Seth could look at it. He perused it carefully, and after making one or two suggestions for minor changes, pronounced it acceptable. Seth seemed to make it a point to appear at various functions at which it might be supposed the Misses Beckett would be present and, in addition, visited the house in Portman Square with such regularity that Lady Beckett mentioned the circumstance to her daughter in a cautionary dissertation.

"Mr. Lindow seems to have formed a decided partiality to you, dearest," she declared one morning at the breakfast table. Garbed for the day in twilled cotton, embellished by a dimity fichu, she bobbed her head vigorously as she sipped her coffee. "I would take some care in your dealings with him." She picked at the lace of the table cover for a moment. "I know that at one time we thought he might be an eligible parti for you, but I have been talking to your father and he says . . . well, his social status is such that . . . I am afraid he is quite ineligible."

Eden swallowed her irritation at this pronouncement.

"We are friends only, Mama. I am certainly not thinking of marriage," she added mendaciously. "Mr. Lindow and I merely have some interests in common, and he finds in my company a pleasant diversion from the press of his business activities."

Her mother agreed with unflattering swiftness. "Yes," she said briskly, "I have been asking around a bit, and there has been no talk of his seeking a bride. Not that there is much talk of him at all. Really, despite his connection with the duke, he seems a complete nonentity. I wonder just what his financial situation is," she continued speculatively. "Being the adopted son of the duke, one would think he must be worth something, but if he were, surely he would achieve more of a . . . well, more of a *presence* in the Polite World. And one rarely hears of his attending the more important gatherings."

"Since we are rarely seen at such functions ourselves," interposed Eden tartly, "how would we know if he was there or not?"

Lady Beckett reddened. "Don't be impertinent. Did I not say, 'rarely *hears*'?"

"In any event," continued Eden, "it seems to me that Seth's—that is Mr. Lindow's status in the *beau monde*, as the adoptive son of the Duke of Derwent, is more than secure. In any event, it is hardly our concern. I consider him a friend—nothing more and nothing less."

"Mm. The fact remains, he is a commoner of low birth. I hope a word to the wise will be sufficient, my dear, as I'm sure it will be. You are not a young flibbertigibbet to be swayed by the attentions of a gentleman. That is," she concluded in a flustered rush, "he is not precisely a gentleman, but—oh, you know what I mean."

Which sentiment so put Eden out of charity with her mother that she swallowed the last of her coffee in a gulp and left the room with an indignant rustle of skirts.

She ascended the stairs, to be met by Zoë, coming down to the first floor.

"Good morning, dearest. I suppose you have already breakfasted? Is Mama—?"

"Yes," replied Eden shortly. "I believe she is just finishing."

"Oh, good. I wish to speak to her about the gown we purchased last week for the Wellerton's ball. I'm going shopping with Melisande Cooper and her mother this morning, and I wish to purchase some ribbon for it. I'm undecided what color I should choose." She laughed. "We may say what we like about Mama's sense of fashion, but she does have an unerring eye for color."

"Indeed," replied Eden, her good humor gradually returning. She surveyed Zoë. Her sister had not been entirely silent on the subject of the Marquess of Belhaven, but somehow this proved more reassuring to Eden than if she had forborne to speak of him at all. She only uttered his name, however, in the most casual manner, commenting on the latest *on dit* in which he featured, or the latest scandal attached to his name. She received her gentleman callers with a pretty enthusiasm, and had even received with every appearance of pleasure the marked attentions of the very young Viscount Hadley. Eden was beginning to conclude that her infatuation with the marquess, if it could be called that, had mercifully been as brief as it had been intense.

Eden wondered if the same could not be said for the marquess's foster brother. To her distinct disappointment, her friendship with Seth proved to be just that. Since the visit to Kensington Palace, his behavior toward her had been exemplary—one of courteous affection, with no hint that he wished their relationship to progress to a more intimate level.

What, she speculated, had been his response to the kiss that had so shattered her well-ordered existence? She had felt a union with him that she had never experienced with another soul. Had he felt the same?

Was he, she mused, laughing at herself as she did so, even now thinking of her, and of the moment they had shared in that blossom-scented bower?

She would have been astonished to know that Seth was doing precisely that. He had retired late after a meeting with the other directors in one of the duke's companies. Now, as occurred so often lately, he had difficulty in finding sleep. Instead, he lay staring at the canopy above his bed, seeing before him a lifted face, framed with a mahogany sweep of hair, misty eyes clouded with passion.

He had kissed many women. What man reaching his age and station in life had not? The kiss stolen in her studio had stirred him. He had been utterly undone by the embrace in Kensington. If he had not been restored to sanity by the sound of approaching voices, God knew what the result might have been. In another moment, he might have tried to take her right there on that secluded path. What, he mused further, with a quickening of his pulse, would have been her response to such an attempt? Her icy little speech on the way home indicated that she would have given him short shrift. However, he believed that something in her had cried out to him in that stabbing instant of communion, that she, too, had experienced a consuming fever in the blood, a desperate wanting to become part of him.

God, what was happening to him? Ever since the episode with Melissa, he had been careful to confine his amours to certain kinds of women—women of easy morals who understood the rules. Certainly, this group included a few highborn ladies; however, he had not desired a permanent relationship with any of them. Nor did he wish one now, he told himself. In any event, Miss Eden Beckett was not the sort to slip into a discreet affair of the sort that was so common among the *beau monde*. No, Eden was of the marrying kind, and, as he very well knew, that meant a man of her own class—a gentleman with whom she would live a life of gentility and produce a future generation of little ladies and gentlemen. She and her genteel family would inhabit a world where the son of an army sergeant might be tolerated, but would never be fully accepted.

True, she had spoken to him of his own worth, and she appeared genuinely convinced that a man could create his own way in the world, but he knew very well that her high-sounding principles were merely a vague ideal, with no application in the real world of arranged unions and the awareness that wealth and privilege were only for the chosen.

So, what was he to do about the delectable Miss Beckett? He had already decided to take himself out of the business of procuring a wife for Bel. He had yet to confront his father with this decision, and he did not look forward to the occasion with pleasure. The Duke of Derwent was not accustomed to having his will thwarted. All that aside, however, he had made his decision, and thus he could simply expunge Eden from his life. He was surprised at the pang this thought caused. Lord, the girl had sneaked into his life when he wasn't looking, and had become more important to him than he could have dreamed just a few short weeks ago. Eden had become a friend, and he did not have so many of those that he could afford to discard one.

No, he would continue his relationship with Eden, provided she had not concluded after his behavior at Kensington that she wished to have nothing more to do with him. He turned into his pillow, his resolution firmly in place. Somewhere within him, a well of despair brimmed, a knowledge that he could never hope to be more than a friend to her, but he ignored this thought as frivolous. Love could be bought, after all, and when and if he felt the need for a wife, he would simply select one of his own station. After all, he had the wealth to make such a choice without fear of rejection.

At long last, he slept.

Chapter Sixteen

Over the next few weeks, Eden found herself increasingly busy. Mr. Rellihan sold three more of her paintings and asked if she could not provide him with a few more. Much to her pleasure, she was now possessed of a fund of money that boded well for her future independence. True to his word, albeit with marked disapproval, Seth accompanied her to the prestigious precincts of Coutts' Bank, where he introduced her to its proprietor. Although this gentleman expressed some surprise at her request to open an account under a fictitious name, the presence and apparent patronage of her companion worked a powerful magic. In short order, her mission was accomplished, and she stared dazedly at her account book, already approaching four figures.

"Oh, Seth," she breathed a little later as she held the book reverently over the table of one of the coffeehouses that dotted London's financial district. "This is going better than I ever dreamed. Why, in a year or two, I shall be able to move into my own domicile—ruler of my own destiny—mistress of my fate!"

Seth smiled, but a hint of concern flared in his dark gaze. Unconsciously, his hand reached out to grip hers. Eden made no move to withdraw it.

"My dear . . ." Eden made no response to the appellation. "I cannot think it proper to keep your new venture a secret from your father. No, no," he continued as Eden opened her mouth. "Do but listen. Even if you do accrue enough money to move into your own home, such a course may still be closed to you. Do you not realize that you may do nothing without his permission? Once he realizes that you have sufficient funds to make yourself independent, he need only demand that they be turned over to him. He can and most probably will refuse to allow you to leave his home. He could kick up all sorts of unpleasantness,

including having you declared mentally incompetent, to prevent you from reaching your ambition. It would be much better
if you were to acknowledge your present activity to him and try
to persuade him into accepting your goals."

Eden grimaced. "You obviously don't know my father very
well. Persuading him into any course of action once he has set
his face against it is like trying to batter through the walls of the
Tower."

"Nonsense." Seth smiled expansively. "Look at Zoë. Look
and learn. That little minx could talk Lord Beckett into riding
naked through the streets of Coventry."

Eden stiffened. "I am not Zoë," she said shortly. "As you
may have noticed, I am not endowed with golden curls and a
winsome smile, nor do I hold the promise of acquiring a substantial *parti*. My only hope of happiness is to pursue my own
path." She laughed ruefully. "Goodness, that sounds like a line
from a very bad play, does it not?" Her expression grew serious
again. "Nevertheless, I plan to keep my successes to myself and
watch my little pile of guineas grow." She glanced swiftly up at
him. "You will not take it upon yourself to tell Papa what I am
doing?" she asked anxiously. "You did promise, you know."

"Of course I know." Seth's eyes sparked. "I am not likely to
forget when I have given my word. I am merely saying I believe you're mistaken."

Eden relaxed. "Warning taken and noted," she said, smiling.
She lifted her nose in a spurious air of condescension. "Never
fear, my good man. You will be rewarded amply for your efforts
on my behalf. I shall leave you a substantial bit in my will of
my gargantuan pile of earnings."

With that, Seth apparently decided to be content, for he
turned the conversation to other matters as they sipped the re-
mainder of their coffee.

Over the next week, Eden worked apace on the portraits of
the Weirhaven children and received commissions to start in on
two more portraits. She attempted to curtail her social activities, but Mama would have none of it.

"Eden, you must come with us this evening. To be invited to
Lady Childers's musicale is a real coup. We met at the duke's
dinner, but she did not seem interested in pursuing an acquaintance. I was never more surprised in my life to receive her invitation, because I know for a fact that the Meechams did not get

one, and Lavinia Meecham has known Lady Childers for this age."

"Yes, but Mama, why must I be there?" Eden asked impatiently. "It is Zoë we're trying to push off, remember."

"Because she always feels more secure when you're there. She still does not know many of the young people in that set, and nothing can be more lowering than standing about by oneself with no one to talk to."

"You will be there."

"Yes, but I shall be seated with the matrons. It would present an extremely odd appearance for me to be flitting about the company like one of the youngsters. Besides—" She paused and shot a quick glance at her daughter, nervously twisting one of her many bracelets. "Well, it was the oddest thing. I encountered Lady Shipstead the other day at the new silk warehouse in Leicester Square. You know, the Duke of Derwent's sister. She asked me if we would be attending Lady Childers's musicale and seemed extraordinarily gratified when I said yes. Eden," concluded Lady Beckett in a puzzled voice, "she said that she had particularly enjoyed meeting you at the duke's dinner party and looked forward to seeing you again. What do you make of that?"

"Why, I'm bound to say I don't know what to make of it, Mama," replied Eden, equally baffled. "Are you sure she said my name? Perhaps she had me mixed up with Zoë. She hasn't spoken to either one of us above a few times."

Lady Beckett frowned dubiously. "Perhaps, but she seemed quite emphatic. At any rate, you really must come, Eden."

Some hours later, Zoë seconded the demand, with the result that when the Beckett family sallied forth to the Childers town home on the following Tuesday, the elder Miss Beckett was among their number.

To her pleasure, she discovered that Seth was in attendance as well. She warmed at his expression of delight as his eyes met hers from across the room. Since she had spent the afternoon in his company, their greeting was brief and informal.

"You said nothing this afternoon at the foundry," he said after hurrying to her side, "to indicate that I might see you tonight. By the by, I hope you enjoyed our somewhat unusual outing."

Eden smiled widely. "Indeed, I did. What a marvelous idea to visit your father's foundry. I've never thought of viewing such an establishment."

"I did not know what you might think of it. Most females of my acquaintance would not have considered so much as setting a toe in a great dirty, noisy factory, much less demanding to be shown about the place."

"You must know me well enough by now, my good man, to realize that I haven't a grain of feminine sensibility. I found the place fascinating. It seems to me that more gently bred women should be given the opportunity to visit our factories and workshops. We would all benefit greatly from at least a moderate understanding of the industries that provide us with our carriages and houses and . . . and all the other necessities we take for granted."

"Oh, very well said, Madame Firebrand. Are you next going to tell me that your fascination with the wheels of progress were not wholly connected with the drama of the furnaces and the rivers of molten metal you were sketching so furiously?"

Eden laughed. "Indeed, I did find that aspect compelling. If I ever decide to do one of those panoramic extravaganzas so popular now, I think I'd like to try to reproduce such a scene. I think," she mused further, "that with the men caught in the blaze of light from the furnaces, toiling so inexorably, it would be rather like creating a vision of hell."

"I'm sure the workers would agree with you. But, come, this is not a topic for such a frivolous gathering. Are you enjoying the musicale?"

"Oh, yes," was Eden's enthusiastic if somewhat breathless reply. It seemed to her that their conversation was taking place on two levels. One consisted of the light prosaic chatter that one always managed at these events. Under the surface, however, Eden was aware of an undercurrent, swift and dangerous, that seemed to flow between them. It was as though everything that had transpired between them since the first day he had appeared at Clearsprings seethed thickly to pull them toward one another in a vortex of wanting. She shook herself and continued brightly. "Lady Childers has apparently spared no effort to provide her guests with the best entertainment in the city. I thought the violinists particularly talented."

"Indeed, my lady is famous for her musical parties. I do not see your father here, by the way. Did he not accompany you?"

"Oh, yes." Eden glanced around. "He must be in the card room. Mama and Zoë, as usual, prevailed on him to come. Mama does not like to attend a function like this without masculine support. She still feels rather uncomfortable in such exalted company."

"Good heavens, Eden, your father is a peer. He and his family must be at home in any social gathering."

"I suppose, but I must say it came as a surprise to receive Lady Childers's invitation. And then—oh, did I tell you? Mama told me that your aunt was especially insistent that we come."

Seth frowned in sudden suspicion. "Did she? I was unaware that she had interested herself in your affairs."

"Yes, I thought it quite odd, too, but . . . Oh, my gracious, what is *he* doing here?"

Seth's gaze followed Eden's to behold his brother enter the room. Stopping only to greet his hostess, he made a path directly for Zoë.

Chapter Seventeen

Zoë turned slowly with studied casualness as Bel approached her, but it was as though Eden could reach out and touch the tension that fairly radiated from her sister's body.

"Good Lord," exclaimed Seth. "I had no idea he planned to put in an appearance here. At least he seems sober. On his best behavior, actually," he concluded, watching as Bel lifted Zoë's hand in his to press a kiss to her gloved fingertips.

Seth growled, "Are his attentions toward your sister becoming bothersome?"

"I don't know," replied Eden slowly. "To my knowledge, they have not seen each other since the episode at Covent Garden. There can be no doubt he is taken with her. Whether he feels something deeper, I cannot say."

Seth snorted. "I doubt that Bel would recognize a deep emotion if it bit him. What about Zoë? Do you think—?"

"Yes," said Eden unhappily. "She has confessed to being . . . well, smitten. I can only hope it is a passing fancy—on both their parts."

After conversing with Zoë for a few moments, apparently in the most unexceptionable manner, Bel turned to greet his aunt, who had hurried over to grasp his arm insistently. Zoë swung back to her friends. Eden and Seth parted as well, and Eden had barely entered into conversation with another lady of her acquaintance when Lady Shipstead approached, her arm tucked into that of her nephew. Bel smiled dutifully as the countess expressed her delight at encountering Miss Beckett. Her brother, the duke, had intercepted Eden earlier in the evening to express similar sentiments. Eden had then observed the duke deep in animated conversation with Lord Beckett, causing Eden to wonder once again what it was about the Beckett family that seemed to have endeared them so to the Derwents.

"It's a dreadful crush, of course," Lady Shipstead said in a high, breathless voice, plying her fan vigorously, "but these things always are. It's my belief that Honoria calculates the number of persons who can comfortably be accommodated in her rooms, then invites three times that many. Bel, you remember Miss Beckett, do you not?"

Eden nodded coolly and offered him two fingers. Bel bent gracefully over her hand, but refrained from kissing it. He shot her a bland glance that did not hide the mischief glittering beneath it.

"How very nice to see you again, Miss Beckett."

Eden said nothing, merely nodding rigidly.

"Are you not afraid your neck will snap when you do that?" asked Bel innocently. Eden gasped, and Lady Shipstead rushed in to fill the ensuing appalled silence.

"Did you enjoy Monsieur Dubonnet's performance, Miss Beckett? I vow, I have never heard the pianoforte played with such feeling. What a coup for Lady Childers to acquire him for her musicale, for he turned down an engagement at Woburn, I understand." Lady Shipstead rattled on at some length in praise of M. Dubonnet before apparently running out of information on the subject. Another awkward silence fell on the little group until Lady Shipstead, undaunted, tittered nervously. "My dear," she said to Eden, "you must join us for the string quartet that will be playing immediately after supper—in the ballroom, I believe." She whirled to face Bel. "You *will* sit with me for the performance, will you not, my dear?" Her tone was honeyed but contained an unmistakable edge.

"I am sorry, Aunt," he replied smoothly, gently removing his arm from beneath her hand. "I shan't be staying for supper. I'm promised to a group at White's and shall probably spend the rest of the evening there." Smiling benignly, he murmured, "Miss Beckett," before easing himself back into the swirling throng of guests—like an eel, thought Eden, sliding back to his ocean haven after a visit to the shoals.

Lady Shipstead's face creased in what looked very much like a thwarted pout. Goodness, what plans had Bel ruined by his precipitate departure? Surely, they could not have involved her own humble self. How very odd. She watched speculatively as Bel made his way about the room, his behavior entirely proper, greeting friends and acquaintances of the family. To her vast relief, he did not seek Zoë's attention, and she eventually lost sight of him.

Nor did she see Seth again until supper was announced. She had been claimed for this intermission in the musical program by a Mr. Wiggam, a gentleman of some five-and-forty summers. He held a position in the Exchequer and was said to be an influential Whig. They had been introduced at the duke's dinner party, and the gentleman had made it a point at every function attended by both to claim her attention for at least part of the evening. Eden enjoyed his easy air of address and his breezy good humor.

As they descended the stairs to the dining chamber, Eden caught a glimpse of Lady Weirhaven, the mother of her current portrait subjects. With the well-known perversity of events, plus the rise in her social status thanks to the duke's still unexplained interest in the Beckett family, Eden had seen the countess at a number of *ton* gatherings, but had successfully avoided her. On this occasion, she scurried down the stairs, to Mr. Wiggam's obvious startlement, and was ensconced in her chair when Lady Weirhaven was seated at a safe distance.

Seth, she noted, had escorted Maria, the Viscountess Fanstead to the meal. The viscountess was an acknowledged Beauty, willowy of form and possessed of classic features. She was also reputed to maintain the most casual of relations with her accommodating husband. Her affairs were notorious throughout the *beau monde*. Eden was annoyed at the spurt of jealousy that shot through her at the sight of Seth's dark head bent over the viscountess's auburn curls.

She determinedly ignored Seth's presence throughout what had become an interminable evening. She laughed at inane witticisms until she thought her face would splinter, and she exchanged mindless tidbits of scurrilous gossip with the matrons gathered on the fringes of the gaiety. As ordered, she sat with Lady Shipstead during the string quartet's virtuoso performance. The music was exquisite, but, perhaps because of the heat and the crush of the number of those in the audience, Eden soon developed a thundering headache that stayed with her until, at long last, the family took their departure.

Inhaling deeply of the cool night air, she participated little in the animated chatter taking place between Zoë and her mother.

"Dearest!" exclaimed Lady Beckett. "I could not help but notice that the Viscount Hadley is becoming most particular in his attentions. And I thought it extremely auspicious that his mama made it a point to converse with you at length."

"I just wish he possessed a trifle more . . . dash," said Zoë, a slight pout in her tone. "He told me he much prefers his seat in Warwickshire to Town, and would not come here at all except that he is interested in politics and sits in Parliament religiously. That's all he speaks of, and I must own I'm getting heartily sick of it."

"You could do a lot worse," grumbled Lord Beckett. "I've been hearing good things about young Hadley. He's a loyal Whig, and he's making a name for himself. He may be up for an important position in the near future."

"In which case," breathed Lady Beckett, "you would find yourself in Town for most of the year."

"Mm, there is that." Reflectively, Zoë plaited the fringe adorning her reticule.

Eden suppressed her distaste at Zoë's single-minded drive toward wealth and status. On the other hand, if the idea of marrying a viscount on his way up the political drainspout was an antidote to her attraction for the undesirable Marquess of Belhaven, Eden could only applaud her sister's goal.

"In truth," she said to Seth the next day, "I could wish her to elope with the man tomorrow if it would keep her out of the clutches of your wretched brother. No offense," she added hastily.

"None taken," he replied, chuckling.

He had come at Eden's request that they begin the oil portrait of him she had suggested at Clearsprings. He sat with her now in her studio as she mixed a batch of paints. He watched her appreciatively, her slim form enveloped in a sturdy cotton apron. Her hands moved swiftly and capably as she manipulated bladders of paint and bottles of thinner, as well as an assortment of small paddles, palette knives, and even brushes until she attained just the blend she sought.

The early afternoon sun slanted through the garret windows to brush her cheeks with gold and to touch the depths of her dark hair with flaming highlights.

He jerked himself to attention as she continued speaking while she settled him prosaically into position. "His attitude toward her last night was far from loverlike. He was merely polite, as any other young man attending a function at which he would just as soon have avoided. I must say," she added suddenly, "your aunt, Lady Shipstead, was most cordial. She actually smiled at Zoë, and she was charm personified with me. And I saw your father chatting with mine as though they were lifelong cronies. Have you any idea what brought about this sudden benevolence toward us on the part of your relatives?"

Seth's stomach plummeted. Good God, his father must have confided his plans for Eden to his aunt, and the two of them had already begun their campaign to bring Eden into the family as Bel's wife. Seth had put off talking to the duke, for he knew their conversation would degenerate quickly into an unpleasant confrontation, but he must not let this go on. Lord, what had possessed the old man to take matters into his own hands? Usually, he was content to let Seth arrange such matters. Had he sensed Seth's reluctance to be a part of the unsavory business? Seth laughed shortly. Not that that had ever given the old man pause before.

Shaking his head in denial of her question, Seth sought a diversion. "What is that you're working on now?" he asked, pointing to a shrouded canvas that stood on a nearby easel.

Eden moved to flip the muslin covering. A street scene stood revealed, a small portion of the great square on which Mrs. Nassington's house fronted. A housemaid could be seen, polish can in hand, rubbing the railing in front of an elegant home. Toward her rolled a sailor, his hand lifted in a flirtatious greeting. Pedestrians in the street included a high-nosed damsel, followed by her maid, carrying a number of packages. An urchin swept the ground before her, while a scissors and knives man trundled along the pavement a respectful distance away. Looking farther toward the square, a dandy on horseback fairly strutted in his saddle as he waved a greeting to a distant acquaintance in a smart curricle. Other shapes, vaguely delineated, filled out the impression of a busy thoroughfare, its inhabitants a microcosm of the city as a whole.

"It's splendid!" exclaimed Seth involuntarily. "I would never have thought that London could provide such a colorful vista, but you have made it all entirely natural. It makes one believe that when the sun is shining, the city becomes almost habitable."

How comfortable this was, Seth thought suddenly. He could

not remember ever enjoying himself so in the company of a woman. With Eden he did not find it necessary to invent conversation. It flowed naturally between them like a laughing stream, frivolous and sparkling and lifting the spirit in an effervescent spray. He was not obliged to ply her with empty compliments or the latest *on dits*. Nor did he need to guard his tongue against a word or phrase that might wound her sensibilities.

Eden, as though sensing his thoughts, sobered and lifted her brows questioningly. A faint flush rose to her cheeks, and he castigated himself for allowing his pleasure in her company to lead him into dangerous territory. Dammit, why did he, known throughout London for his composure and cool objectivity, so lose himself when he was with this perfectly ordinary, if dazzlingly talented, young woman?

"At any rate," he said briskly, "from what you say, it sounds as though you are meeting with great success in your new career."

"Mmm, hmm. I cannot believe how well my paintings are selling. Particularly when only a few months ago Mr. Rellihan was telling me there was no market for my work." She glanced at Seth from under her lashes. "I wonder if my *succés de fou* might have anything to do with an art purchase or two made recently by the Duke of Derwent?"

"I beg your pardon?" asked Seth, striving for an expression of bewildered innocence.

"None of that, now, my lad," responded Eden. "Your aunt happened to mention last night that her brother has acquired the oddest painting and insisted on hanging it in a prominent position in his library. 'Flowers!' she said. 'But, my dear, they look to me like nothing such much as a handful of fireworks stuck in a vase.' A description remarkably similar to what Mama said on beholding my *Summer Poppies*, which, I might add, was among the works I delivered to Mr. Rellihan not two weeks ago."

"My father," said Seth with great dignity, "is a great proponent of the avant-garde. He likes to search out the work of promising young artists who explore new expression. I suppose it is possible that he saw your work in Rellihan's gallery—"

Eden burst into laughter. "Oh, Seth, you are the most complete hand. Your father seems to me as likely to delve into the avant-garde as he is liable to search through the writings of Thomas Paine to augment his library. But, I do thank you, dear friend," she added, once more becoming serious. "I am not above taking advantage of the Duke of Derwent's position in the Polite World—nor of yours. I am quite sure that a judicious remark or two from the duke's perspicacious man of affairs carries enormous weight."

"In some areas, perhaps," Seth replied shortly. "Let me assure you, however, that my influence in the Polite World is nil."

So abrupt was his tone that Eden glanced at him in surprise. "Are you angry that I refer to your standing in society? I meant no insult."

He laughed harshly. "I perceive no insult on your part, but you must know that my status in the *beau monde* is only slightly higher than that of the average tinker."

Eden's eyes widened. "There you go again, denigrating the contribution you've made to the duke's family. Surely, you have earned their respect and that of the rest of the *ton*."

"I am the son of an army sergeant, and I will never be allowed to forget that."

"You certainly won't," Eden snapped, "particularly if you do not allow yourself to forget." She stared at him in astonishment. Did he truly perceive himself as an outcast? Did he not believe himself to be secure in his position as family member to one of the highest-ranking peers in the realm? In addition, he had attained a comfortable degree of success on his own merit. What was he talking about? Son of an army man or no . . .

"I'm sorry," he said awkwardly. "I did not mean to vent my spleen in such a manner. Let us dispense with the dismal subject of my antecedents." He took a watch from his waistcoat pocket. "Actually, I must leave you now so you may put the finishing touches on your street scene. I am due in the City in less than an hour."

"Of course." Eden took up a cotton rag to remove some of the paint residue and gave him her hand. "Will I see you at the concert at Brentwood House tomorrow?" She was dismayed at the pleading tone she heard in her voice, and to her further discomfiture, she put forth a hand to touch his sleeve. "You had mentioned—"

His arm felt rigid beneath her fingers, and his face closed. "No. That is, I'm afraid I'm engaged elsewhere. I'm not sure when I shall see you again. Press of business, you know. No, don't bother," he added as Eden moved to accompany him from the room. "I can see my own way out."

With a brusque nod, he was gone, leaving Eden to stare after him.

Chapter Eighteen

Outside the house, Seth stood for a moment, gasping as though he had just gone ten rounds with Gentleman Jackson. Lord, what was the matter with him? Eden had put forth the merest tendril of invitation, and he had reacted like a maiden about to be ravished.

Slowly, he mounted his waiting curricle, greeting his tiger curtly. He had made the decision to enjoy his friendship with Eden. Had he now been driven to panic at the thought of raising the level of their relationship from friendship to something stronger? No, of course not—at least, not precisely. He told himself firmly that he merely did not wish Eden to grow accustomed to his presence in her life. He had helped her establish a position as an artist. This was not simply because he liked the young woman, but because it was a crime against nature that her extraordinary talent should go unnoticed.

By the time he started up Ludgate Hill on his journey to the Royal Exchange, he had convinced himself that his behavior just now had, under the circumstances, been unexceptionable. Actually, he had behaved wisely in disabusing Miss Beckett of any notion that, despite the intimacies they had shared, he was likely to forget his station in life. Certainly, he had impressed upon her the impossibility of any future commitment between them. He hoped he had not hurt her by his abrupt departure, and he would see her again—here and there and from time to time.

He should have felt relieved, but, searching within, he could find only a dismal, hollow sensation—a frightening loneliness that an hour's worth of negotiations with several stock jobbers did nothing to dispel.

In her studio, Eden puttered distractedly. After a futile few minutes trying to infuse an atmosphere of Mediterranean gaiety into her London street scene, she abandoned the attempt. Cov-

ering the canvas, she retired to a chair overlooking the subject
of her endeavors and stared blankly at the passersby.

What the *devil* had come over Seth? She had merely asked a
civil question, but one would have thought she had suggested
an assignation in a brothel. Well, yes, it must be admitted that
her voice had been warm with invitation, for she had come to
believe that Seth reciprocated her feeling for him. She had,
without thinking, assumed he would welcome her covert suggestion that she looked forward to seeing him again. Perhaps
. . . perhaps she should not have allowed herself to brush his
hand with hers. She rose to pace the narrow confines of the garret room. How utterly humiliating to have thrust her attentions
on a gentleman who did not welcome them! And how shattering, she reflected sadly, to have them so bluntly rebuffed. How
could she have been so mistaken in Seth's feelings for her?

Because the dratted man had kissed her—twice—in a fashion that had left little doubt in her mind that he found her desir-
able. And, like a naive schoolgirl, she had busily begun crafting
air castles that had no foundation in reality. How very stupid
she had been. Well, she told herself briskly, Seth Lindow had
just made it perfectly plain that he had no interest in a romance
with a spinster of meager attributes. And, if that's the way he
wanted it, so be it. Fine. Suppressing with great effort an urge to
bury her head in her lap and wail like an abandoned child, she
rose and returned to her easel. Ignoring the portrait of Seth, she
immersed herself for the rest of the morning in her street painting, and though she was not entirely happy with the results, she
congratulated herself on making progress, in more ways than
one.

Seth's day progressed in much the same fashion. He felt
rather like a man who has lived on the verge of starvation for
some weeks—light-headed, hollow, and unable to concentrate
on matters at hand. Despite the malaise that plagued him, however, he realized that he must address the problem he had refused to face for some days.

He strode into his father's study later that afternoon to find
the duke perusing *The Gentleman's Magazine*. He raised his
head at Seth's entrance with no great sign of pleasure.

"Well, then, I wondered when you'd come to see me."

"Sir?"

"We decided some three weeks ago that the Beckett chit was

the most likely candidate for Bel's offer, yet nothing seems to be going forward. Your aunt, using God knows what method of coercion, had bludgeoned Bel into attending functions where he ordinarily wouldn't be caught dead. I've seen him talking to Miss Beckett—well, both Miss Becketts actually. I've dropped a word or two in Beckett's ear, and he seems receptive, but so far the girl—the older Miss Beckett—seems to show no interest—nor does Bel in her. I am not satisfied with the progress that is being made, and I want to know what you plan to do about this, Seth."

Seth drew a long breath and moved to stand directly before the duke. "I plan to do nothing," he said clearly.

For a moment, the duke said nothing, merely staring disbelievingly at his son.

"Nothing!" he barked, at last.

"Yes, Your Grace. Nor do I intend to in the future. I'm sorry. I regret that things are not working out in your quest to find a bride for Bel, but I must inform you now that I shall no longer take part in that quest."

During this speech, the duke seem to have swollen to twice his size. It was not often His Grace had become angry with Seth in his early years—not because he held the young Seth in particular affection, but because it was obvious he felt no obligation to take a hand in the boy's development. Now, however, his face reddened much in the same fashion it used to on the rare occasions he found it necessary to punish the lad for some childhood transgression.

"What are you saying?" the older man roared.

"Father, you know what we're doing is wrong. After our discussion on the subject of Bel, I did as you asked. I scoured the marriage mart for eligible females, and when I found one, like a faithful beagle, I trotted her out for you and laid her at your feet, so to speak. When it turned out she wasn't suitable, after all, I dutifully turned to her older sister. But then . . ." Seth paused. He smiled painfully. "I suppose I was struck at last with whatever is left of my conscience. Father, we cannot possibly induce her—or any other female—to marry Bel. It would be like staking a lamb to snare a beast of the forest."

The duke drummed his fingers several moments on the desk before replying. "Seth," he said at last, in a voice like splinters of steel, "we've been over this. Bel must marry. He may not make an ideal husband, but, provided she stays out of his way, he has a great deal to offer a young woman. He will have one of the most prestigious titles in the country, he's wealthy, and we're prepared to offer a more than generous settlement on her family. Lord, Beckett fairly slavers when I hint that we might find his daughter acceptable for Bel."

"Dear God, you've done that?"

"Well, I haven't made an outright offer, but I've cast out the merest lure. From what you've told me, he's none too plump in the pocket, and it's my belief he'd very much like to be."

"Yes, I think you're right, but have you considered, Father, the young woman herself? Or any young woman married to Bel? You say she'd have to stay out of his way. That's all well and good, but if Bel decrees otherwise, that course would be closed to her. Father, you know Bel. He'd be like a little boy with a new kitten. In the beginning, assuming he was pleased with his bride, he'd be all attention. But he'd soon begin tormenting her—at first playfully, then in earnest, until she became either a pitiful lunatic or dead. Only when he tired of her would she know any respite, and even then, she'd be at his mercy any time he happened to think of her."

By now the duke was white around the mouth.

"This is Bel of whom we're speaking, Seth. I think you forget that. He is my son. The heir to a dukedom, and it is not for the likes of—"

By now Seth was angrier than he had ever allowed himself to be toward his father. He stepped forward with clenched fists. "I know my place, Father. At your beck and call and service, as I have always been. I know what I owe to you, and believe me, I am grateful, but I . . . cannot . . . do this."

"Curse your impudence, boy. You *will* do as I say!"

"Not this time, Father. I regret this more than I can say, and you may wish to toss me out on my ear. Long ago, I placed myself at your service, and I believe I have been of benefit to you. I have no desire to defy you, but I cannot do this." He paused and said in a softer tone. "I think that on reflection you must see that it would be beneath you to be a part of ruining the life of an innocent young girl. You have an heir, you know. Young Jack is not—"

The duke waved an impatient hand. "Pah! Jack! My brother's son is an effeminate milksop who would bring the line to ruination. For one thing, I seriously doubt if he could bring another Lindow from his loins. In any event, he is not of my blood—although," he concluded with a certain benevolent contempt, "I don't expect you to see the importance of that."

The insult made no impact on the scar tissue Seth had acquired over the years. He merely replied wearily, "Of course, I realize its importance, and I am truly sorry that—for the first time, I think—I cannot reconcile your desires with my conscience."

The duke lifted both hands in a gesture of bafflement. "I must confess I don't understand this womanish display of sensibility. However, I suppose that, in dredging up two reasonably worthy candidates for the position of Duchess of Derwent, you might be said to have fulfilled your task, and I shall have to complete the bargain myself."

"What?" asked Seth in consternation.

"Certainly," the duke replied blandly. "I have met Lord Beckett and begun tentative negotiations. It remains only for me to speak to him more formally and send our attorney to him for a final confirmation. The lawyers can work out the details. I am prepared to be generous, after all. In addition, I've planted the seed in Bel's mind that the elder Miss Beckett would make an admirable bride for him. He laughed, of course, but when he realizes that this time I mean to bring him to the sticking point, I believe he'll capitulate."

Seth simply gaped at his father. It had not occurred to him that once he had withdrawn his assistance in achieving the duke's goal, the old gentleman would plow ahead on his own. The man had not lifted a finger on his own behalf for the last ten years. Why in God's name did he have to start now?

Because Bel's marriage was of prime importance to the line, of course. His Grace's will was not to be thwarted by the recalcitrance of the lowborn orphan he had taken into his home. Seth realized there was no point in speaking further. The duke could be stubborn as a spoiled child where his wishes were concerned. He might let Seth guide him in matters of finance and civic duty, but he would not be swayed in circumstances in which his personal desires were at stake.

Seth contented himself with a curt nod. Jaw clenched, he left the room. Behind him, he heard the duke's expansive chuckle. He returned to his sanctum at the rear of the house and, flinging himself into the chair behind his desk, gave himself up to thought.

If the duke chose to continue negotiations himself, there could be little doubt of the outcome. Lord Beckett would welcome with open arms the son and heir of the Duke of Derwent for the daughter he had previously considered unmarriageable. He might be somewhat disappointed that Zoë had not come up to the ducal standard, but he would no doubt take comfort in the certainty that Zoë would snabble someone on her own who would be almost as acceptable. Beckett, concluded Seth, would be beside himself with visions of wealth and prestige.

And what would be Eden's reaction to her father's demand that she marry the Marquess of Belhaven? Would she cry defiance? Would she go so far as to leave the Beckett menage, relying on her art to support her? Lord, Beckett would destroy her. If she persisted in pursuing her independence, he would simply lock her up at Clearsprings—or in Bedlam—until she capitulated.

At least, he thought, he would no longer be involved with the Beckett family—or, more specifically, the elder Miss Beckett. If his father chose to continue negotiations on his own, so be it. He, himself, at least would be out of it. Eden surely had enough backbone to defy her father if he began an effort to force her into a repugnant marriage. He need not visit the Beckett house, and he needn't force himself to attend the myriad insipid social functions that dotted the landscape of Mayfair like outbreaks of measles.

He need not see Eden anymore.

The words seemed to echo in the silence around him like the last words of a dying man. Good Lord, he had lived without love for most of his life. He had survived, and he would continue to do so. He had proved that he did not require love. He was not even sure what the word meant. Surely, it was not the sentiment done to death in ballads and poetry. Just as surely, it could not mean the prison in which so many of his friends and acquaintances found themselves entrapped—that unhappy state of bondage to the desires of another, catering to the loved one's desires and whims and defending oneself against imagined transgressions.

Yes, he was much better off on his own, as he had always been, and he would soon recover from the temporary aberration of his feelings for Eden. He was a busy man and had plenty to occupy him and to keep his thoughts away from gray eyes like pools of summer mist and laughter that warmed his heart like sunlight on a frozen lake.

Suppressing the ache that somehow seemed almost too much to bear, he rose from his desk. If he was to make an effort to repair the damage he had done, he knew where to start—although he felt the most abject dread at the thought of the confrontation that lay ahead.

Summoning his curricle, he made the short journey from Grosvenor Square to Arlington Street and stopped before a fashionable set of lodgings only a few steps away from St. James's Street. Climbing the stairs, he rapped sharply at one of the doors lining the corridor and was admitted almost immediately. Greeting the manservant who took his hat and walking stick, he made his way into an elegant if carelessly furnished sitting room and moved toward the figure seated before the hearth, immersed in a copy of Blackwood's sporting journal.

"Hello, Bel," Seth said in a tone of utter weariness. "I'm pleased to find you at home."

Chapter Nineteen

Bel's eyes widened in mock astonishment. "Well, by God, Saint Seth coming down from his mountain to mingle with the sinners?"

Seth noted that Bel was apparently sober, although at the moment he was sipping languidly from—good Lord, what . . . ?

"What the devil is that . . . thing?" asked Seth, indicating the enormous mug Bel held loosely in his fingers. It was made of some sort of ceramic, and was covered with a fanciful oriental design, featuring fire-breathing dragons and bolts of lightning. It was glazed with an odd, opaque substance that gleamed dully in the light of the fire. Beside Bel, on a table, stood a matching pitcher.

Bel laughed, raising the vessel with a flourish. "You like it? I think it suits the exotic side of my nature."

Seth uttered a bark of laughter. "It looks like something out of Prinny's palace at Brighton. Where did you get it?"

Seth knew he was grasping at straws to avoid the subject he must bring forth, but, Lord, he didn't want to get into this.

"I won it in a card game a few months ago," replied Bel carelessly.

"I might have known."

"I took it off Charlie Wellbore. I must say it was sweet. Charlie had a streak of luck a few months ago. Won a thousand from me, braying all the while over his skill. For some reason he treasured the set."

Seth allowed himself to be drawn into the current of this innocuous conversation with Bel, pleased that, at least for the moment, he and his brother were having a normal conversation, free of contention or ill will.

Bel chuckled. "It's rather odd, actually. Charlie had just returned from the Continent, where an inventor friend gave this to him. Claimed it's glazed with a newly discovered substance."

Seth grunted skeptically.

"Well, that's what I thought—mere gammon, but the material is unusual. I like the feel of it and the way it catches the light. And, of course, knowing what it meant to Charlie—well, I'm quite taken with it."

Seth drew a deep breath. Time to get to work.

"That's not all you're taken with, is it, brother mine? And whatever takes the Marquess of Belhaven's fancy, he must, of course, possess."

Bel glanced up warily, and his customary expression of ugly discontent settled on his features.

"What are you babbling on about now? And, in case it has escaped your notice, you are not my brother."

"Thank God for that. I'm talking about Zoë Beckett."

Something unexpected and indescribable leapt into Bel's eyes. "What about her?"

"Your attentions to her are causing concern to her . . . her family."

Bel's unattractive laugh brayed out into the room. "Do you think I care a tinker's damn about her family's concern?"

"No, but if I were you, I'd have a care for Father's. He's not happy at your newest inamorata."

"But, Seth, old fellow," Bel said plaintively, "Father is never happy with me. Speaking of which, what is this current maggot he's taken into his brain about my marrying the other Beckett chit?"

"Well, that's the problem, you see. He wants you to marry one sister, ergo you must stop trifling with the other."

"Well, you can go back and tell the old man that I intend to do neither. Good God. How many times do I have to tell him that I do not wish to marry? I'm having a perfectly fine time as I am. Does he think that marriage will somehow turn me into a respectable pattern of rectitude like him?" The marquess belched. "Not bloody likely. And as far as Miss Zoë is concerned, if you think I've been forcing my attentions on her, you're badly mistook. The little twit actually likes me," he concluded in some surprise. "I've got her in my evil clutches, Seth, me lad, and in a few more days, I'll have her in my bed."

Something cold and unpleasant stirred in the bottom of

Seth's gut. Short of tying Bel up like a spring calf and hauling him to The Priory, he doubted there was anything that could sway him from his fell purpose. He assumed his sternest mien.

"Bel, Father is serious this time. He is determined you shall marry. Personally, I would just as soon not see anyone married to you. However, in case you're interested, I have no intention of allowing you either to ruin Zoë or to marry Eden Beckett."

"Really?" Bel drawled unpleasantly. "You have an interest there yourself, oh saintly one?"

"She is my friend," replied Seth curtly, "and I wouldn't wish a lifetime with you on my worst enemy. I give you fair warning, Bel. Abandon your pursuit of Zoë Beckett if you value your allowance, your horses, your low companions, these pleasant lodgings, and all the other frivols that mean so much to you. And, don't even think about marrying Eden Beckett if you value your life."

Bel merely laughed and raised his mug in salute. Seth turned on his heel and left.

Some hours later, upon concluding a piece of business in the City, he took a shortcut through Green Park to a small property he wished to inspect in Hans Town. To his surprise, on crossing the little bridge over the canal, he beheld in the distance Bel's long-tailed gray, Hellion, tethered to a tree on the fringe of a small grove. Next to it stood a gig, in which was seated a young woman in the garb of a lady's maid.

Slowly, Seth guided his curricle in a circuitous route that took him past the gig without being seen, to a position some distance away. Dismounting, he made his way on foot through the little grove. Upon catching the sound of a faint female giggle, he moved forward silently. Soon, his efforts were rewarded by the sight of Zoë and Bel, standing in a secluded bower. They were not embracing, but they stood disastrously close to one another, apparently oblivious to the world about them.

It was equally obvious that Zoë was lost in love's young dream. Her visage as she gazed up at Bel was not one of besotted adoration, but rather she looked as though she had moved to a heightened plane of awareness. Her eyes sparkled, her cheeks, glowed, and she lifted a hand to caress Bel's cheek. It was Bel, however, who truly caught Seth's attention. Never had he seen such an expression of tenderness on his brother's face. He laughed as he lifted his own hand to clasp Zoë's, and for once there was no trace of the ugly sneer that usually marred his features.

Seth's first instinct was to accost the pair, to wrest Zoë from whatever plans Bel had in mind and take her home. This urge was superseded by an equally strong one to drive his fist into the bridge of Bel's nose.

He did neither.

After a moment's struggle with his good sense, Seth began to consider the matter rationally. He was aware that Bel would surely not attempt to seduce Zoë in a public park with her maid in attendance only a few feet away. Nor did he believe Bel would take her to a more appropriate spot, such as his lodgings—at least, not in the middle of the afternoon with said maid in tow.

No good would come of confronting the pair right now. After all, he had no real authority over Zoë, nor over Bel, for that matter. He would go immediately to tell Eden what he had seen. Together, they could then decide the best course of action.

A treacherous undercurrent of excitement swept through him at the prospect of seeing Eden again, which he suppressed with impatience. Good Lord, he was going to see her on a family matter, not an assignation. When would he overcome this ludicrous weakness where she was concerned?

In the days that followed Seth's departure from her life, Eden had attempted to return her life to its usual, placid course. As time passed, and Seth did not appear at Nassington House, she could only conclude that her dismal surmise had been correct. He did not wish to pursue the relationship that had developed between them.

Or had there really been a relationship? If so, she had said or done something to sever that tenuous bond. Perhaps, she had simply misread the connection she had felt with him. She supposed spinsters must be prone to that sort of thing, although she had never imagined anything of the kind with any other man.

Well. She was certainly not going to sit by the fire and weep, nor would she set the latest fashion in sackcloth and ashes. She had a life of her own, after all. She had muddled along very nicely, thank you, without Seth Lindow in her life, and she would contrive just as nicely now. Particularly when she had a great deal with which to occupy herself. To begin with, there

was her career. How she liked the sound of that. Seth had told
her she was being an undutiful daughter in deceiving her father,
and perhaps that was so. She simply did not care. Seth had said
that she was walking a dangerous path, that Papa, if he discovered her secret life, would be very angry indeed. He might con-
fiscate her so-far meager funds and banish her to Clearsprings,
to live on bread and water.

Mmph. She would take her chances. Papa might be angry
with her, but surely he would not go so far as to make her a prisoner in her own home. Would he? Actually, he might very well
be relieved at her setting off on her own. She would be one less
mouth to feed, and perhaps he might even grow to be proud of
her accomplishment. After all, it was not a sin against society. It
was not as though she was setting herself up to be a . . . barris-
ter, or some such. Several female artists had managed to make a
good living for themselves without being ostracized from society. Miss Jane Austen, she understood, was a clergyman's
daughter, and still in good standing. There was Angelica Kauf-
mann, for example, and Elisabeth Vigie-Lebrun, the celebrated
French artist. Of course, what might do very well for a French-
woman might not be considered acceptable for a proper English
female.

In any event, she had gone to some lengths to keep her name
a secret. Perhaps with the assurance of her continued
anonymity, Papa would be more amenable to her selling her
daubs.

And then there was Zoë. The girl was behaving in an extremely odd manner lately. She was still an engaging, willful
sprite, but now she was unwontedly pensive. She vanished into
her room on increasingly frequent occasions and would not be
seen for hours. She declined her sister's company on shopping
expeditions, but would depart in the morning with a friend, or
simply her maid for company and reappear just in time for dinner, burdened with packages.

She was apparently becoming disenchanted with her current
crop of admirers. At Lady Winslow's ball, she quarreled with
the Viscount Hadley, to Mama's intense displeasure. Now, she
seemed not to care that the rift still stood unhealed, and when
the viscount made tentative peace overtures, she ignored him.
In addition, Zoë no longer perused bouquets and trinkets sent to
her with the eagerness she had formerly displayed.

Eden knew a twinge of foreboding. Zoë never spoke of Belhaven, although she might comment idly if his name came up. She turned aside Eden's casual queries with a shrug of her shoulders, and an interrogation of her maid, Beadle, proved fruitless.

Eden turned her mind resolutely from the problem. After all, was she her sister's keeper? Zoë was an adult—theoretically—and thus must be allowed to lead her own life.

She was leaving the house one afternoon for Weirhaven House when she was surprised to encounter Seth mounting the front steps.

He smiled, a polite curving of his lips that held none of the warmth to which she had become accustomed. She nodded courteously and waited for him to explain his presence. He seemed somewhat discomfited, but raised his hat.

"Good afternoon, Miss Beckett. I hope I have not come to call at an inconvenient time."

Really! The gall of the man. Did he think to find her with her nose pressed against the drawing room window, desperately hoping he would appear? She carefully ignored the fact that she had done just that for a good fortnight after his last visit.

"Yes, I'm afraid so," she replied coolly. "I was just on my way out."

"But I have come to see you," he said in what could only be considered a plaintive tone.

"How very unfortunate." Eden's tone remained even, and she allowed not the slightest hint of encouragement to creep into her voice. "I'm afraid I have an appointment for which I am already unforgivably late."

"I see." Seth spoke with an icy politeness to equal her own.

Eden nodded coolly and proceeded to her carriage. Once inside, with a gesture to the coachman, she clattered away without a backward glance. Seth stood, indecisively, on the front steps of Nassington House. What was he going to do, now? He *had* to apprise Eden of what he had seen in Green Park.

Horsley coughed discreetly, and bending an insouciant smile on him, Seth turned to exit Portman Square.

When Eden returned a few hours later, tired from an afternoon spent before her easel with the obstreperous Weirhaven daughters, and in no better mood than when she had left the house, Seth was no longer on the premises. Eden had hoped that perhaps . . . She thrust the thought from her mind and re-moved bonnet, gloves, and pelisse in mechanical fashion.

Making her way upstairs to her chamber, she began prepara-tions for yet another ball, this time at the home of the Marquess of Hunstanton and his lady.

Some hours later, the festivities at Hunstanton House were in full swing when Seth made his entrance. At the top of the great staircase, he was greeted with flattering cordiality by both the marquess and the marchioness before proceeding into the ball-room. His eyes searched the chamber. Hunstanton House was the last place on the planet he wanted to be tonight, but he rather thought the Beckett family would be putting in an ap-pearance. Surely, he could successfully waylay Eden in the crush of guests and whisk her off for a private conversation. Ah, there she was, gowned in one of what he had come to term her "spinster rig." It appeared to be the same shapeless sack in which she'd been garbed the first time he had seen her. Lord, how could he have failed then to perceive the delicate beauty that lay beneath the unpromising exterior. Tonight she was very pale, her head held proudly atop her slender neck. Her gaze swung to him almost immediately. Seth hastened toward her.

Once more she treated him to a cool smile. At least, she did not speed off in the opposite direction. After a routine exchange of pleasantries, he ventured to lay a hand on her arm.

"I wonder if I could have a word with you—in private," he murmured in as importuneless a tone as he could manage. Nonetheless, her arm grew rigid under his.

"As I recall, there is an alcove concealed behind that ghastly potted plant in the corner. If we're quick, we can lay our claim before some other couple desirous of privacy snabbles it." As he had hoped, the lightness of his words brought a slight relax-ation to the tightness of her lips. He slipped his hand under her elbow and propelled her gently toward the alcove.

Eden felt as though she were moving in a kaleidoscope. The individual components of the ballroom, as well as the throng of guests, seemed to whirl about her in a confused splash of color and noise. What was Seth about? After his crude dismissal of her and his subsequent disappearance from the face of the earth, why was he now seeking her out with the persistence of a housewife seeking a bargain at the butcher shop? For she was sure his only reason for attending the Hunstanton ball had been to speak to her. His nearness was having its usual effect on her, and her flesh burned under his fingers.

The alcove proved to be furnished conveniently with two small satin-covered chairs.

"There now." Unthinking, Seth took Eden's hand into his own, and although color rose to her cheeks, she did not withdraw it.

She lifted her gaze to Seth. "What was it you wished to impart to me?"

Seth's expression grew serious, and he tightened his hold on Eden's hand. He took little time in telling his tale.

"Oh, dear God," breathed Eden when he had finished. "I had no idea—although I suppose I should have known," she concluded bitterly. "Once Zoë comprehended that Bel was forbidden fruit, she would, of course, lose no time in hurling herself into his arms. I could just strangle the little widgeon."

"I hesitated to approach Bel, for anything I might say or do to him would only serve to cement his determination to seduce Zoë."

Eden shuddered at the word. "You're quite right. It is up to me to keep Zoë under lock and key until we remove to Clearsprings once again." She paused, arranging carefully in her mind the words she wished to speak. "I . . . I thank you, Seth, for coming to me with this information. I know you are busy, and . . . and you do not ordinarily attend these things." She swept her arm toward the ballroom.

"Not at all," Seth replied stiffly. For an instant, a swift, hungry expression leapt to his features. "It's good to see you, Eden. I've missed you." He spoke the words painfully, almost unwillingly.

Eden experienced a spurt of indignation. She lifted her eyes to stare directly into his.

"Have you?" she asked dryly.

Gazing into her eyes, Seth felt enveloped in a chill gray mist. He wanted only to gather Eden in his arms and beg her forgiveness for his cavalier treatment of the past weeks, but no. He must remember his resolution to put his feelings for Eden away from him. Lord, he did not know it would be like severing an arm. He groped for a new subject.

"You don't think you should tell your parents of Bel's . . . pursuit of Zoë?"

"Oh, no!" she exclaimed involuntarily. "That is, yes, I suppose I should, but I've never tipped the double, if you will forgive my vulgarity. I've always managed to handle Zoë's transgressions on my own without betraying her trust. If I were to do so, I fear she would never confide in me again—although she certainly has not been open with me in this latest series of escapades. Still, my main leverage with Zoë has always been that she knows I'll keep her little secrets."

Eden sighed. "If I have to go to Papa to keep her from ruining her life, I will, but I would much prefer to handle the situation myself. I shall simply be obliged to increase my watchfulness."

"I'll try to keep an eye on Bel, as well, although that will be difficult. He goes to pretty extravagant lengths to avoid me."

"Do you take him to task so often, then?"

"No. At least, not so frequently as he deserves. Not that I have the slightest influence over him, being, of course, beneath his notice."

Eden looked at him quickly. There it was again, that bitterness when he spoke of his adopted family. "Is your father here tonight?" she asked idly.

"Yes, I believe so. At least, he told me he intended to make an appearance. I'm not sure why," he added a trifle uneasily. "He and Lord Hunstanton are not the best of friends, and they rarely appear at the same functions."

A silence fell between the two at this point, and Seth seemed to realize for the first time that he held Eden's hand in his. He released it as though he had just been informed she had the plague, then reddened as though realizing his gaucherie.

"Perhaps," he said in a strangled voice, "we should rejoin the company."

Eden wanted to cry out for an explanation of Seth's sudden coolness over the last few days, but she tightened her lips. One had one's pride, after all. He may have felt obliged to warn Eden of Zoë's mischief, but he seemed in no way inclined to resume the relationship that had unaccountably become as the breath of life itself to her.

"Why, there is the duke now," she remarked as they moved into the ballroom. "Good heavens, he's speaking to Papa—again." She swiveled to face Seth. "Do you have any idea—oh, look, the duke is urging Papa from the room—toward one of the salons. What in the world—?"

But Seth had drawn her farther into the crowd of dancers. The orchestra was just swinging into a boulanger, and he hastily drew her into a set for the spirited dance. She had no opportunity for speech with him until the last strains of the music had faded away. By that time, Seth had begun another topic of conversation, one which, Eden suspected, he had rehearsed during the course of the dance in order to forestall any more questions about the duke's behavior with her father.

It was some time before she saw her father again, but shortly before the supper hour, she observed him approaching Mama with an air of barely suppressed excitement. Drawing his wife aside, he spoke briefly in her ear, with the result that Mama dropped her fan and placed a hand to her breast. An expression of beatific joy spread across her placid features, and she glanced quickly about the room as though searching for someone. Her gaze did not cross that of Eden's, and after a moment, Eden shrugged and turned away, only to bump into Lady Shipstead.

"My dear Miss Beckett," said the countess, fairly bubbling over with bonhomie. "How very nice to see you. I must say you are in looks."

Which left Eden in some doubt as to her ladyship's eyesight. However, the countess stayed to chat for several minutes before moving off to another conversation, and her ladyship took pains to speak to her in passing several more times that evening.

She had hoped that Seth might ask to take her in to supper, but looking around, she rather thought he must have left the premises. She would, of course, have refused his offer to escort her to the dining room, but now, any enjoyment she might have taken in the evening darkened and died. She was at least saved from the ignominy of trooping into supper with the group of maiden ladies and matrons who had been seated along the walls of the ballroom. As the moment approached, her company was solicited by Mr. Horace Wicheldon, a widower with a quiverful of unruly children for whom he was desperately seeking a mother.

She observed Zoë enter the chamber on the arm of young Lord Gundrip. She laughed gaily up into his face, but her eyes were blank and disinterested. Supper took a mere eternity to pass, and the rest of the evening was spent watching Zoë. Eden almost expected Bel to put in an appearance, but he remained mercifully elsewhere. At last, when Eden's head was fairly ringing with empty smiles and inane platitudes, the Hunstantons' guests began drifting back down the stairs and toward the front door.

The Duke of Derwent, who had smiled at her from a distance several times during the evening, was among the first to leave, with his sister on his arm. Both the duke and her ladyship nodded cordially as they made their way to the door. Eden wondered if somehow word had reached them of her modest success in the art world. She could think of no other reason why the Lindows should single her out for such condescension.

It was some time before the Beckett carriage made its way along the street to the front portal of Hunstanton House, and Lady Beckett and Zoë declared themselves heartily sick of standing about on the pavement while others were taken up.

"At least it isn't raining," remarked Eden prosaically.

"Never mind the weather," growled Lord Beckett in Eden's ear as they mounted their vehicle at long last. "When we arrive home, come to my study. I must speak to you privately."

Wondering, Eden contented herself with her own thoughts during the short drive home. Zoë, bidding the others a brief good night, scurried up the stairs. Lady Beckett, her eyes bright with a secret excitement and her hands fairly vibrating in the air, hugged her daughter.

"Oh, my dear child, what a marvelous evening this has been!" With this cryptic expression, she kissed Eden's cheek with extraordinary vigor and hurried upstairs after Zoë.

Shaking her head in puzzlement, Eden made her way to the back of the house. Lord Beckett was right behind her and he hustled her into the room.

"Well, missy," he said, rubbing his hands as he made directly for the brandy decanter, "I have some most excellent news for you."

His smile curved so broad that his face resembled a split melon. Eden could only stare at him in wonderment.

"How would you like, m'dear, to be the Marchioness of Belhaven and the future Duchess of Derwent?"

Chapter Twenty

Eden simply gaped at her father.

"What are you talking about, Papa?" she gasped faintly.

"I had an interesting conversation with the Duke of Derwent tonight at Hunstanton House. Nothing has been settled yet, but he is most impressed with you, m'dear—so much so that he is considering you as a bride for his heir."

"Me?" The word came out in a strangled croak. "His heir? You mean Belhaven?"

"None other. To be frank," he added kindly, "I rather had the impression that Zoë was their first choice, but she didn't measure up—not surprising. Lovely girl, of course, but a little bumptious for a future duchess."

"B-but . . . are you sure you heard him aright? What in the world could have led His Grace to so much consider me—or Zoë—for the position?"

"Why, it was Lindow, of course."

"Seth?" asked Eden, puzzled. "What could Seth possibly have to do with recommending a bride to the Duke of Derwent? Did he see something in Zoë during his visit to Clearsprings? I cannot believe that he would suggest an innocent like Zoë for such a position. For Seth," she explained earnestly, "sees Bel clearly for what he is, even though the two are brothers."

"Huh, much you know," retorted Lord Beckett. "If I read His Grace right, Lindow's purpose in coming to Clearsprings was not merely to purchase a few nags, but to make an appraisal of Zoë's qualifications as Belhaven's bride."

This time Eden was bereft of speech. He could not be serious! Seth? She had wondered at his purpose in coming to Clearsprings. But . . . his visit a complete fabrication? She turned again to her father, who stood rocking on his heels in self-congratulation.

"Are you sure?" she asked again, faintly. "I . . . I mean, it seems so impossible. Even if the duke had decided it is time for Bel to marry, why would he find it necessary to send Seth to scour the countryside for a bride? Surely, if Bel could be brought to the same notion, it would take only a twitch of the duke's little finger to bring prospective maidens lining up from Land's End to John O'Groats."

Lord Beckett cleared his throat. "Um, as to that, the duke wasn't specific, but I gather that the youngster has got into a spot of trouble recently. Nothing but youthful high spirits, I'm sure, but he's acquired a rather unsavory reputation. I understand that some of your niminy-piminy, milk-and-water misses won't give the lad the time of day."

"Yes, that's true," said Eden tonelessly. "An unsavory reputation is putting it mildly. Most parents," she added stringently, "would be unwilling to turn their daughters over to the tender mercies of the Marquess of Belhaven."

"Umph," replied her father, flushing slightly. "Well, I would not be so hasty, nor would any person of sense. That particular title comes with a fortune beyond my—that is, our wildest dreams."

It seemed to Eden that she had been plunged into a nightmare, where light and shadows whirled about the room in a harsh, almost physical presence, and where nothing made sense. She was having difficulty concentrating. "Papa— Surely you don't mean to allow Zoë to marry Belhaven!"

She almost used the word "coerce," but it struck her that, in light of recent discoveries, it would take little to send Zoë flying into Belhaven's evil influence.

"No, I don't. Didn't I just tell you? It's *you* the duke wants for his heir. Apparently, after looking Zoë over—I have to tell you, the duke was a little in his cups and said perhaps more than he should—he and that hatchet-faced sister of his decided she wasn't biddable enough. Or some such. At any rate, they decided *you* would fit the bill admirably."

"Oh, God." Eden swallowed the bile that rose in her throat. She wanted to scream her denial. She realized with stunning suddenness, however, that she had no time now to indulge in the agony of recrimination and betrayal on whose edge she teetered so precipitously. She was, she knew, in a struggle for her very existence.

She straightened abruptly and glared at her father. "I'm not going to marry Belhaven, Papa. From what I know of him, I might very well be signing my death warrant."

"Tchah! You sound like a heroine in one of those stupid books you and Zoë are always reading. You'd have to be out of your mind to turn down an alliance with the house of Lindow."

Eden turned to face him directly. Dear God, please let her say the right thing to Papa, before his will hardened any further.

"Papa, I have always been a dutiful daughter. I love you and Mama and Zoë dearly, but I cannot do this. I cannot believe you would ask it of me." Beneath her words lay the almost shattering pain of Seth's duplicity, a wound she knew would never heal, but she forced it from her consciousness. The hurt would be addressed later.

To her surprise, Lord Beckett merely chuckled. "Feminine nerves, m'dear. You just sleep on it, and by morning, I'm sure your good sense will tell you of all the advantages to such a union. You'll be set for life—a by-God duchess."

He was fairly dancing in place before the crackling hearth.

"By Jupiter, I'll be set for life, too. I'll be someone now. No more the country baron clinging to his pittance in obscurity. And Zoë—there will be no question of her snabbling her peer."

"And what about me, Papa? You may speak of titles and wealth and your plump purse, but would you buy them all at my expense? Do I mean so little to you that you would sell me as a brood mare to a man who, from all reports, is completely unbalanced?"

"Tchah!" said Lord Beckett again, more explosively. "I'm sure the reports of his escapades are just the usual tittle-tattle that is spread about any young buck these days."

"Papa, everyone knows what Lord Belhaven is—a degenerate who has gambled away his sustenance, ruined several gently bred young women, and is strongly suspected of beating his own groom nearly to death."

"All rumor, I'm sure. Marriage will no doubt settle him down. In any event, we do not need to discuss this further right now. I have an appointment with His Grace tomorrow morning, when we will discuss settlements." Another smile erupted at this lovely word. "Then Belhaven will no doubt come to you and do the pretty. You and your mama can talk of dates and wedding journeys and all that folderol."

"Papa—"

Lord Bartlett lifted a meaty hand. "No more talk now. You go on up now and seek your bed. You may expect a busy day tomorrow."

He opened the door in a dismissive gesture, and the next moment Eden found herself in the corridor, staring at the paneling. Somehow, she made her way upstairs and sat still and cold through her maid's ministrations, but when she slid into bed, she lay for some moments staring into the darkness before rolling over to bury her head in her arms.

Had Seth actually set out to find a bride for his wretched brother among the dwindling number of gently bred maidens who would consider marrying Bel? Then, having made up his list, perhaps narrowing it down to a select few, taken a trip to the country for a cold-blooded assessment of Zoë's suitability? Dear Lord, she had thought him a friend to her family!

And what was it Papa had said? She could feel the blood buzzing in her ears as she contemplated her father's theory that, having found Zoë wanting, he transferred his attention to herself. Of course. Seth would have perceived almost immediately that Zoë would not fit the ducal requirements, for the Derwents would want a submissive bride, one who would not complain of her treatment at Bel's hands. They would no doubt want a female content to remain immured at the family seat, producing the requisite heir and spare without protest, and making no further demands on any of them.

Who better to fill Seth's needs than quiet, colorless Eden Beckett, whose stated desire in life was to remain in the country surrounded by her flowers and her paint pots. Dear God! Eden had managed to maintain her composure before her father, but now she wanted to scream her despair. Seth was her friend! He had become her confidante and, she had come to realize of late, her love. And now, Papa had told her, in that odiously oily, satisfied voice, that Seth had been appraising her sister's possibilities—and subsequently her own—as though they were minimally acceptable breeding cattle. What she had taken for an interest in her and her artistic aspirations was nothing more than research on his part. He had no doubt mentally recorded with relief every syllable that confirmed his opinion of her as a reclusive doormat—a poor, sniveling hinny who would do as she was told and put up with any abuse the villainous Marquess of Belhaven saw fit to heap on her. Dear Lord, Seth was willing to fasten her into a life of bondage merely to satisfy the Duke of Derwent's whim.

And she, basking in an unaccustomed glow of a little masculine attention, had risen to his every lure. She had poured out her heart and soul to him, revealing every facet of her dreams and aspirations. How he must have laughed at her blushful, naive confidences. No wonder he had expressed his disapproval of her intention to set up her own household. We couldn't have that, now could we?—the prospective bride of the Derwent heir haring off on her own to pursue a career as an artist. He had humored her, no doubt with a view to discarding her plans on the trash heap, once he had her safely buckled to Bel.

Lord, she had infused her voice with blatant invitation the last time she had received him at Nassington House. He must have been horribly embarrassed and possibly concerned that she was trying to force him into a compromising position. No wonder he had bolted like a hunted hare. And no wonder he had scurried back to her side to seek her assistance in keeping Bel and Zoë apart. An affair with Zoë at this point would throw a spanner into his carefully calculated plans for Bel.

Eden fairly trembled with self-loathing and humiliation. She had allowed the snake to kiss her! She had responded with wanton abandon to his advances. Of course, that was before he had determined that it was her humble self rather than her flamboyant sister who would be led to the slaughter. No doubt he saw no harm in a little dalliance on the side in the pursuit of his duties. How could she have been so taken in?

Over the course of an interminable night the question rang in her ears in a dozen different versions, each one more unpleasant than the last. She longed to sob out her hurt, but found she was unable to cry. Dry-eyed and icy with anguish, she considered her future. It had seemed so promising just a few hours ago, but now it had turned to ashes. When she arose with the dawn that slowly limned the outlines of the room, she was unrefreshed, curiously empty, and lonelier than she could ever recall being in her life. Lonely and bitter, angry and hurt, and wishing with all her heart that she had never met Seth Lindow.

The morning brought no relief. She sought out her father, in hopes that she might sway him before he set out for his interview with the duke. She failed utterly. Not only was Papa even more set up in his rosy plans for the future of the Beckett family, but he would brook not even the appearance of opposition from his daughter.

"Dammit, Eden," he said irritably, "here I present you with news that would have any other young woman dancing in the chandeliers, and all you can do is whine. I tell you, I won't have it, do y'hear? I will not have it! When I have returned from Derwent House, I shall inform your mother and your sister of our good fortune, and you will put a good face on it. You will, by God, be happy!"

With this, he slammed out of the house. Eden was left to contain herself as best she might until Papa returned, deigning to inform her of her future.

Feeling that she must either get out of the house or burst, she returned to her bedchamber to change clothes for a brisk walk. She found it hard to concentrate and found herself on several occasions, staring into space, holding a shoe motionless, or her scarf half flung over her shoulder. At last, she was ready to make her way to the park, but she halted suddenly on the staircase.

Zoë!

Good heavens, she had been so absorbed in her own problems, she had completely forgotten Zoë's involvement with the wretched Belhaven. So conditioned was she to putting her sister's affairs before her own, that she did not hesitate in whirling about to mount the stairs once more.

Zoë, of course, was still deep in slumber, but Eden bustled about the room, flinging open curtains and shutters.

"Wha—?" mumbled Zoë, burrowing beneath her pillows. "Ed'n, is that you? What the *deuce*—?"

"Language, language, dearest." Eden tugged vigorously on the bellpull. She then plumped down on the bed. "Now, then, wake up. Beadle will be here in a moment with chocolate, and then we can have a comfortable coze."

"A *what*?" Zoë pulled the covers over her head. "Eden, have you gone out of your mind? What time is it?"

"It is time to open your budget, sister mine. There will be no day-long shopping trips, or visits to old friends for hours. I want to talk to you—and you are going to talk to me."

"Won't," mumbled Zoë, sounding very much like her six-year-old self.

"Will," retorted Eden in an exchange unused since childhood.

A few minutes later, seated in an armchair near the bed, with Zoë settled in a nest of pillows, sipping chocolate, Eden opened negotiations. "I know what you've been up to with Belhaven."

Zoë jerked spasmodically, causing her to spill some of the chocolate, but she said only, "I beg your pardon?" widening her eyes in azure innocence.

"Don't try your little ways with me," retorted her sister. "You've been sneaking off to meet him! I think it's you who have lost your mind."

Zoë's lips curved in an odd smile. "Perhaps I have."

"Zoë!" gasped Eden in consternation. "What have you done?"

Zoë shrugged, white shoulders rising from the embroidered lawn of her night rail. "Good Lord, Eden, I haven't done anything. Except—well, yes, I did go out to meet Bel," she admitted, picking at the coverlet defiantly.

"And it's not the first time, is it? Oh, Zoë, I do not mean to fratch at you, but you are traveling toward disaster."

Zoë's musical laugh rippled from the warren of silken bedclothes. "Don't be absurd, dearest. I know what I'm doing. Bel is . . . amusing. That is all. He makes me feel treasured and . . . well, seductive."

"Oh, Lord," muttered Eden, nauseated.

"I knew you would not understand."

"Zoë," continued Eden patiently, "the man is poison. Have you not heard the things—"

"I've heard a great deal of nonsense. Oh, I know," Zoë said, a little wildly. "He has done some things that are not quite, er, *comme il faut*. Well, perhaps somewhat beyond that," she added as Eden snorted, "but he is not a bad person—not truly. There is something . . . something I feel . . . inside him that gets in the way of his real self, and . . . Oh, I cannot explain what I mean. It is as though he is under a wicked spell."

"And you are his fairy godmother? Sent to kiss the frog and turn him into a prince?"

"Of course not," replied Zoë with such quiet dignity that Eden felt ashamed—and not a little frightened.

"Zoë, is your heart truly engaged? I mean—you're not going to do anything stupid, are you?"

Zoë stiffened, but a moment later, that strange smile again curved her lips. "Please don't worry, Eden. No, I'm not going to do anything stupid. I promise."

With that, Eden knew she must be content, for Zoë flung aside her coverlet and swung her legs over the side of the bed.

"What do you say to a spot of shopping?" she asked brightly. "It's been quite a while since you and I invaded Leicester Square. I have nothing to wear to Lady Brumborough's soiree next week, for I simply will not appear in public again in that ghastly little gros de Naples tunic."

Eden sighed, rose, and made her way downstairs to await her sister's appearance. The sick heaviness in her heart was in no way alleviated, but having an immediate purpose gave her some respite from the pain she knew would be her companion for the rest of her life.

It was necessary to get through breakfast first with her Mama, who was in a state of utter bliss.

"Oh, my dear, I am *so* happy!" she repeated over and over until Zoë entered the breakfast chamber. Apparently, her lord had instructed her that the news was not to be spread about the household until matters had been formally settled.

At long last the sisters sallied forth to the precincts of Oxford and Bond streets and the silk warehouses of Leicester Square. It was some hours later that Eden returned home with Zoë, the carriage ladened with packages, to find her father waiting for her. She had dreaded this confrontation and steeled herself for what was to come. She stared at him curiously as he bore down on her, for his expression was not one of exultation. His face was contorted in raw fury.

"Ah, you're home are you, missy? And about time, too."

To Eden's complete astonishment, he grasped her arm and shook her violently.

"What the devil do you think you're up to, missy? You march right into my study, for you and I are going to have a talk. Yes, indeed, a talk," he growled, bending to glare furiously at her, "about what you've been doing with your damned paints! Did you really think you could plunge the family into a scandal and not have to answer for it?"

Speechless, Eden allowed her father to half pull and half drag her into his study.

Chapter Twenty-one

Pale and shaking, Eden stared at her father across the desk. He thrust an empurpled face toward her.

"Haven't I always been a good father to you? Haven't I always provided for you? Ain't I done everything I could since you was a puking babe to help you grow up right? And is this," he continued without waiting for an answer, "how you repay me?"

Eden could only stare dazedly at him.

Had something gone wrong in his negotiations with the Duke of Derwent? A faint light shone through her cloud of depression. But what was that about her paint pots? A stirring of apprehension made itself felt deep within her.

"The duke?" she whispered.

"Oh, yes, I saw the duke," snarled Lord Beckett, "and we arranged your betrothal to his heir all right and tight. No thanks to you." He swallowed convulsively. "I can't believe you've been going behind my back!" By now, he was fairly trembling with rage. "You've been painting! For money!"

If Eden had not been sitting, she would have fallen. Dear God, not content with causally delivering her into bondage, Seth had now betrayed her in a wholly different fashion. The universe spun around her as she listened to her father's next words.

By now, he had regained a modicum of composure and, while he still loomed over her from his side of the desk, the ominous color in his cheeks had faded somewhat.

"By God," he sputtered, "I have a good mind to take a cane to you as I used to do when you were a spotty-faced brat. To think," he added in some puzzlement, "you've actually managed to sell some of your daubings. And you're doing portraits, too, I understand."

"Where . . . where did you hear this?" whispered Eden through the lump that had risen in her throat to all but rob her of breath.

"Why, I was having a pleàsant conversation with His Grace at Derwent House. In his library. I glanced about the room, and there, hanging on the wall, was one of your god-awful daisy pictures! The duke saw me staring and said, as chirpy as you please, 'Oh, do you like it? It's a recent acquisition. Not my usual taste, but I understand the artist'—a female, for God's sake—'is making quite a name for herself.' I couldn't believe my ears! And to boot, he said young Lindow had purchased it on his behalf! I've been thinking about that, missy, and I'll wager he did it as a favor to you. Aha." He nodded at Eden's stricken expression. "I was right, wasn't I? And all the while I thought him such a fine young fellow. I even thought of him as a mate for you, at one time. Where was I? Oh. I must have blurted something inadvertently at that point, for he gathered almost at once that I was acquainted with his female artist, and he winkled your name from me almost immediately."

"Oh," said Eden faintly.

"Oh, indeed. I must say, he was most understanding. I thought he might well break off our negotiations at once, but when I assured him the paintings would be withdrawn and you would not peddle any more, he took it all in good spirit. Even told me a tale on one of his daughters who, he said, at one time had ambitions to be a novelist, if you would believe. I asked him where he'd got your daisy painting, and after we'd concluded our business, I nipped around to this Rellihan's gallery. I couldn't believe my eyes when I saw four more of your daubs hanging on his wall. Good God, I don't know how the man stays in business if that's what he considers fine art. When I asked about the pictures—I didn't give my name, of course—he emptied the sauce boat over me, trying to tell me you're one of his most successful young artists and all that balderdash. That's when he told me about the portraits. He actually asked me," concluded Lord Beckett, beginning to swell again, "if I'd like to have him approach Miss Baird—evidently that's the name you're going under, and thank God you had sense enough to make something up—for a study of me or my loved ones. It was all I could do to keep from ripping the fella's tongue out by the roots.

"I surely would have ripped the damned pictures off the wall, but that would have involved an explanation—that is, I suppose I would have had to give him my name eventually. At any rate, missy"—his glower intensified—"that will be all we'll see of Miss Abigail Baird's wretched pictures in Mr. by-God Rellihan's fancy gallery." He swung a meaty hand to point at her. "Just how much money have you made from your sales?"

When Eden told him, in a barely audible voice, his eyes bulged like plums popping through a pie crust.

"Good God! How many of the things have you flogged?"

"Just three, Papa."

"Good God," he said again, in a tone of genuine bafflement. "There must be more loose screws in this town than I suspected, willing to part with their gelt for a few gaudy splotches of paint on a canvas." He rubbed his hands together.

"Well, what I'll do is return to Rellihan's place tomorrow and retrieve your daubery. I'll explain to him very carefully that should he ever divulge your name, he'll be meeting me at the business end of a horsewhip. Now, what we're going to do right now is go to Coutts' bank and take out all the money you've stashed there. Get your bonnet, girl, we're going into the City."

"Bank?" Dear Lord, this was worse than she had envisioned. "How," she faltered, her lips ashen. "How did you find out about the bank? Did Seth tell you—?"

For the first time, Lord Beckett's furious color faded, and an uneasy expression crossed his features. He waved his hand airily, however. "Yes, that's it. Lindow told me. I . . . I confronted him after the duke told me who'd purchased the painting."

No, thought Eden dully. She really could not bear this. Not only had Seth chosen her as the sacrificial goat for the duke's purposes, he had given her up to her father's wrath. In the space of two days' time, he had wiped out her life's dream. He didn't just not love her, he must truly hate her to have done this to her.

"I said, come along, Eden," barked her father.

"But Papa," she whispered, "it's my money. I earned it!"

"Hah!" barked Lord Beckett mirthlessly. "Your money, indeed. You are not entitled to so much as a farthing of it. Surely, you can't have arrived at your advanced age without realizing that you have nothing but what I say you may have. I've paid for everything in your possession, from your reticule to the paintbrushes you so wickedly used to your own advantage, and by God, they're mine. And so is that nice little pile of earnings you've accumulated, so let's get on with it."

"Papa, please! I . . . I had no wish to defy you! I merely wish to be independent, to live on my own and not be a burden to you."

If Eden expected to soften her father's attitude with this art-less speech, she was doomed to disappointment. If anything, he grew even angrier.

"Independent! What kind of talk is that for a gently bred young woman. Out on your own? Before my agreement with the duke, I planned for you to live at Clearsprings with your mother and me, where you could be a comfort to us in our old age. I figured if I couldn't get you married and turning out grandchildren, at least you'd be around to be of some good to me!" He rubbed his hands. "Luckily, things have turned out much better than that."

The words flayed her, but such was her anguish that she scarcely heard them. She was conscious only of an engulfing blackness that presaged the end of her precious dreams. Her hopes of fulfillment and accomplishment had been thrown from a cliff to be trampled and left to lie shredded and bleeding into the dust. And it was Seth who had taken them, along with her heart, into his slender, capable fingers and casually tossed them from that pinnacle. But why had he done such a thing? The words swirled around her like dry leaves in an icy vortex. How could he? they sounded in a rustling moan. To what end had he so betrayed her?

"Papa, I don't know what Seth may have told you. I . . . I am sorry to have caused you distress, but I feel it is my right to . . . put by my own money to—"

"Yes," interposed Lord Beckett dryly, "to go off on your own like one of those wretched free-thinking women that set every-one's backs up. Well, I won't have it, Eden. What would people say? That Beckett cannot support his own family? That his el-dest daughter is forced to peddle her wretched scrawls to put bread in her mouth? Speaking of which," he said, descending abruptly from his lofty rodomontade, "your little nest egg will come in very handy just now. The way your mama and your sis-ter have been spending the ready since we arrived in London would drive Golden Ball Hughes to the poorhouse."

"No, Papa," said Eden resolutely. "I must speak further with you on this. I know you perceive my actions as a direct assault on your authority, and I meant it as nothing of the kind—or at least," she added, incorrigibly truthful, "I did not intend to cause you discomfort. This means a great deal to me, Papa, and I do think you might at least hear me out. I have never asked you for anything beyond the physical support any parent is obliged to provide for a child. The money I earn—"

"The money you earned," interposed Lord Beckett sharply. "Past tense. Eden, I wish to hear no more of this nonsense. Where did you get these fool notions, anyway? Whoever heard of a gently bred female leaving her parents and her home to go haring off on her own? No, not another word." He paused for a moment, then continued not unkindly. "You are behaving as though this is the end of the world. It is not as though you are to be sentenced to a life of penury if you do not sell your paintings. Am I a tyrant? Do I beat you every day and order you to do my bidding?" He shifted uncomfortably. "Well, yes, I do have the ordering of your life, but it is only for your own good. I do my duty by you, Eden, and I expect you to do the same." He held up a hand as Eden opened her mouth once more. "We will leave now for the bank."

"We can't," declared Eden. "Look, Papa." She gestured to the clock on the mantelpiece. "It's too late. The bank offices close at five o'clock, I believe, and it's just going on six."

Lord Beckett grunted in annoyance. "Well, tomorrow morning then. First thing." He turned to level a hard stare at his daughter. "I will not be cajoled out of this, Eden, so do not think to try any of Zoë's tricks on me. I am still very angry that you would so forget your rank. I have still not determined whether or not to punish you for this outrageous behavior."

He turned on his heel and strode from the room, slamming the door behind him with considerable force. Eden sank back into the chair and gave herself up to dismal reflection.

She knew further remonstrance with her father would be useless. In all her seven-and-twenty years, she had never known him to change his mind once it was set.

It was not as though she hadn't known how it would be if Papa were to discover her purpose. Men of his stamp saw it as their God-given right and responsibility to regulate the lives of the women in their family. She might talk herself hoarse, but she knew that tomorrow morning on the stroke of nine, she would walk into the portals of Coutts' Bank on her father's arm. A few minutes after that, her precious account would be a thing of the past and Papa would no doubt convey her meager little hoard to his own bank with all possible speed.

A sense of desolation swept over her. She was trapped. Even if she were able to avoid marriage to the wretched Marquess of Belhaven, she would be fastened into the role of spinster daughter in her father's household, at the mercy of his whims and at the beck and call of Mama and her sisters. She would forever be dear-Aunt-Eden-who-never-married-you-know. Even on his death—although, God forbid, she loved the hidebound old tyrant and did not wish him ill—he would probably consign her to the care of some other male. Her sister Meg's husband, perhaps, or her Uncle Henry Beckett, Papa's younger brother.

All because of Seth's faithlessness. How could she bear it? She wanted to run from the house, screaming her desolation and her betrayal. She wanted to run to Derwent House, to rage her hurt to Seth Lindow.

She recalled their day at the bank, the hope that had soared in her breast like a young eagle—the laughter she had shared with Seth, and the absurd, high-hearted jokes. How could he have destroyed her happiness with such easy cruelty?

On reflection, she rather doubted that his actions had been deliberate. She could think of nothing she might have done or said that would kindle such enmity in his breast. It was simply as though he had formed a brief *tendre* for her and then the flame had blown out with a careless puff. He no doubt thought little of it when the duke and her father called him in to ask about the particulars of her contract with Mr. Rellihan. He had already made plain his disapproval of her bid for independence. She could almost see him shrugging. Perhaps he even smiled ruefully at the brevity of her escape from the shackles of family obligation.

She drew a shaking hand over her eyes. What would be—?

"Eden!" It was Zoë, who rushed into the room, white-faced and shaking. "Eden, where have you been? I've been looking all over for you. Dear God, I have such dreadful news!"

She flung herself into a nearby settee, drawing her sister down beside her. In one trembling hand she held a scrap of paper, which she waved wildly under Eden's nose.

"I have just received a note from Bel! He says—oh, Eden, I can scarcely credit it! His papa has ordered him to marry. To marry *you!*" she fairly screeched the word, as though Bel had just been sentenced to hang.

"Yes, I know," whispered Eden through dry lips. She related her conversation with Lord Beckett, omitting the portion that dealt with Zoë's perceived unsuitability for the position of Marchioness of Belhaven.

Zoë jumped to her feet once more. "Bel says not to worry, that such a thing will never come to pass—that he will die before he would marry y— Oh. I did not mean . . . of course . . . But . . ."

Eden would have smiled if she had not been so close to releasing the tide of tears that rose behind her eyes. "No, I know you did not. You need not fear. I shall not marry the marquess—not that you will be marrying him, either."

"Oh. No, of course not," agreed Zoë quickly. "But, you know how Papa is. He will bore at you and bore at you, and you were never able to stand up to him. I never could, either, but I learned how to get round him. You did not."

"That's true, my dear, and it is time I began to do so—stand up to him, that is. I shall never learn your tricksey ways, but I shan't allow him to bully me in this."

Zoë smiled tremulously. "That's very well said, Eden, and I hope you will be able to withstand Papa's tactics. However, I shouldn't be surprised if he whisks you off to Clearsprings to live on bread and water until you capitulate."

Eden's returning smile was grim. "I shouldn't wonder if you're right, but since it wouldn't profit him anything to actually let me starve to death, I need only outwait him."

Zoë shivered and glanced once more at the note, making it clear she placed her trust elsewhere. With a sigh, she paced the floor for a few moments before halting abruptly before the fire. "I cannot face Mama right now. I believe I'll go to my bedchamber to . . . to write some letters. I shan't be down to dinner."

"But what about tonight? We are to go to Lady Medster's musicale."

"Oh, bother! Well, it won't be an untruth to say I have a thundering headache and I cannot go."

She swept from the room, leaving Eden to stare into the embers in the hearth. She wished only to sink into the pit of desolation that beckoned, but she had reckoned without Mama.

"Eden! I have been looking for you everywhere!" that lady exclaimed, bustling into the room a few moments later. "I have been wanting to get you to myself for a comfortable coze all day. I want to tell you again how happy I am for you. Who would have thought that you would become a married lady before your little sister. And to a duke's son!"

"Indeed, Mama—to a duke's son."

Lady Beckett gazed uncertainly at her daughter. "B-but, you are not pleased, dearest?" She paused, plucking at the lace that adorned her bodice. "You are not thinking of the ridiculous stories circulating about the Marquess of Belhaven, are you? I . . . I'm sure they are all malicious gossip."

"That's not what you were saying last week, Mama."

"Oh. Well, yes, but I had not considered, then. Just think, Eden. Even if he . . . that is, you will be a marchioness—a duchess some day. You will have clothes and jewels and become a leader of society."

"Something to which I have always aspired," replied Eden dryly. "Mama, you are confusing me with Zoë."

"Oh, dearest!" cried Mama distressfully. "You know I wish only for all my children to be happy. Do you not think you could be happy with all that lovely money? Why, you could paint to your heart's content—and grow the finest roses in the country."

Again, Eden was forced to smile despite herself. But . . .

"Mama," she said gently. "I am truly sorry to disappoint you and Papa, but I am not going to marry the Marquess of Belhaven. The man is a monster, and I sincerely pity any woman unfortunate enough to be wed to him. I do not plan to be that woman."

With this, she disengaged her hands from her mother's clutching fingers and took herself off to her own chamber, where she remained for the rest of the evening. Taking a leaf from Zoë's book, she invented a headache and sent her regrets to her mama that she would be unable to attend the Medster's musicale. Mama visited her chamber to dither and commiserate and left finally to storm society's bastion once more, this time in the company of Mrs. Fenmore Wibberly, a wealthy widow, whose acquaintance Lady Beckett had been cultivating for some weeks.

Eden expected to sleep little that night, but the events of the day had exhausted her. Soon after blowing out her candle, she fell into a slumber that was deep, if troubled. Nightmares tore at her sleeping mind like shafts of flame rising from her own personal hell, but she did not open her eyes the next morning until Makepeace, her maid, entered with her morning chocolate.

She had barely imbibed her first sip of that beverage when Beadle, Zoë's maid, rushed into the room without so much as knocking. She was flushed and breathless, and her eyes stared wide as cartwheels.

"Oh, miss! It's Miss Zoë! She's gone!"

Eden simply gaped. "W-what?"

"Miss Zoë's not in her bed. It ain't—hasn't been slept in all night. She's gone, Miss Eden."

Beadle approached Eden's bed, waving a crumpled bit of paper in her hand. "She left a note."

Eden accepted the scrap in trembling fingers and read the information conveyed there.

Dear Mama and Papa and Eden,

I hope I have not overset you, but I have run away with the Marquess of Belhaven. We are going to be married! Is that not famous? I know, Papa, that you have made different plans—regarding Bel and Eden, but I hope you won't mind this substitution!!! I know you want me to be happy. And I love Bel. Please do not try to follow us. Bel has everything planned, and he says you won't be able to find us. We will return in a few days, and then I'll be a married lady—and the Marchioness of Belhaven!

Y'r loving daughter,
Zoë Beckett

For some moments, Eden could only stare incomprehendingly at the note, as though it were written in a foreign language. Then, to the accompaniment of Beadle's sniffs, she threw back the covers and pulled on a dressing gown. Hurrying down the corridor, she entered her mother's bedchamber, where her ladyship's maid was just drawing back the hangings.

Waking her gently, she apprised Lady Beckett of Zoë's disappearance. The lady responded as expected.

"Never say so! My little girl in the hands of that ravisher of innocent maidens?" she screamed, conveniently forgetting her malicious gossip theory. "Oh, was any mother so beset?" She cast a cursory glance over the note and screeched once more. "What is to be done, Eden? Oh, my darling, my pet—ruined! Or—oh, Eden, do you think he truly means to marry the gel? No, of course not. Oh, heavens, we shall never be able to hold our heads up again in polite society. Oh, that wicked girl."

She clasped and unclasped her hands, and clutched at Eden. She issued a barely comprehensible flurry of contradictory orders to her maid before swinging once more to her oldest daughter. "Papa!" she moaned. "He will go into apoplexy! But—oh, you must tell him at once, Eden. He will know what to do."

Eden, who had been thinking furiously on her own, rang for the housekeeper. That lady, who had undoubtedly been waiting for just such a summons, bustled into the room almost immediately. Eden impressed upon her the need for keeping the current situation a secret from the rest of the household, and handed over the two maids to her care. Then, gently, but with great firmness, she turned back to Lady Beckett.

"No, Mama. We must not tell Papa. Not just yet. You must keep him in the dark on this for as long as you can. In the meantime, I shall pursue Zoë on my own."

"Pursue her?" Lady Beckett twisted the bedclothes she clutched in both hands. "But— Oh, Eden, do you know where they have gone?"

"No," replied her daughter shortly. "But I think I know who might."

With that, she spun on her heel and left the room. Returning on the run to her own chamber, she dressed hastily. Ordering the family's traveling carriage and her maid and a footman to accompany her, she packed a few essentials in a small portmanteau. In a few moments she was on her way to Grosvenor Square. Much as she was loathe to do so, she knew well to whom she must turn for help.

Chapter Twenty-two

When she drew up some minutes later at her destination, Derwent House stood silent in the early morning sunlight. Accompanied by the footman, she ascended the steps of the house, pulling firmly on the doorbell. It was some moments before the door opened narrowly to expose the unwilling features of the Derwent butler.

"Yes, I know, Bentick," she said firmly, grateful that the fellow's name had popped into her mind. "It is very early, but the circumstances of my, er, visit, are most unusual. Please inform Mr. Lindow that Miss Eden Beckett is here and wishes to speak to him on a matter of great urgency."

Bentick's suspicions were apparently unallayed, but the authority with which Eden infused her voice seemed to sway him. With obvious reluctance, he opened the door an inch or two wider.

"The family's still abed, miss," he said brusquely. "I have not seen Mr. Lindow as yet. If you would like to leave a message, I shall see that he is given it as soon as he comes down."

"I'm afraid that will be unsatisfactory. I must speak to him now. Please open the door. I have no wish to stand any longer out here in the street."

At this, the footman, who was one of Eden's staunchest supporters at Nassington House, placed a large hand on the door and pushed inward. This resulted in an equal and opposite reaction from Bentick, and a struggle ensued.

"I can't possibly rouse Mr. Lindow," panted the butler, "and if you two do not cease and desist, I shall be forced to call for reinforcements. Your behavior, I am bound to say, miss, is outrageous. This is the residence of the Duke of Derwent, and we are unaccustomed to such goings-on. Now, if you—"

"What is it, Bentick?" inquired a voice from inside the house, and Eden sagged with relief.

"A female, sir," replied the servant, his voice stiff with disapproval. "She wants to speak to you, but I was just sending her on her way."

"Seth!" called Eden in a low voice, whereupon footsteps could be heard hastening toward the door, which was peremptorily flung open. Seth moved through the aperture, and at sight of her, a spark of something she could not name leaped into his eyes and was as quickly extinguished.

"Eden!" he exclaimed with what seemed to her sensitive ears a strained cordiality. The next instant, she was startled as he added, "My dear, come in."

My dear?

Eden brushed past the butler and spoke icily to Seth. "I apologize for my . . . my unorthodox appearance at your home at this untimely hour. Believe me, if it were not absolutely necessary for me to speak to you, I should not dream of doing so."

Casting her a puzzled glance, Seth murmured to Bentick, who promptly dissolved into the early-morning gloom of the house's interior and from thence vanished into its nether regions with the footman.

On the short journey from Portman Square to Derwent House, Eden had rehearsed both her speech and her demeanor. She was extremely reluctant to seek help from Seth Lindow. For that matter, she never wanted to see or speak to him again, except perhaps to hurl at him her outrage and her betrayal and her hurt. In her preoccupation with what she would say to Seth and how she would say it, her sister's predicament had not faded, precisely, but had taken up for the moment a secondary position in her consciousness. She resolved to not so much as mention his perfidy, his black-hearted ruination of her future— her dreams of independence and the cruel hoax he had played on her and her sister.

Now she followed him as he led her to the rear of the house and his study. Having reached his sanctum, where candles already burned on a paper-littered desk, he inquired politely if she would like some refreshment.

Seth stared at Eden in some bewilderment. Since their encounter at Hunstanton House not two days ago, he had thought of almost nothing else. He had missed her abominably in the

weeks since he had bid her his discreet farewell. He had known
his departure from her would leave a void in his life, but he
hadn't realized just how painful it would be. When he had
greeted her at Huntstanton House, it was as though he had come
home to a loved haven. She had been cool then, not surprising.
Now, however, her gray eyes brimmed with—no, not just hos-
tility, but with what looked very much like hatred. What could
have happened in the intervening hours to create such an expression of frigid contempt on her delicate features?

"No, I don't want anything. Thank you," she replied in response to his offer. "Frankly, I would rather be anyplace on
earth at this moment than here with you, but a . . . a crisis has
arisen, and I believe you are the only person who can help me."

He took her hand in his to draw her down next to him on a
settee in one corner of the room, but she snatched it away.
When Seth sank awkwardly into a chair behind the desk, she
seated herself primly across from him.

"Zoë is gone," she began without preamble. "Carried off by
your brother."

"Good God!" breathed Seth. "He abducted her?"

Eden flushed. "No. There is little doubt she went with him of
her own free will. Apparently, Belhaven promised her marriage."

Seth muttered something unintelligible. "Yes, he's used that
ploy before—with distressing success. How long has Zoë been
gone?"

"I'm not sure. Her flight was not discovered until her maid
went into her chamber this morning. She must have left last
night after the family was abed." She lifted her eyes once more
to Seth, and once more he was struck by the enmity in her stare.
"I thought you might know where he has taken her."

Seth rose from behind the desk to pace the floor. After a moment, he said, "Yes, I believe I do. He usually—that is, he has a
hunting box north of here, not far from Northampton, near a
village named Olney. The house is some miles from the village
and quite secluded."

"Perfect," replied Eden bitterly. She, too, stood. "Thank you
for your help, Mr. Lindow." She turned toward the door.

"Wait!" cried Seth. "Where are you going?"

"To Olney, of course. I'm not sure precisely where it is, but
I'll find it."

"But—" Seth began, then halted abruptly. He moved swiftly to Eden and grasped her by the shoulders. To his astonishment, she flinched at his touch. "Eden, what is it? I . . . I know you have cause for affront, for I will admit I've behaved rather shabbily over the last fortnight or so, but you seem more than angry. Please tell me."

For a moment, Eden said nothing, but she went very pale. "I cannot believe you are such an insensitive boor that you do not realize—" She laughed shortly. "But, after your recent behavior, I should not be surprised. Yes, I am more than angry. Right now, I do not have time to discuss the matter with you. However, when I have found Zoë and pried her from your brother's wretched clutches, I shall be more than happy to sit down and have a comfortable coze with you on the subject."

Seth drew back, startled. She looked as though she would like to strike him. With that peculiar union he always sensed with her, he felt the pain that radiated from her very core. Had *he* done this to her? But, how? He must make her confide in him. He had vowed that he would not allow himself to love her, but he could not bear to see her like this. First, however . . .

"Eden, wait. I will go with you."

When she lifted a hand in negation, he continued hurriedly, "It will take you hours to find Bel's lair, even after you reach Olney, since you haven't been there before. In addition, although it's only a few hours' drive to get there, it may be necessary to spend the night. Let me go after them, Eden. Return to your home and wait. You may trust me to accomplish the thing to Zoë's advantage."

He started as she spat a sound of derision. "Trust you? I will go to Zoë myself, and I prefer to go alone."

"I told you," he said, stunned at her response, "it will probably be necessary to spend the night away from London. You have no chaperon."

"I brought my maid," Eden said shortly.

"Do you really think an abigail will suffice?"

"I am a spinster, Mr. Lindow. My reputation will scarcely be considered. Now, please let me pass."

"Besides all that," Seth continued, as though she had not spoken, "Bel can be extremely dangerous when he's in a rage, and I know how to handle him."

This, at last, seemed to give Eden pause, and in an attempt to lighten the atmosphere, Seth quirked his mouth into the semblance of a grin. "It is less than a day's drive, so if we start now, we should arrive by afternoon. We can while away the tedium of the journey by enumerating my flaws."

No answering smile rose to Eden's lips. Instead, she merely stared at him blankly through eyes that were like a winter landscape. Without a word, she allowed him to open the study door for her, and preceded him through it.

When they reached the hall, Seth tugged on a bellpull near the door. "I will instruct my valet to pack a few things. It will only take a moment."

True to his word, it was only a quarter of an hour later that he handed Eden into the Beckett traveling coach and climbed in behind her. He settled back on the squabs, but his hopes for an elucidatory conversation with Eden were doomed by the presence of Makepeace, who perched stiffly on the edge of the carriage seat opposite him.

They proceeded to the Holyhead Road, and as soon as they left the bustle of London and passed into the countryside, Eden closed her eyes and laid her head against the squabs. To his attempts at conversation, she uttered only monosyllabic responses until at last, discouraged, he subsided and stared gloomily out the window.

Lunch at the Three Tuns in Dunstable was equally silent, and by the time they left the main road at Newport Pagnall, Seth had given up any attempt to coax Eden from her self-imposed withdrawal. He merely made the observation that their destination lay an hour or so ahead. He noted that at this information, the tension in her slim form increased.

When they reached Olney, they left the road and made several turnings through fields and leafy lanes until at last they approached a weathered gate at which Seth directed the coachman to turn in. In a few moments, they pulled up before a comfortably sprawling, ivy-clad structure. The aged brick glowed in the afternoon sun, giving the house a welcoming aspect—which was belied by Eden's drawn features as she peered out the window of the coach. Two horses stood near the door, a groom at their heads preparing to take them to the stables.

"Would you like to remain here?" asked Seth, once more taking her hands in his. This time, apparently absorbed in the sight before her, Eden did not withdraw them. "It looks as though the master of the house is in residence. Let me ascertain whether or not Zoë is here as well."

"No," Eden replied unequivocally. "I will go in with you. If Bel is here, so must be Zoë."

Seth opened his mouth to remonstrate, but after one glance at Eden's set face, he clambered from the coach and turned to assist her to the ground. He kept a hand under her arm, although her frame was stiff and unyielding under his touch. A knock on the door produced a surprisingly swift response from a man whom Seth recognized as Henry Broom, the servant who, with his wife, looked after the lodge in Bel's absence.

"Yes, indeed, Mr. Seth, my lord is here. He and his lady just returned from riding and are in the drawing room."

He turned to lead the way through the casually furnished interior of the house.

"His lady," whispered Eden through pale lips.

Seth said nothing, but increased slightly the pressure of his hand, still under her arm. What would they find in the drawing room, he wondered with some uneasiness. A semi-orgy in progress? An hysterical Zoë pleading with Bel to be released? Perhaps he might have already regretted having brought Zoë here and had begun abusing her physically or emotionally. Seth swallowed hard as they reached the drawing room door, upon which Broom scratched before opening it wide.

It came almost as an anticlimax to behold the Marquess of Belhaven, garbed in riding gear, in the act of pouring a glass of wine for his guest, wearing a riding habit and seated sedately on a velvet settee. Both turned with no appreciable aspect of guilt at the entrance of the newcomers.

"Eden!" cried Zoë delightedly.

"Seth!" exclaimed Bel simultaneously, with equal pleasure.

Eden plunged into the room like an incendiary rocket. She fairly leapt at Bel and, before he was able to marshal his defenses, she slapped him with such force that he nearly fell over backward. Then she rushed to her sister and flung herself down beside her.

"Zoë, my dearest Zoë. Are you all right? Has the beast harmed you? Oh, Zoë, how could you? How could you do this? How could you be so swayed by a honeyed tongue that you would abandon your family? You are ruined, Zoë! At least you were very nearly ruined. There is still time, though, dearest. We will—"

Bel, who had recovered his equilibrium, moved to stem her vituperation, but he was halted by Seth, who snarled, "Put one finger on Eden, and I'll flatten you into the carpet—which I should do, in any event. Good God, Bel, what the devil are you about? Zoë is a mere child—an innocent, and gently bred. How could you deliberately bring such a one to her ruination? How do you think . . . "

Bel said nothing, but exchanged a long glance with Zoë. Then, to the utter astonishment of their visitors, the two broke into peals of laughter.

"Zoë!" cried Eden, again.

"Bel!" echoed Seth in thunderous accents.

"Oh, Eden, do sit down," said Zoë at last between giggles. "You look like that ridiculous female in the monument to Morality in our village square. I am not ruined, and I am *not* going home with you." She raised her gaze to that of Bel, and in her eyes was such an expression of tenderness that Eden nearly cried out in dismay. "For you see," she continued, a pronounced hint of smugness in her tone, "I am now the Marchioness of Belhaven."

"What!" gasped Seth and Eden in unison.

"We were married this morning," said Bel, speaking for the first time. For once, he was neither smirking nor scowling. His countenance was open and expressive almost of joy. "Father told me yesterday of his plans for my betrothal to Miss Beckett." He turned to Eden. "I hope you will not take this amiss, but I told him I was in love with Zoë and nothing would prevail upon me to marry you. Father would not listen," he continued bitterly. "He said Zoë was utterly unsuitable. When he clung buckle and thong to his blockish notion, I was ready to put a period to my existence. No offense," he assured Eden again.

Dazed, Eden waved a hand in negation.

Bel dropped a kiss on Zoë's hair. "I knew," he continued with a smile, "that my love for Zoë was returned. Thus, I nipped right out of the house to Doctors Commons and applied for a special license." He chuckled, an open sound that Seth had not heard from Bel's lips since he was a child. "There was a regular blizzard of papers to fill out," Bel continued, "but I muddled through it. The license in hand, I sent round a note to Zoë to tell her what had happened."

"Oh, Eden," interposed Zoë. "It was so romantic. He said that his life would be meaningless if he had to spend it without me. Bel proposed an elopement! He wrote of his love and said he had made all the arrangements. He said it was only for me to agree to make him the happiest man in the world."

She glanced around expectantly, but her two listeners sat silent and stunned.

"So," continued Zoë, "when everyone was asleep, I stole out of the house. I was a little frightened at being out alone so very late at night, without even my maid! But, my darling Bel was waiting for me on the corner. He scooped me into his carriage, and we clattered off into the night. Oh, Eden, it was like something out of the pages of one of Mrs. Radcliffe's romances."

"Very like," murmured Eden. "And are you telling me you and he are actually married?"

"I can show you the marriage lines if you wish," interposed Bel, an edge to his tone. "And I mean to tell you, if the two of you are going to sit there with your Friday faces and ruin our wedding day, you can both go to perdition. Or at least back to London."

Eden almost cried out in her distress at Bel's words. Zoë—innocent, headstrong Zoë—married to Bel. The girl had no idea what she had let herself in for, of course. According to Shakespeare, she thought dismally, love looked not with the eyes but the mind, but in Zoë's case, love had been completely bamboozled by the senses. Her little sister had been captivated by golden curls and blue eyes and an air of wickedness and would regret her decision for the rest of her life if something was not done.

"Zoë," she said at last in ringing tones, "this will not do. You cannot stay with this man." She gestured with contempt to Bel, whose jaw was beginning to thrust forward in an expression with which she had become only too familiar. "You will return home with me now, and Papa will see what can be done about having this so-called marriage annulled. I do not know what this will involve, but—"

Bel advanced on her, but even before Seth surged forward to intercept him, he halted. His face was white, but he spoke with reasonable calm. "Zoë will stay here—with me, her lawful husband. Our marriage was performed in a church, all right and tight, by the village vicar. He wasn't happy about it, but I had the license, and Zoë is of age now. The vicar's sister and her husband, who were visiting at the time, were witnesses. The lines are recorded in the registry and—" He smirked. "If you want to know, our union has been consummated."

Zoë was blushing furiously, but she rose to stand close to Bel. "Yes, we are husband and wife in every sense of the word, so you may as well make the best of it, Eden. I acquit you of jealousy at my good fortune, particularly since you must have thought yourself almost wed to him yourself, but—"

"Jealous!" The word exploded from Eden. "Dear God, you silly little widgeon, I would as soon have found myself betrothed to Attila the Hun! If you think for one moment I raced up here in the company of a man I . . . of a man I loathe, in a fit of pique . . ."

Loathe? Seth nearly reeled. He had sensed Eden's inexplicable enmity, but to hear her phrase it so baldly was like a blow taken in battle to some vital spot. He *must* get to the bottom of this.

Now was not the time, however. Gazing at Eden, he realized that her nerves had been stretched to the snapping point after a sleepless night, a long, worry-filled journey, and the jarring news that had awaited her at its end.

Zoë, too, was apparently startled at her sister's unwonted vehemence, for her eyes widened. "Really, Eden—"

"Eden," said Seth almost simultaneously. "As repugnant as the idea must be to you of a runaway marriage on the part of your sister—and I will freely admit, the situation is far from my liking, as well—I'm afraid we're going to have to accept it."

Eden whirled on him, ready to do battle, but Seth stepped forward to place both hands on her shoulders. "Please, my dear, do not do this to yourself. You must allow yourself a period of calm reflection. It is still early in the day, and we have time to make decisions. Zoë, why do you not take Eden upstairs where she may refresh herself. Then we can decide what must be done." Over Eden's head, he shot a minatory glance at Zoë, who moved to take Eden's arm.

The look Eden turned on Seth was anything but reconciled, but she allowed Zoë to lead her from the room.

"Phew!" Bel grinned and gestured Seth to a chair. "What a

termagant." He poured a tankard of ale for Seth from the pitcher Seth had seen earlier in his lodgings in London, and filled the matching mug for himself. He flung himself into a chair opposite the one taken by Seth. "I'm thinking of taking Zoë to The Priory in a few days," he said, rather in the manner of one throwing down a gauntlet. "It is only right that she become acquainted with her new home. I'll have to notify Aunt Shipstead to meet us there to do the pretty—be with her to receive the county gentry and all that."

Seth uttered a mirthless bark of laughter. "Is this really you, spouting proprieties?" Seth paused a moment, then blurted, "Good Lord, Bel, what possessed you to marry the chit?"

Bel set the goblet down carefully and rose to stand over his brother. "Seth, I'll thank you to remember you're speaking of my bride. If you can't infuse some respect into your tone, you will leave my house."

Surprised, Seth stared up at Bel. His eyes, as they always did when he was displeased, had turned from blue to a menacing gun-metal gray, but there was no sign of the rage that usually displayed itself at the first sign of his displeasure.

"All right," Bel said after a pause. "At first, I planned to seduce Zoë—just like all the others. But, on reflection—well, I just couldn't do it. For, you see, Zoë isn't anything like the others. She loves me. She really loves *me*. Not the heir to the Duke of Derwent—although she freely admits being much taken with the idea of becoming a duchess some day—or a dashing profligate with blue eyes and yellow curls, but me, Charlie Lindow, with all my faults and flaws. You might as well get this through your head, Seth. I love Zoë. Given my record, I probably won't make the best husband in the world, but I'll try to make her happy. And nothing you or Papa or Zoë's family can do will change that."

Seth felt almost shamed. Bel's voice rang with a simple sincerity he had never heard there before. Could it be that Zoë—flighty, self-absorbed, pampered Zoë—would prove to be Bel's redemption?

He could scarce credit the idea, but could see no point in antagonizing Bel further at this point. Sighing, he sought to lighten the moment. His attention was caught by the dull gleam of Seth's mug. It seemed to wink mockingly in the shaft of late afternoon sunlight that slanted through the long windows of the drawing room.

"I see you brought your new toy with you." Seth gestured toward the cup. "You must be extraordinarily taken with it."

Bel chuckled, an uncomplicated expression of contentment that stirred Seth unexpectedly. "Mm, yes. As you see, I use it not just for ale, but wine and spirits as well. Actually, I've come to look on it as a good luck charm of sorts. I met Zoë not long after I acquired it, and since it's been in my possession I've . . . well, I know it sounds absurd, but I feel . . . not happy exactly, but better—more at peace with myself and the rest of the world. Partly, I guess, because my headaches have diminished appreciably. It's a pure blessing to be free of them once in a while."

"Were they truly so bad?"

"God, yes. Some days, I thought I might scream with the pain. I took laudanum—even tried opium—with little success."

"I didn't realize," murmured Seth, thinking that there was possibly a great deal about Bel that he had not known. He smiled. "In that case, you'd better take precious care of it. It's strange-looking stuff. You say the glaze is made from some sort of metal?"

"Yes. Discovered in the last year or so. It starts with an L, I think. Liddimum . . . or Lyrium . . . or, no! Settler called it lithium. Said it means stone in Greek."

"Ah," murmured Seth. "Appropriate."

The conversation turned to more general topics, then, and it was not long before Zoë and Eden returned. Eden was still pale and drawn, but appeared composed and resigned to her little sister's new status. Bel announced his plan to bring Zoë to The Priory and invited Eden and Seth to join them.

"You might as well stay with us, now that you've arrived." He turned to Seth. "There's no hunting now, of course, but if you'd like, we could probably bring down a few rabbits."

"Yes, I'd love to act as chaperon," put in Zoë with a grin.

"Oh, no!" replied Eden. "I must return home. Mama and Papa will be beside themselves. I must tell you, I am still not convinced that this absurd marriage—"

She was interrupted by the sound of loud, angry voices boiling from the direction of the front hall. As they drew nearer, the duke's booming baritone could be discerned, responding irritably to another, apparently in the throes of a furious tirade.

"I tell you," roared the latter, "I shan't be put off! If m'daughter is here, by God, your boy is going to marry her, if I have to—"

The drawing room door flew open and two gentlemen, much disheveled and distraught, burst into the room.

"Father!" cried the Lindow brothers in unison.

"Papa!" screamed the Beckett sisters, blanching perceptibly.

Chapter Twenty-three

For a few moments, chaos reigned in the drawing room of the Marquess of Belhaven's hunting box. The voices of six highly wrought persons were raised in cacophony. The most incensed of these was undoubtedly that of Lord Beckett, who, upon entering the room, strode to his youngest daughter and proceeded to shake her until her head seemed in danger of flying from her shoulders. Next, he moved to the marquess, and, were not for Seth's intervention, would have pummeled him insensible.

"You bastard!" bellowed his lordship, oblivious of the ladies present. "Did you think to ruin my daughter? My precious jewel? By God, sirrah, you are a scapegrace and a cad, and you will wed her or suffer the consequences."

"By God, indeed he will not!" roared the duke. "At least . . ." He paused in some confusion. "He *will* marry your daughter, but not *that* flibbertigibbet!" He pointed an accusing finger at Zoë.

At this, Bel entered the fray, advancing on his father in a menacing fashion. Seth was forced to abandon Lord Beckett, transferring his protection to the duke. Zoë and Eden took up the slack by wrapping their arms around their father and gradually forcing him backward, and eventually into a chair.

Seth then addressed himself to calming the duke, and at last the two gentlemen each were forced to a modicum of reason in comfortable chairs at a prudent distance from one another.

"Now, then," said Seth, "it seems there are one or two misapprehensions that must be cleared up. First of all—" He bowed to Lord Beckett and the duke. "Allow me to present to Your Grace and my lord, the Marquess and Marchioness of Belhaven." He swept an arm in the direction of Bel and Zoë, who had retreated to a settee, where they sat, arms entwined.

At this, disorder broke out again. The two older gentlemen once more leaped to their feet and began speaking both at once. Bel rose.

"It is true, Father," he said to the duke. "We were married early this morning, in church. By the vicar. With a valid license. We are," he continued, warming to his subject, "husband and wife in the eyes of God and the law, and there's nothing you can do about it." He glared pugnaciously.

At his words, however, the belligerence suddenly evaporated from Lord Beckett's countenance.

"Married?" His small eyes glittered. "Zoë, you and the marquess are married? Why, that makes you——"

"Yes, Papa." Zoë bounced from the settee to dance across the room to her father, whereupon she dropped a kiss atop his thinning hair. "Is it not famous?" she caroled. "I am the Marchioness of Belhaven and shall someday be the Duchess of Derwent. Not that I am in a hurry to claim my position," she assured His Grace kindly.

"Married!" roared the duke. "I won't have it! I don't care if you stood up in St. Paul's with the Archbishop of Canterbury in attendance, I'll find a way to scotch it. I'll have it annulled! I'll——"

"I'm afraid that's impossible, Father," interposed Seth. "Zoë is of age and, no matter what you might think, of sound mind. Bel informs me that the union has been, er, consummated, and I believe, from the number of by-blows we're already supporting, he cannot be proved impotent. Now, then——" He bent to speak low in the duke's ear. "It seems to me this circumstance solves our problem nicely. Zoë may not be the bride you might have chosen for Bel, but she is gently bred and Bel appears to have formed an affection for her that may, if we are fortunate, prove lasting. The thing to remember here is that Bel is actually married and with any luck will produce a son or two in short order. I think you should accept this with good grace."

Eden could only watch in cold wonder as Seth, obviously with long practice, manipulated the duke into a state of reasoned calm. The older man was actually smiling by the time Seth turned away from him to face the rest of the company.

She stood for a moment, apart from the group, irresolute. As horrified as she was at the thought of Zoë married to Bel, there was little she could do, particularly since Papa was obviously in transports at the news.

At any rate, perhaps she could prevail upon the duke and her father to return to London. She could accompany them back to town, thus avoiding the journey with Seth.

But, no. She turned her attention back to the now convivial group to find that the duke and Papa had phased into a mood of mutual congratulation.

"I knew this would all work out satisfactorily," said the duke with what Eden could only consider a fatuous grin. He poked Seth slyly in the ribs. "I'll wager you had it planned out all along, you crafty young devil. Convincing me that while Bel might not suit Miss Zoë"—he dropped a wink at Seth in appreciation of his diplomatic phrasing of the situation—"he might do very well for Miss Beckett."

Seth, with one horrified glance at Eden, turned white.

"N-no!" he croaked, but the duke plowed on. "When all the time you knew how things stood between Bel and Miss Zoë." He rubbed his hands together. "I think this calls for champagne. Have you anything decent in your cellars, my boy?" he asked Bel.

Broom was sent for. His response was so prompt, it might have been supposed he was lurking in the corridor, waiting for the sound of the bell. The champagne was ordered, and in a few moments, plans were under way for a celebratory dinner at the local inn.

Eden had never felt so conspicuously isolated and unwanted. She had not needed confirmation of Seth's duplicity, but hearing the words spoken so casually by the duke caused a well of pain to open in her heart that threatened to overwhelm her. She felt she had to get out of this place. She looked around wildly and moved toward Bel. Perhaps she might prevail upon him to put a carriage at her disposal to get her back to town.

She was intercepted by a solid obstacle in the form of Seth Lindow. His face was still pale, his eyes stricken.

"Eden," he said, his voice low and intense. "What you just heard was not— That is, if you'll just let me explain—"

"No explanation is required, sir," Eden replied tightly. "I had already been apprised of your machinations on your father's behalf."

"What!"

"His Grace was good enough to divulge them to my father, who relayed them to me as he sought to impress upon me my good fortune in being chosen as your brother's bride."

"Oh, God." Seth thought he would be sick. He grasped Eden's arm. He had to make her understand! "Eden, please. I must speak to you."

"I can't think why. You have achieved your ends. You have found a bride for your wretched brother. That in doing so you have destroyed the life of an innocent young girl will, of course, not weigh with you. No, thank you, Mr. Lindow, I do not wish to listen any further to your persuasive speeches. They have done enough damage to this family." *And to me!* she almost cried out. Instead, she drew herself up coolly. "If you would request of the marquess the use of a carriage to return me to town, I would be most grateful."

"No, wait, Eden. You must let me— Look," he continued desperately as Eden continued to gaze at him as though he had just crawled out from beneath a lettuce leaf. The trouble was, he reflected gloomily, she was right. His behavior had been beneath contempt, and how he was to restore himself in her esteem he had no idea. He only knew he must try. "Please just give me fifteen minutes. If you still wish to leave then, I shall arrange the whole thing."

Eden glanced at the group conversing genially nearby. She had no wish to create a scene, and she supposed she could listen to Seth for fifteen minutes without becoming physically ill. Twisting her arm from his grasp, she nodded, and followed him from the room.

A few moments later, she was seated in a wing chair in what was apparently a library, although only a few books rested on the shelves that lined the room. Seth paced the floor before her.

"Eden," he began at last, "I can't deny that what my father said was true. I suppose you were also told that my purpose in visiting Clearsprings last month was not just to buy horses but to meet Zoë."

"Yes." Eden found it difficult to speak beyond the tears that gathered in her throat, but she managed to keep her voice steady. "Not just to meet her, of course, but to assess her points."

Seth squirmed, but having decided to tell her the whole, he plunged ahead. In a few moments he bared everything from his conversation with the duke all those weeks ago, to the wearisome day he had spent trying to talk the duke out of his plans for Eden.

"You see," he concluded miserably. "You had come to mean . . . a great deal to me. I could not deliver your sister to my father's ambitions, and I certainly could not see you wed to Bel."

"I see," said Eden woodenly. "I perceive I am to blush prettily and say thank you. Do you really think that makes all well?"

Seth swallowed. "No, of course not." Although this, of course, was precisely what he had hoped. He felt empty suddenly, and cold. How could he make her understand the motives that had led to his blind obedience to his father's wishes? He sank down on the chair opposite her.

"Eden, I have no excuses to offer. I wish I could say that I was somehow coerced into this infamous scheme, but I entered into it more or less willingly. You see"—he shifted in his chair—"as distasteful as I found the whole project—I've explained to you before, I made a vow—"

"Yes, I know all about your vow," snapped Eden, "and the motives that prompted it. Are you telling me that once you decided that Zoë would not suit, and having found a dull, submissive spinster to fill the bill"—Seth flushed a dull red—"that you completely abandoned the whole scheme because you had formed an affection for me?"

Seth drew a deep breath. "No," he said slowly and deliberately. "By that time I had realized that I am in love with you."

Eden gasped, feeling the blood drain from her face. How could he say such a thing to her? Only a few days ago, she had longed to hear those words on his lips, and had even thought they might be forthcoming in the not too distant future. Then he had given ample evidence that whatever feelings he might have nourished in his bosom had withered to a careless disregard.

"How *dare* you?" she whispered brokenly.

She watched as Seth sagged in his chair. "I'm sorry," he said in a low voice. "I had thought perhaps—I know someone of my status could never aspire to your hand, but I wanted you to know what was in my heart." He rose. "I have done you a grievous harm, and I wish I could undo the damage I did."

"What are you talking about?" murmured Eden through stiff lips. "What is this idiocy about your status?"

He stared at her blankly, as though she had asked why the sky is blue. "Why, I am lowborn, of course," he replied with a hint of impatience.

In one of those increasingly inconvenient moments of identification with Seth, she felt his pain as though it were a shaft through her own spirit. It was as if his anguish were a reflection of her own. Good Lord, he was serious! Could it be that he really loved her! For a moment, she was almost overcome with a dizzying sense of happiness, which was smothered almost immediately at the recollection of his most recent betrayal. How could a man love a woman and still destroy her happiness so completely and so carelessly?

"For heavens' sake," she said angrily, "for a man of such vaunted sense and perspicacity, you are speaking perfect nonsense. You are a gentleman, Seth. That is apparent in every fibre of your being. No, it is not your status that I find unacceptable. And I do understand the importance you attach to that ridiculous vow. No, it is that other. I do not understand how you can stand before me, mouthing words of love, when—"

"What other?" asked Seth blankly

Eden felt she simply could not go through all this with him. "Please, Seth. I can't—"

She was interrupted as the library door flew open to admit her father.

"There you are! I've been looking all over for you. Come along, we're going back to London."

"W-what?" Eden stammered in bewilderment. "But I thought you were going to dinner with—"

"That was before I remembered I want to get to that bank! If we leave now, we can still get there before closing, otherwise we shall have to wait until Monday morning."

"Bank?" interposed Seth, perplexed.

"Yes," snapped Lord Beckett. "Do not think I have forgotten, Eden, what I said to you yesterday. No daughter of mine is going to live on her own, eking out an independence by peddling paint daubs."

For a moment, Seth stared at Lord Beckett, then at Eden. "He knows?" he asked incredulously.

"Of course, he knows." Eden's reply was caustic. "Since you were so obliging as to tell him."

"But I didn't!"

"What? But Papa said—"

Both turned to gape at Lord Beckett, who had paled suddenly.

"Oh," he said, beginning to back out of the room. "Demme, I forgot—

"But how could he have known if you didn't tell him?" The words burst from Eden. The dizziness she had experienced earlier returned, increased in magnitude and intensity. What was happening? Could it be? A sudden suspicion rose in her mind, and she whirled on her father.

"Papa, what have you done?"

Stung by the harshness in his daughter's voice, Lord Beckett resorted to bluster. "I didn't do anything!"

"You told me that Seth had related to you—"

"Yes . . . well, that wasn't precisely how it was."

Eden knew a wholly unfilial urge to hit her father over the head with a blunt instrument. "Just how was it—precisely?" she asked, spitting out the question word by word.

"There's no need to take me up so, Eden." Lord Beckett took refuge in the disappearing shreds of his dignity. "I am your father, after all."

"What have you done?" Eden asked again, this time her voice resounding like that of an avenging goddess.

"Well, it wasn't me at all. It was the duke. We were conversing—as I told you—in his library. I'd just discovered your painting hanging there—" He paused as Seth gave a startled exclamation. "I asked where he'd got it, and he said Mr. Lindow had purchased it. When I asked where, he took me to a little office in the back of the house and began looking through the papers stacked on the desk."

"Good God!" said Seth explosively. "You and Father were rummaging through my papers?"

"Well, I didn't know they was yours. And, anyway, as the duke said, since you're his man of business, and since we were in his house, everything there was rightly his to begin with."

"Indeed," growled Seth.

"We found the bill of sale for the daisy picture and another besides." He halted again, this time at the small sound uttered by Eden. "They all bore the name of that Rellihan feller and his address. And I tell you, Eden," continued Lord Beckett, the picture of paternal disapproval, "His Grace was more than somewhat taken aback at the thought that such a gently bred lady was going behind her papa's back to earn her own money."

Eden thought she might simply explode in an unbecoming burst of blood, bone, and emotion! Seth had not betrayed her! Her father had managed that feat all on his own! She cast Seth a look of such jumbled emotions that he almost smiled.

"Anyway," concluded Lord Beckett, the bluster returning to his voice, "we'll be going now. If we stand here nattering much longer, closing time will be on us again, and I don't intend to wait another needless day for what is rightly mine."

"I see," said Seth, and Eden was startled to note that he spoke, apparently, in the best of good humor. "You will, my lord, of course do as you see fit, but I must tell you it will present a very odd picture indeed to the rest of the world."

"Eh?" Lord Beckett glared suspiciously at Seth.

"It is not uncommon in this day and age for perfectly respectable ladies to pursue careers in the arts. Look at Miss Austen—a clergyman's daughter. She had sold, I think, five or six novels before her death a couple of years ago. And look at Lady Caro Lamb—although the word 'respectability' can hardly be uttered in the same breath with her name, she is a peeress. She published *Glenarvon* to enormous success, and I understand she's working on a second novel."

"Yes, but they didn't go haring off on their own with their money."

"No, of course not. However, there is nothing in it for a lady of mature years to set up her own establishment with a suitable companion."

"Mm, I still say it won't do."

"In any event," Seth went on, an odd note in his voice, "even if you do elect to empty your daughter's present account, you will be unable to do so in the future."

"Eh?" barked Lord Bartlett again. "What are you talking about?"

Seth paused a moment. He exchanged a swift, unreadable glance with Eden before he continued speaking. "Because very soon she will be a married woman, and as such no longer under your control."

Eden could only stare at him. Her knees gave way, and she plumped down into the chair behind her. Her gasp of astonishment was no less heartfelt than that of her father.

"Married!" they both exclaimed in the same breath.

"Yes," said Seth firmly. "To me."

"But, you . . . you are a soldier's son!" spluttered Lord Beckett.

"But, a very wealthy one. And, I have been told, I'm a gentleman."

"Nevertheless, I won't have it."

"I can understand," Seth returned mildly, "your reluctance to lose such a treasure." He smiled warmly at Eden, who continued to gape at him, feeling that she must look as mindless as she felt. "No man is worthy of her, of course. However, I must remind you that she does not need your consent."

What Eden recognized as his acquisitive expression began to creep over Lord Beckett's face. "Wealthy, you say? How wealthy?"

Eden's toes curled in distaste. "Really, Papa!"

"I do not think we want to discuss this before a lady, but I believe you will be pleasantly surprised," replied Seth, nothing but the blandest courtesy in his voice.

Lord Beckett stood uncertainly. It was obvious that he was not happy at this turn of events, but he did not want to offend a son-in-law who might turn out to be a boon. And then, reflected Eden cynically, it looked as though the spinster daughter he had despaired of some years ago might finally be taken off his hands.

"I suppose you mean to let her make a fool of herself over this painting business?" he asked, his tone heavy with sarcasm.

"I do not propose to *let* her do anything. She is an adult, perfectly capable of making her own decisions. However it is my intent that she should paint until her fingers fall off if she so desires, and she may sell her work on the steps of St. Paul's if she likes."

Lord Beckett made no response, but stared at Seth as though he had just entered the room stark naked.

Eden thought it time she intervened. She rose from the chair into which she had sunk, boneless and trembling, a few minutes before. She was not, she conceded, in much better straits now. "Papa," she began, but Seth moved quickly to stand at her side.

"Actually, I had just finished proposing when you came in. Although your daughter has given me reason to believe my suit will prosper, I still await her answer. I wonder if I might beg your indulgence to leave us alone for a few minutes."

Eden inhaled sharply in indignation, but the prospect of getting rid of her father, even temporarily, was so appealing that she remained silent. Lord Beckett, his mind still apparently on Seth's utterance about wealth, remained for some length, shuffling uncertainly from one foot to the other like a dog hopeful that the roast on the table will be his eventually, but not at all sure this will come to pass. At last, with a pontifical "I'll talk to you later, missy," he stamped from the room.

Eden whirled on Seth. "What do you mean by this?" she exclaimed. Sizzles of happiness still shot through her at the knowledge that it was not Seth who had revealed her efforts to establish herself as a successful artist. But to blurt out a proposal of marriage, merely, she was sure, to silence her father, if only for a moment. How could he? After professing that he loved her. For surely he could not have been speaking the truth on that matter, either—could he? He had not disclosed her secret, but he had used her shamefully—as he had Zoë. He had admitted as much. He'd apologized and proffered his reasons for behaving so abominably, but—no, she could never trust him again.

These chaotic thoughts and more tumbled through her mind in the few seconds in which she stood gazing into his eyes—eyes in whose depths two flames seemed to leap.

"I'm sorry to have been so precipitate," he said softly, his hands on her shoulders. "On the drive here, I had an opportunity to think at some length, and by the time we arrived, I had come to the conclusion that I've been a fool. For all my adult life I have pandered to the duke's interests, completely submerging my own inclinations merely to ensure that he became even more obscenely wealthy and powerful than he already is."

He began a slow stroking motion on her neck, which she found so distracting she could hardly attend to his words.

"I have you to thank for that, for it was you who made me realize that whatever debt I owed to the duke, I paid in full a long time ago. It is time, I realized, that I look to my own interests. It was weeks ago that those interests became irrevocably bound to a beautiful, gifted artist of my acquaintance, and on the two occasions when I allowed my growing passion for her to spill over into what was not quite proper, I came to believe that she—you—had come to look on me first as a friend, and then, I hoped, as something more."

He had moved closer to her, and the fingers on one hand cupped the back of her head, while the other brushed tendrils of hair from her cheek. She knew she should have stepped back with an appropriate exclamation of outrage, but she could not have moved at that moment if so ordered by the Prince Regent.

"Long ago I had drummed into me the impossibility of one with my background aspiring to the hand of a lady, but a few minutes ago, you destroyed that fallacy in one sentence. I hope you meant what you said, my dearest love, because—oh, Eden—" He bent to brush his lips along her cheek. "I do love you so, and I cannot envision the rest of my life without you."

Eden lifted her face to receive his kiss. When his mouth came down on hers, urgent and seeking, she felt her defenses crumble and melt like the last of winter's ice in the heat of a spring sun. She arched into him, joy surging through her so fiercely she thought he must hear it in the beat of her pulse beneath his fingers.

When he withdrew his mouth a moment later to trail kisses that burned along her jaw and onto the line of her throat, she whispered brokenly, "Oh, Seth, my darling Seth, I love you, too. I have been such an idiot."

He smiled tenderly. "No, it is I who claim that dubious distinction. I am still of the opinion that you could do much better in your choice of husband, but having successfully cozzened you into accepting my humble self, I plan to marry you with all possible speed."

"But, what will your father say?"

Seth grinned, permitting himself the pleasure of placing his lips just there, where a curl fell enticingly against Eden's temple. "I expect he will be displeased that I have allowed a distraction in my life. However, he will have much more than that upon which to vent his spleen."

He drew back slightly to gaze directly into her eyes. "For I plan to terminate my employment with His Grace as soon as we leave this room—effective immediately."

"Oh, Seth, that's wonderful. You can lead your own life now!"

"With you at my side, my one and only love. How do you feel about living in the wilds of Warwickshire for the rest of our lives? I have a reasonably decent property there, needing only a rose garden to make it a paradise on earth."

Eden laughed into his face. "Ah, I see, this whole scenario is nothing but an effort to acquire a gardener with no expense to yourself."

Seth kissed her again, this time slowly and with great care. "Wench! I'm done with grand plans and designs. I'm marrying you because I can't think who else would have me."

"Nor I," replied his love obligingly, "but whoever she is, I'm prepared to scratch her eyes out."

"How territorial of you, m'dear. I like that in a woman—particularly one who is married to me, which by the by, I plan to arrange as soon as possible."

Eden, secure in the circle of his arms, chuckled. "Then we'd better divulge our plans to our respective families. I imagine my father has already imparted the news of our betrothal to your father."

"He will be amazed, no doubt, at your condescension," returned Seth, "but the news will pale, I think, at the information that he will have to find a new man of affairs."

"Indeed," purred Eden, her eyes sparking mischievously. "You will be much too busy with certain other affairs to consider those of the duke."

Upon which, her beloved swept her into his arms for one more searing kiss before leading her out of the library and into their new lives.

Author's Note

Readers of Regency romance being a perspicacious lot, I'm sure many of you will have noted the reference to lithium in these pages as the probable reason for Bel's dramatic emotional improvement at the end of the story. While I am certainly not claiming that his ceramic mug and pitcher, glazed with lithium carbonate, were responsible for the alleviation of some of poor Bel's symptoms, I will observe that lithium was discovered in 1817 in Sweden by J.A. Arfvedson. It was not produced in quantity until the 1850s, and did not come into general use until this century.

The metal now is applied in many purposes, but its use in the treatment of mental disease did not come about until the 1970s. Thus, neither Bel nor his loved ones, even if the concept of bi-polar disorder had been understood in the Regency period, most certainly would not have comprehended its efficacy in relieving the symptoms of his affliction.

Thus, I will freely admit that in hinting at Bel's improvement because of the problematic leeching into his system of the lithium carbonate in the glaze of his mug and decanter (the same form of the metal employed in glazes and as a medication for mental disease) I am stretching fact almost to snapping point. However, the operative word there is "almost." I maintain that such an event, although unlikely, *could* have happened , and what is fiction, if not the realm of "what if?"